MAKE HER PAY

MIRANDA RIJKS

INKUBATOR
BOOKS

Published by Inkubator Books
www.inkubatorbooks.com

ISBN (eBook): 978-1-83756-304-3
ISBN (Paperback): 978-1-83756-305-0
ISBN (Hardback): 978-1-83756-306-7

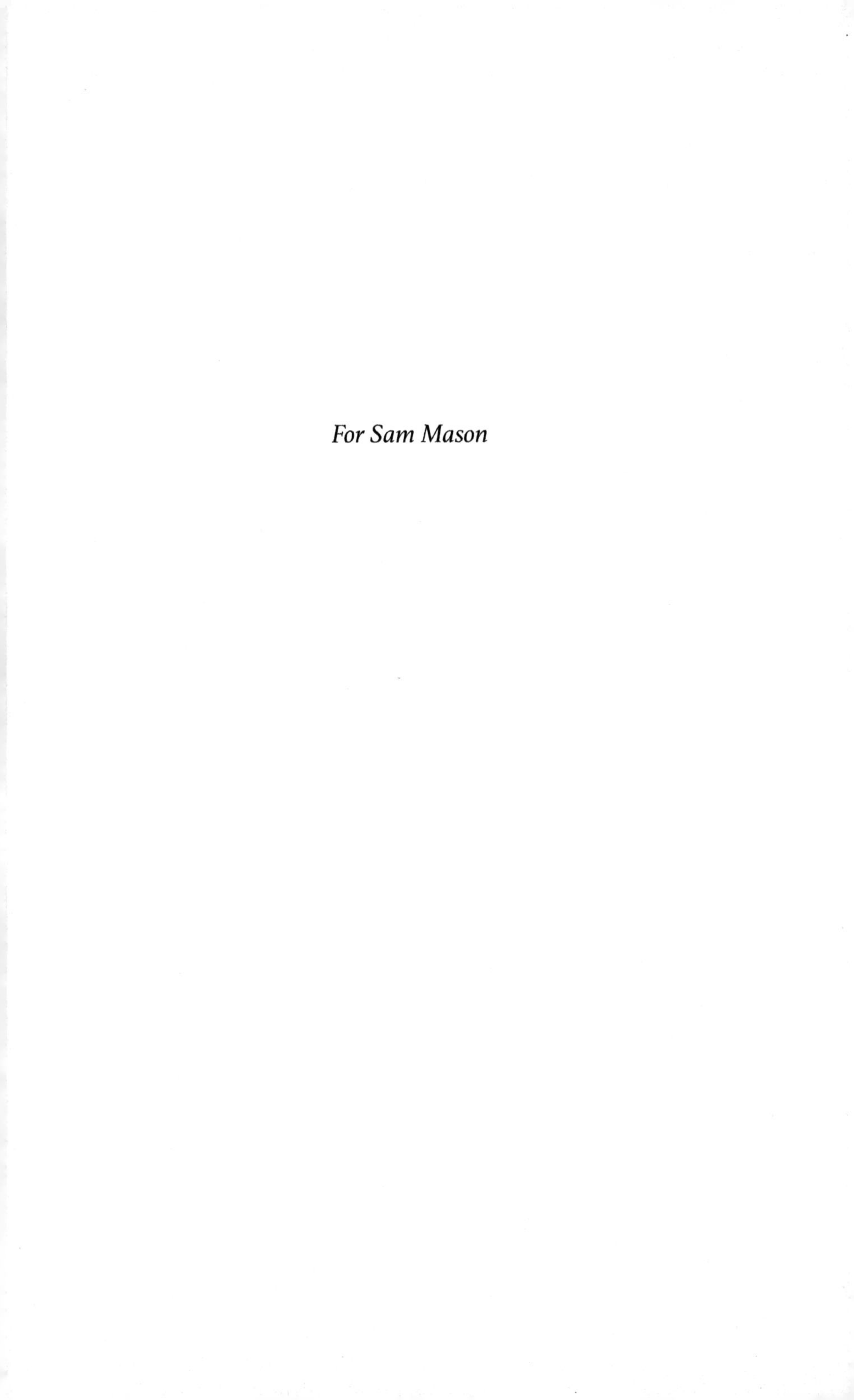

For Sam Mason

PROLOGUE

They say your life flashes in front of your eyes when you're dying. Mine didn't. There were bright, blinding lights that burned my retinas. A terrible choking fear that made my gut clench as I realised I'd lost control. A roar in my ears of screeching engines, crunching metal and splintering glass, along with the pounding of blood. And the smell. That terrible stench of burned rubber and diesel combined with blood. When did the silence come? Seconds or minutes later? Seconds probably because complete blackness descended quickly.

My life didn't flash in front of my eyes because in that first moment, I wasn't dying. That came later. Much later. For the lucky ones, death is swift and decisive. A relief. But I wasn't a lucky one. I deserved the pain and the suffering and the slow descent to the end. At least I thought that initially when I first came to and understood what I had done. But then I assumed help was just moments away, that I'd hear the welcome sound of sirens, that strong and capable hands would ease my broken body away from the wreckage. That

I'd be transported to hospital where I'd be put back together again by talented surgeons and kindly nursing staff.

Except no one came.

I read somewhere that when you have a horrific accident, adrenaline and endorphins mingle together to create a chemically altered state that masks pain. It's true, for a short while. Although maybe it wasn't a short while because time bent and distorted. Night gave way to day and back to night again and with the grey light came hope followed by suffering. Such overwhelming torturous agony that is utterly indescribable. In those few moments of lucidity, I thought about my life, but there was no cinematic scrolling of highlights, just the terrible realisation that death would be my salvation. The birds were singing. I wanted to scream at them to shut up. And when that final blackness descended, I was truly grateful.

1

LEONIE – 10 YEARS AGO

'The caterers have arrived!'

Mum's voice is shrill as it echoes through the cavernous house. I know for a fact that she's drunk the best part of a bottle of wine, and their fancy guests aren't due to be here for another hour at least.

I'm sitting on a sun lounger next to the turquoise swimming pool, painting my toenails with neon orange nail varnish. You can count on one hand the number of days in the year it's warm enough to sunbathe. If only we had a holiday home in Ibiza or Majorca, but no. My parents, Brenda and Gus Wilding, choose to holiday in Northumberland, the northeast corner of England. Mum walks through the open bifold doors. She's wearing a new maxi-dress in pinks and reds, and it's too low-cut and emphasises her saggy boobs. It's gross.

'You need to get ready,' she says, squinting at me in the sunlight, which isn't even that bright.

Dad appears and stands next to her. His floral shirt

stretches over his fat stomach. 'And whilst you're at it, pack up your things. We're going home tomorrow.'

'What?' I jump up from the lounger, rescuing the nail varnish just in time. 'You said we were going home on Thursday,' I exclaim, a knot of dismay building in my stomach.

'Nope. Change of plans. I've got to get back for a meeting with the solicitors on Monday, and your mother has some charity do.'

'Stop scowling.' Mum squints at me. 'If the wind changes, your face will stay like that. You'll get wrinkles.'

I ignore her stupid comments. 'But I want to stay.'

'"I want" doesn't get.' Dad speaks in a mocking tone.

'I'm sixteen, not a kid anymore! Why do you both treat me like an idiot?' My voice rises in volume as I put my hands on my hips. 'I'll stay by myself and get a train home.'

'No, you won't.' Age isn't doing Dad any favours either. He's jowly and balding with eyes that are too small for his large, circular face. 'You don't get a say in the matter, missy,' he says. 'I know exactly what you're thinking. This is my house, and I've no desire to see it trashed by a bunch of irresponsible teenagers.'

'It's not going to get trashed. It'll only be me staying here.' Which, of course, is an outright lie. I'm already mentally planning how Ollie can stay the night with me, and how perhaps we can have a party. A pool party for twenty or so of his friends, perhaps. That would be manageable.

'You're coming home with us whether you like it or not,' Dad says, crossing his arms across his broad chest.

'That's not fair, Dad! Millie stays at her parents' second home when they're not there.'

'I don't care what Millie does or doesn't do. Firstly, you'd be stuck out here in the middle of nowhere without transport, and secondly, you're too young. Hop to it and pack your bags.' He stares at me then. 'And whilst you're at it, change into something more suitable for the party. I don't want any daughter of mine looking like a slut.'

That's a low comment, even for Dad. I stride through the living room, stomp up the stairs and slam my bedroom door behind me. I know it's petty, but I'm raging. I do not want to go home.

My parents bought this house eight years ago and then spent a fortune modernising it. I know we're lucky to have a second home because my parents never fail to remind me that I'm spoilt. Mum comes from the picturesque city of Durham and always dreamed of returning to the northeast. Because Dad's business is southern-based, that wasn't going to happen, so he indulged her by buying this place. Fortunately, I've got friends up here, and not *just* friends. I'm in love. Not the obsessive, infatuation kind like Millie and Ciara; this is proper love. Ollie is nineteen and in his first year at Exeter University. We got together three weeks ago at the bonfire party on the beach at Whitley Bay, and I've decided that I'm going to lose my virginity with him this week. Except now my bloody parents want me to go home tomorrow, and that means I might never see Ollie again. The thought makes tears spring to my eyes and creates a deep longing in my gut.

Dad has a real estate business, developing and building residential homes in London and the southeast. He and Mum are always talking about opportunities and investments and boring stuff about planning permissions. I zone out. My brother, Sam, literally bailed out. He's two and a half years older than me, and although I wouldn't admit it to any of my friends, I think he's cool. He stuck a finger in the air to Dad and has gone off traveling for a year. He sends me postcards from exotic places like Marrakech and Gabon, which is really sweet because he could just text me. How I wish I were with him.

I mope around in my bedroom, listening to the music starting up (they've got an actual DJ playing ancient songs; I mean, how lame is that?) and watch some of the guests arrive. They're all alike: the women in strappy sandals and sundresses showing off their fake-tanned limbs, and the men in ridiculous patterned shirts and shorts. All I can think about is Ollie. He messaged me earlier, said he was going out for supper with his parents and cousins, but could we meet up tomorrow? And now I'm expected to be back home in the south. We live miles away from each other in the UK, and once he's back at uni, I know I'll be forgotten. I send him a message.

What time will u b back from supper? We can meet somewhere later.

Ollie's family is from Northumberland, and his house is about a fifteen-minute drive away, too far for me to walk at night. Ollie has an old Golf, but he pranged it a few days ago, so right now he doesn't have a car.

'K. Meet u in churchyard at 11.

And now my heart is racing. We'll do it tonight, I just know we will, and it'll be amazing. We'll find a field somewhere, or perhaps we'll even do it in the graveyard with all the ghosts watching us. Or maybe not, that'll be too creepy. And then a better idea pops into my head.

Dad shouts up the stairs, 'Come down, Leonie. I need the next generation of Wilding Properties to be seen.'

I grit my teeth. Dad never shuts up about how I'm going to take over his business one day, and our family will become an empire. It's not like I'm even interested in houses. I want to do something worthwhile like Ollie. He's studying geography and wants to save the world from overheating. I'm going to study history of art at Oxford, if I get in, that is. Dad thinks it's a good compromise, as I'll get to learn about aesthetics, and that might help him one day. Personally, I think that's bollocks. I want to save artefacts for the nation, a bit like the Monuments Men in World War Two, who saved national treasures from the looting Nazis.

I glance at my watch. It's only 7.30 pm, so I'll show my face at this hideous party, and then, when everyone is drunk, I'll sneak off.

A couple of hours later, I'm desperate to get out. The women are all braying and laughing too loudly. I've no idea where Mum is, but Dad is deep in conversation with two men, and now he's got his phone out and is showing them something. Pictures of one of the London mansions he's developing, no doubt. I thought a party was for having fun, not trying to stitch up some business deal.

With everyone outside, milling by the pool, the house is quiet and dark when I tiptoe upstairs, careful to make sure no one is watching me. I walk barefoot along the corridor, my feet silent on the wooden floors, and push the door open into Mum and Dad's bedroom. It's a huge room, which makes the bed look small. The windows are the full length and breadth of the wall and lead out onto a glass veranda with views over the garden to woodlands beyond. I don't switch the light on, but tiptoe over to the chair in the corner where Mum dumps her handbag. I rifle inside it until my fingers are clutching her car keys. Mum has a black Range Rover here, and Dad a red Porsche. Only the best for my parents.

I slip back into my bedroom and switch the light on in my marble bathroom. I'm wearing more makeup than normal, and double-check that the red lipstick hasn't stuck to my front teeth. I peel off the dress I've been wearing this evening and put on a spaghetti-strap top that shows off my modest cleavage, and a very short denim skirt. At the last minute, I decide not to wear any underwear. It feels exciting and wicked.

So here's the thing. I don't actually know how to drive – or more like I haven't passed my test yet. I've had a couple of lessons at home, but those were on a shift car. Mum's Range Rover is automatic, so it should be much easier. The only thing I'm nervous about is its vast size. I hurry downstairs, and when I'm sure no one is looking, I open the door to the garage and slip inside. It's cooler in here, and my trainers squelch on the painted concrete floor. The light comes on automatically, and my heart starts pounding. I press the unlock button on the key and slide into the driver seat. Mum's seat is too far forwards, and it takes a moment to work out how to send it further back. She's one of those nervous drivers who sits hunched over the wheel, her fingers gripping the steering wheel too tightly. I'm never going to be like that. Driving is freedom, and I can't wait until I get my own car. Dad's promised me a car for my eighteenth, assuming I pass my test, which of course I will.

Mum always reverses her car into the garage, which is just as well, as it makes my job that little bit easier. I put the car into drive and gently place my foot on the accelerator. It jerks a bit, but nothing happens. *Shit.* Then I remember: I have to release the park button. It's not that easy getting out because my parents' guests have parked all along the driveway, but it's well lit up, and I drive at a snail's pace, the car beeping wildly at me if I get too close to anything. Eventually I'm at the end of the drive, the main road in front of me. My palms feel moist on the leather steering wheel, and my heart is pounding. I didn't think it would be that scary.

'Come on,' I say aloud to myself. 'You're a Wilding. You can do anything you put your mind to.' Normally I hate Dad's motto, but right now, I need the positive thinking. I indicate to the left and put my foot down on the accelerator. The headlights throw wide beams across the road.

And then I let out a squeal. I'm driving! I'm actually driving, and it feels amazing. Ollie is going to be so impressed. I can't wait to see his face, his beautiful eyes widening and his jaw dropping open as I pull up into the church car park and hop down from the Range Rover. I jab at some buttons, but can't work out how to switch the radio on. Never mind. I'm going quite slowly at twenty-five miles per hour, but I need to be safe. I let out another whoop. But then headlights appear in the rear-view mirror. They're getting closer... like really close, and they're flashing at me, blinding. What the hell? I swallow hard. Is it the police? How do they know that I'm driving without a licence? And then there's the honking of a horn – so not the police, because they'd put a siren on, wouldn't they? Is it because I'm driving too slowly? *Shit. Shit.* I put my foot down on the accelerator, my fingers gripping the wheel so tightly. I can feel beads of sweat on my upper lip and under my arms, and tightness across the back of my neck. This is unfunny. Why the hell doesn't the jerk just overtake me?

My phone starts ringing, but I can't do anything about that now. I drive faster, hunching forwards, but the lights behind me are so distracting.

No!

I scream.

It all happens so fast. There's another car approaching. In a split second. Lights blinding me front and back.

On my side of the road.

I wrench the steering wheel to the left and swerve. The car bounces from side to side. There's a screech of metal. Brakes. I slam my foot down hard. The headlights of the other car jump up and down and disappear. I bring the Range Rover to a halt in the middle of the road.

No. No. No.

This can't have happened.

I squeeze my eyes shut, but I'm trembling violently, my teeth rattling in my jaw. Where's the other car? Where has it gone?

Without thinking, I yank the door open, and I'm running to the side of the road, the headlights from the Range Rover lighting up the pitch-black night.

'Leonie!'

I freeze.

What the hell is Dad doing here?

'What the fuck have you done?' His voice is ice cold. He's next to me, his thick arms around my shoulders. 'Leonie, what have you done?'

I wrench myself from Dad's clutches and run down the steep bank, slipping and sliding in the slippery grass, my bare legs getting scratched from scrub and branches.

Dad's shining a light down towards me, swinging it in an arc and beyond. And then I spot it. A crumpled heap of metal at the foot of a tree down the verge in a cluster of woodland. It's fizzing and cracking, steam rising from the twisted bonnet, the lights still on, illuminating shrubs and low-lying trees.

'Get back!' Dad shouts at me. 'Don't touch anything.'

I stand still and stare with horror.

There's a body. A pair of legs with heavy black boots, like Doc Martens, visible underneath a mangled-but-open car door. A body. A body that isn't moving. I edge forwards, and then I scream. In the low light, a mangled, bloodied face and eyes that glisten and stare. Dad clatters down the hillside and appears at my side. He puts an arm around my shoulders, squeezing me so tightly it hurts, and he places the palm of his hand over my face, blinding me.

'We need to get him out!' My voice is a whisper now. Dad's hand smells of beer, and my stomach turns. He releases his palm from my face and forcibly swivels me around so I can't see the carnage.

'Don't say a word. Turn around. Go back to the Range Rover and wait for me.' His fingers dig into my shoulders.

'No! We need to help.'

'You caused this catastrophe, Leonie.' Dad's voice is trembling with rage. 'What the hell were you doing stealing your mum's car? You're not insured! You haven't even passed your driving test. Get back to the car. *Now.*' He shoves me towards the bank. I glance over my shoulder and see that he's using the torch on his phone to view the wreckage. I'm whimpering now; I can't help it.

'Shall I call 999?'

'Do nothing,' Dad barks at me. And then the light from his phone is burning my eyes. 'It's too late,' he says. 'He's dead.'

I collapse onto my knees and howl, but Dad is having none of it. He grabs my arm and literally tugs me back up the bank. 'Shut the hell up, Leonie. We need to get you out of here. Don't you understand the implications of what you've done? If the police find out you were driving illegally, your life will be over. And I mean *over.* No university, no friends, no fucking future. You'll be banged up in prison for the next decade. The shame on us, on me and your mother, on the business.' His voice fades away, but his fingers are gripping my upper arm so hard, I can feel the bruises welling up.

He pulls open the passenger door of the Range Rover and shoves me inside; then he walks around to the driver's side, starts the car up and pulls it over onto the verge. 'Wait here while I move my car.'

The roar of his Porsche in the silent night air is deafening. I watch in the rear mirror as he parks his car right up on the verge, underneath the branches of a massive tree. The next thing I know, Dad is back in the driver's seat of the Range Rover.

'We need to help him. That man.' My voice quivers. 'Call an ambulance.'

'I've already told you, it's too late. We've got to get you home.'

He starts the engine and drives a couple of hundred metres before turning the car around in the entrance to a field. And then we're driving homewards. I stare out of the window, trying to catch a glimpse of the wreckage of the other car, but I can see nothing in the dark. I can't stop the tears, the whimpering. I glance at Dad. His jaw is set forwards, and there's a vein pinging in the side of his forehead.

'I'm sorry,' I whisper.

'You could have ruined this family.'

'What are you going to do?' I ask.

Dad pulls into our driveway. The house is lit up like a Christmas tree, but it seems so crass now. Guests' cars are still parked around our drive, and everything is just... normal. Yet how is that possible? How can everything have changed in the space of fifteen minutes?

The garage door opens up and over as we approach.

'Dad, shouldn't we have called an ambulance?'

I can see the sinews through Dad's flabby neck. He turns towards me, his eyes narrowed, his voice low and threatening. 'This is what is going to happen, Leonie. You are going to make your way up to your room, and you will stay there. You will never think about or discuss this accident ever again. Your university plans and the plans for working in our family business will not be derailed. You will not mention this to your mother, to your brother, to anyone ever in the future. Do you understand?'

I don't move.

'If you go to prison, the stain on my reputation will be devastating, and I'm not prepared to let that happen. You'll leave me to clear up your mess, and we will never, ever talk about this again. Give me your mobile phone.'

I hesitate, wondering where it is, but then glance down in the passenger footwell. My small handbag is there. With trembling fingers, I open the clasp and hand Dad my phone.

'Now go. Take the back staircase to your room and stay there. *Capiche?*'

I'm shaking so much I struggle to open the car door, but when I do, I race up to my room, tears and snot running down my face, blurring my sight. I shut the bedroom door behind me and collapse on the bed and sob. It's so cold. So very cold, so I pull the duvet over me and bury my head in the pillow.

I've just killed a man.

I've taken someone's life, just because I wanted to see my stupid boyfriend, who isn't really my boyfriend anyway. That poor person. His poor family. How will I ever live with my conscience? I go over that moment again and again. The lights blinding me from behind. Was that Dad? And then the other car. I swear it was on my side of the road, but was it really? Could I have imagined that? The swerving, the screeching, that terrible thump. Those thick black shoes and the immobile legs.

I hear footsteps outside my door, then the sound of a lock closing. *What the hell?* I rub my sore eyes with my knuckles and pad over to the door. I turn the handle and pull the door towards me. It's locked. Dad has locked me in.

As I sink to the floor, it hits me. Dad didn't ask how I was. Not once in our conversation did he check to ask if I was hurt.

2

LEONIE – NOW

The sun is high in the sky, and the sea is sparkling, looking more like the Mediterranean than the English Channel. I'm driving along a private road in an exclusive estate in Angmering, a village on the south coast, wedged in between Worthing and Littlehampton. The properties here are sumptuous, the ones facing the seafront so exclusive, they rarely come onto the open market. I suppose it's a little like the Hamptons in the States, not that I've ever visited, with huge houses in eclectic styles. Second homes for the mega-wealthy. I drive slowly as the seafront comes closer, and then my satnav tells me to take the first turning on the right. Sandcastle House. The sign at the front is discreet; the electric gates, not so. I press a button lit up in blue light on the metal keypad, and the gates silently slide apart. My heart always thumps a little harder as I approach a new property. It's the prospect of a deal, combined with an awe as to how the very wealthy live – and, if I'm being completely honest, nosiness. I love that my job takes me into people's homes, or rather, rich people's homes. It's not like I've ever had to slum it myself, but these houses are often at the billionaire rather than the millionaire level.

I run a business called Castaway Property Search. We find homes for wealthy people who are time poor, and famous people – and sometimes infamous – who value their privacy and would never contemplate living in a house that has been on the open market. I expanded my team of two to five this year, and I'm really proud of what we do. This year, we're on track to hit seven figures in sales, and I'm on speed dial with all the leading estate agents in the south of England. There's only one fly in the ointment, and that's Dad. He's my boss.

Yes, I had all of those plans to break free and work for governments, protecting valuable artefacts in war zones, but the fantasy never merged with the reality. I got into Oxford, got my degree in history of art, and then I did what Dad wanted and expected of me: I joined the family business straight out of university. To my surprise, I enjoyed working in the property world; I just didn't enjoy being barked at twenty-four seven by my father.

Frankly, I've no idea how his staff have stayed so loyal to him. I can only suppose that their hefty salaries buy their loyalty. No one could accuse Dad of favouritism, though. Oh no. He started me right on the bottom rung of his business, working in admin, photocopying, taking notes and making coffees. Then I was shipped off to a building site, shadowing a site manager, being wolf-whistled by the builders. Eventually, when I told Mum I wanted to leave, he moved me to the sales and marketing department. Yet despite working hard for five years, Dad refused to pay me what I felt was a fair wage.

'Can't abide nepotism,' he said. 'What'll the others expect if I up your pay just because you're my daughter?'

I was offered another job at a rival house developers, and when Dad found out, it was as if a nuclear bomb had exploded. I didn't really want to work anywhere else, but I did want autonomy and fair pay. So, as a compromise, I suggested I set up a property search arm. Dad dismissed the idea, but somehow Mum talked him around. He gave me a fancy office and a five-thousand-pound start-up fund. I actually think he expected me to fail, or even subconsciously wanted me to, but I didn't. Castaway Property Search is a success, yet still Dad doesn't recognise it. I suppose I should be used to the snide remarks and the rolling of his eyes, but it still hurts. Maybe it always will. I'm not sure I'll ever understand Dad. It's almost as if he's jealous of my success, yet he's a fifty-one percent shareholder, so if I do well, it reflects straight back on him. I park the car and stare at the house. Dad would like this one.

Sandcastle House bears absolutely no relation to a sandcastle. There are no turrets, no moat and nothing in a honey colour. I wonder whether the name is a legacy from a previous incarnation of a house on this site, because otherwise, the naming must be ironic. For this is the most modern of structures, brutalist even, with granite stone covering the walls and massive glass windows, darkened so it's not possible to see inside. The house is huge: three storeys high, with a vast glass atrium that extends cathedral-like up to the blue sky. Parked outside the anthracite grey door, which itself is at least double the size of a normal front door, is a shiny black Tesla. I park my BMW next to it and climb out of the car. Despite the sun and azure sky, there's a chilly breeze. I shiver as I stride to the door.

It opens before I ring the bell.

'Oh,' I say, immediately flustered and taking a step backwards.

A man walks out and stands so close to me, I catch a drift of woody aftershave.

'Apologies,' he says, extending his hand. 'I'm Markus Klausen. We spoke on the phone.'

I automatically put out my arm, and he clasps his hand around mine. His palm is cool and smooth, and he gently squeezes my hand, holding onto it for a fraction too long. I glance at his face, and his eyes gaze into mine. They are clear blue, pale yet rimmed with dark lashes. His eyes crease into a smile, and he lets go of my hand.

'You must be Denise.'

'Actually, no. My colleague Denise spoke to you on the phone, but I'm Leonie Wilding, the managing director of Castaway Property Search.'

'It's a pleasure to meet you, Ms Wilding, and I'm honoured that you chose to come today. Welcome to my humble abode.' He nods slightly.

I follow him into the atrium. While it looked impressive from the front of the house, inside it's even more so. Light pours in from the glass ceiling, and there's a view through the full width of the house, giving a glimpse of the sea in the distance. Yet despite the grandeur of the house, it's Markus who captures my attention. I feel his eyes on my face, my body, and every time I glance at him, there's a glint in his eye – a knowingness, if there's such a word. He's an extremely handsome man, with his starched white shirt open a button too low, hinting at a smooth, toned and bronzed chest. His dark jeans have a crease down the front, and they fit snugly over his muscular thighs, tapering down to slim ankles and shiny brown leather brogues.

He's saying something to me, but I miss the words.

'Sorry,' I say. 'I'm in awe of your house.' My laugh sounds forced, and I hope that the blush I feel on my cheeks doesn't give away the truth: that I'm in greater awe of this man than I am the house. I need to pull myself together. This is ridiculous. I don't do crushes or even relationships. My focus is on business. My heels clip-clop on the marble floor as I follow Markus Klausen through the hallway into the vast living room. The concertina glass doors run the full width of the room, giving a panoramic view over the sea, bringing the inside in. The room is tastefully decorated in the palest of hues, looking as if it has been designed by a top interior designer.

'You have amazing taste,' I say. 'Or your wife perhaps?'

'I don't have a wife.' His eyes bore into mine, and I have to look away. 'I used the services of a decorator. Would you like to see the kitchen?'

I nod and follow him through to the next room. It's even larger than the living room. The kitchen side of the room has an island unit made wholly out of white marble with grey veins, a double sink set in the middle with gold taps. There is a bank of four ovens, and the fridge is the largest I've ever seen, and I've seen plenty of oversized fridges in my time. Beyond the kitchen area is a glass table with fourteen metal-framed dining chairs. A chandelier made from thousands of sparkling diamantés hangs over the table, throwing dazzling spectrums of light.

'Wow,' I murmur. 'I'm surprised you want to leave this place.'

'It's too big for just me. It used to...' His words fade away.

'Well, now it's just me, I want to downsize and move away from the memories.' He stares out of the window towards the sea. An air of sadness settles on him, and I wonder what sort of loss he's suffered. Is Mr Klausen a widower, perhaps? I reckon he's late thirties – which seems too young, if that's the case. As we walk around the rest of the downstairs, passing through a study lined with bookshelves, a gym, a small indoor swimming pool and a vast utility room, I keep an eye out for family photographs. Strangely, there are none.

Upstairs, there are five bedrooms, all with en-suite bathrooms. The three on the rear side of the house have glass balconies with fabulous views stretching along the coastline and out to sea, where the banks of wind turbines on the horizon catch the light as they turn around and around. This house is immaculate, almost unlived in. I can think of at least four or five families on our books who would love this place. Londoners searching for their weekend house, or the odd investor wanting to rent it out on a weekly basis.

'And what are you looking for, Mr Klausen?' I ask.

'Please call me Markus.' There's a hint of a smile edging at his lips. 'I don't want anything like this. A two- or three-bedroom apartment in central London, ideally. I'm an investment banker and want to reduce my daily commute. A view of the Thames would be nice, along with underground parking and a roof terrace or balcony.'

'Have you started looking?' I ask.

He shakes his head. 'I just haven't had the time. I'm hoping that's what you'll do for me. Find me something perfect.'

'With pleasure. I'm very confident we'll find you a buyer for Sandcastle House and somewhere for you to downsize to. Do you have a preferred area in London?'

'Kensington or Chelsea, ideally.'

'Near our office, then,' I say unnecessarily. 'And budget?'

He looks away for a moment. 'Between three and five million.'

So he's good-looking and wealthy, a fine combination. But then I chastise myself. Even if this man was interested in me, the last thing I'm looking for is a relationship.

'Do you think you can help?' He tilts his head to one side and briefly bites on his bottom lip. That look makes my knees weaken. I shake my head. *Get a grip, girl!*

'Absolutely, we should be able to help. And I hope that we can find you a buyer for this beautiful home. Is your purchase in London dependent upon selling this property?'

He smiles coyly. 'No. Although I want to be shot of this house, as lovely as it is. Too many memories.'

'Of course. Can you show me the exterior?'

We walk around outside, where the wind whips my hair into my face, and I have to hold my skirt down to stop it from blowing upwards. When we're done, we end up back at the front door.

'Thank you very much,' I say, putting my hand out.

Markus Klausen hesitates, and I wonder if I've done something wrong.

'I know I shouldn't ask, and it's extremely unprofessional, but is there any possibility I could take you out for a drink?'

I'm totally flummoxed. I've had clients flirt with me, but never before has anyone asked me out like this – and, in particular, no one as handsome as Markus Klausen. I open my mouth, but I stumble over incoherent words like a complete idiot.

'I'm sorry, I shouldn't have asked,' he says, stepping backwards and grimacing with embarrassment. 'You're probably married or in a long-term relationship, someone as beautiful as you.'

'It's very kind of you, but I try not to mix work and pleasure.'

'Of course not. I should never have asked. Please forgive me. I'm sorry.'

And then it's as if he can't get me out of the house soon enough. Markus shuts the door quickly and disappears inside.

I can't stop thinking about Markus Klausen on the drive back to London. What has gone on in his life to make him want to leave that stunning house? I imagine his cool palm in mine and give a little involuntary shiver as I think about the chemistry, because there *was* chemistry, and it clearly wasn't just me who felt it. It isn't until Zac calls me to let me know that long-standing clients of mine, Mr and Mrs Cohen, have put in an offer on a grand house in Hampstead, and that the offer has been accepted, that my mind moves away from Markus Klausen.

Castaway Property Search's office is on the sixth floor of an office block in Knightsbridge. It's small, with just two rooms, but the location couldn't be better. And, exceptionally for central London, the office comes with two underground parking spaces. I could never have afforded the office, but Dad was insistent that if I was going to set up a property search business, I had to have the very best address money could buy. And as Dad has a lot of money, Knightsbridge it was, turning Harrods into my local shop.

But just because Dad is rolling in wealth doesn't mean that I am. I was determined to make my own way, and now I pay full rent and rates, plus the salaries of Zac, Mum – who works part-time – Denise, our new office manager, and Erin, our new search agent. If you first met me and knew about Mum and Dad, you'd think I was just some little rich girl, playing around in the kingdom of the wealthy. And yes, I could have been that person, except my conscience wouldn't let me, and to be fair to Dad, he didn't afford me any special treatment at work. I haven't touched a penny of my trust fund, and I don't intend to. If I have kids one day, the money can be theirs, or maybe I'll give it all away to a deserving charitable cause. But wealth is like a sticky coat. When we have it, people cling to us in the hope that our good luck will pass on to them. It gives us an air of impermeability, but it's a truism that money can't buy you everything. I'm not sure it's brought me happiness or luck, yet if I was ever bold enough to articulate that out loud, I know I'd be accused of being ungrateful. I guess it's a security blanket, but one I hope I never have to use.

The traffic into London is dreadful. By the time I arrive at the office, Mum has left, Zac is packing up, Erin is out, and Denise is typing rapidly.

'A drink?' Zac asks.

'No, I'm tired.'

'So a drink is exactly what you need, then. You up for joining us, Denise?'

She glances up. 'Give me five, and I'll meet you there. I just want to finish off these invoices.'

I sigh. There's no point in arguing with Zac. He's my best friend. We met at university, our rooms adjacent to each other in our halls of residence, and we've been inseparable ever since, except one small awkward period of about a month, eight years ago. We were at a nightclub. Neither of us were drinking, and I was feeling sad and lonely, although with the passing of the years, I can't remember why. Zac's relationship was on the rocks, but at that point, it wasn't quite over. As the music slowed down, he put his arms around me, and for the first time, I didn't push him away. That night, we slept together. Afterwards, we were both racked with guilt, agreed that it was a mistake and our friendship was more important. In the intervening years, Zac has had a string of girlfriends, mostly unsuitable, while I have focused on my business.

Eighteen months ago, Zac was made redundant from his sales and marketing position, and when I suggested he join me at Castaway, he leapt at the chance. They say you shouldn't mix friends and business, but it's worked for us. Zac is charming with our clients and has a great instinct for a deal. Unlike me, he's happy to cold-call, and will even resort to door knocking if need be. I owe the large upturn in our profits to my best friend.

Denise, on the other hand, is a newer friend. She joined our business recently as our first-ever office manager, in charge of accounts and all admin, yet it's as if she's been part of the team since the very beginning.

It's dark and raining, the lights of Knightsbridge glistening, the air heavy with fumes from cars and buses despite the low-emissions zone. We make our way to a small pub tucked behind the Victoria and Albert Museum, so hidden it's only frequented by locals.

'Lime and soda?' Zac asks me as he strides up to the bar. He's six feet two inches, with blond hair that curls over the collar of his starched white shirt and startling blue eyes that see more than they should.

'Thanks.' I'm a cheap date, and sometimes I wonder why I still don't drink alcohol. Would it really loosen my lips? I decided a decade ago that I would never put myself in a position where I might lose control; much to the bemusement of my fellow students, I was teetotal. I never touched drugs, either. It wasn't, and still isn't, worth the risk. Zac thinks he knows everything about me, except he doesn't. I have never told him about the accident; never explained that I killed another human being, never let him know that my dreams are fractured and terrifying. Never admitted that I dread spending the night with someone, in case I sleep talk and my subconscious brain shares my darkest secret.

'How was the coastal house?' Zac asks, placing my lime and soda in front of me, a beer for himself and a white wine for Denise, who arrives just as Zac sits down.

'It's foul out there,' she mutters, peeling off her raincoat. 'Thanks for the drink, Zac.'

'I was just asking Leonie how she got on this afternoon.'

My mind leaps to Markus Klausen, and despite myself, I can feel my cheeks redden.

Zac peers at me. 'Got something to tell us, Leonie?'

Damn. He knows me too well. 'No!' I laugh. 'It's just the owner was exceptionally good-looking, and he asked me out.'

Denise claps her hands. 'Did you say yes?'

'Of course not,' I reply. 'I can't mix pleasure and business.'

'Oh, come on,' Zac says, rolling his eyes at me. 'Everyone meets their partner through work.'

'I met my ex through my last job,' Denise says. 'Our boss was so annoyed we started dating, she moved our desks so that we were facing each other. Every time I glanced up from my computer, there he was, filling my field of vision.'

'Eww, awkward,' Zac says.

'Yeah. The relationship didn't last long. It's one thing

choosing to be with someone day and night, another being forced into it.'

'Clever tactics,' I add. 'But Markus Klausen is a client, so it's different.'

'No, it's not! There's nothing to say you can't date a client.' Zac turns to Denise. 'Do you realise this woman hasn't been on a date in five years?'

'Jeez,' Denise says, running her fingers through her damp, blonde hair. 'But why? You're gorgeous.'

'I've been too busy with the business.' That's a lie, of course. I just don't want to be vulnerable, to put myself in a position where I might be hurt, or to get so close to someone, I'll feel I have to tell them my sordid truth.

'Have you ever had a long-term relationship?' Denise asks. I wonder when we morphed from being colleagues to friends and shuffle awkwardly on the chair.

'The answer to that question is no,' Zac answers for me. 'I think you and me have got some work to do.' He winks at Denise.

3

CARRIE

'You're late. Again.'

I try to sneak past Fiona, my witch of a boss, but she has eyes in the back of her head, with antennae that focus on me and my supposed misdemeanours. She even looks like a witch, with her dark grey hair pulled back in a bun and a hooked nose.

'Sorry. The bus didn't show.'

'It's your final warning, Carrie. If you're late again, I'll ring the agency and ask for a replacement.'

When she turns her back on me, I stick my middle finger up in the air and hope she doesn't really have eyes in the back of her head. It might be childish, but it makes me feel better. Susan, who sits next to me and has worked for the company since it was set up twenty years ago, tuts loudly. She dislikes me as much as I dislike her, treating me as if I'm some dumb kid. I've never bothered to tell her that I have a first-class honours degree in business and, once upon a time, ran a company that made this place look like a backwards dump. There's no point, because then I'd have to share my story and watch the pity distort my colleagues' faces as they realise how very low I've sunk. I prefer to keep myself to myself.

I work in admin for a mail-order clothing brand, which, if you live in the UK, you'll have heard of, because they send out way too many catalogues. And don't believe a word of their promise to plant a tree for every catalogue printed. You've probably bought from them; I did, once upon a time, when I had money to spare. I'm in the returns department, which is depressing in the extreme. The offices are in a portacabin-type building bolted on to a massive warehouse, which is the fulfilment centre. Frankly, I'd rather be in there, bantering with the guys who race their forklift trucks up and down the loading bays. But no, I sit in front of a computer all day long, my eyes squinting and my scarred shoulders tight with knots.

I don't even decide what gets refunded and what doesn't. That's Susan's job, and she loves the power it gives her, tutting and moaning with what people try to get away with – hiding the tag, wearing the item and then returning it covered in foundation or lipstick or even mud. Good luck to them. If I needed something half-decent for a night out, that's what I'd do, because who's got the money these days to treat themselves to a new dress? All I do is scan the return barcodes and make sure they're properly logged.

Truth be told, I don't find it easy to hold down a job. I get bored too easily, and then I open my big mouth and offend someone, the boss, normally. Perhaps I've acquired ADHD or something similar as a result of my injuries, because I sure didn't have a problem concentrating in my previous life. I also get panic attacks, and I've had horrible withdrawal symptoms coming off the drugs, which has meant I've had to take weeks off work, relying on benefits.

The thing is, I'm still the same person deep down, and I want to work. I want to earn my own way to get out of the dump that's my current life. It's just I haven't got the energy. Every few months I start again, full of good intentions, and then things go awry.

'Carrie.'

I'm zoned out. I think I just logged the same return three times, but what the hell. It'll be Amber Scott's lucky day.

'Carrie!'

I yank my earphones out. 'Yeah! You don't have to bloody shout at me.' I glower at Susan.

'Don't swear.'

I roll my eyes. What is she, the morality police?

'It's Tom's birthday, and we're doing a collection. Fiona is buying him a present, and we're all going for a drink at the pub.'

'Sorry, but I don't have any spare change to give to someone who does a sarcastic wolf whistle every time I walk past him.'

'Don't be so miserly. You got a present on your birthday.'

'If you're talking about the sickly strawberry-smelling liquid soap that was discounted to £2.99 at Superdrug, then yeah, thank you very much, but no thank you.'

I put my earphones back in and turn my back on Susan. Okay. I'm being a cow, but I don't have any spare money. I've barely got enough to eat, let alone pay the bills, and that's living in a shared dump. If I could be generous, believe me, I would. It's just generosity is in short supply these days, both on the giving and receiving front.

On the dot of 5 pm, I switch off my computer, and I'm out of there. It would be easier to take the tube home, but the underground isn't good for me. I had a panic attack on the Circle Line about a year ago. I was convinced I was dying, unable to breathe, the walls of the train caving in on me, all of those strangers' faces distorting into terrifying masks. I'm not risking it again, so I take the bus. Or more like three buses, because the connections are crap. That's London for you. Sometimes I reckon I could fly to Italy and back in the time it takes me to get home.

I live in a crappy shared apartment in Peckham. There are four of us, and I've got the smallest and worst room by far, with barely enough space to move around my lumpy single bed. I stomp into the flat and am hit by the stench of Indian cooking. Don't get me wrong, I love a good curry. But my roommates, and Kayla in particular, don't know how to cook, so whatever is going on in the kitchen is being massacred. There's thumping music coming from the living room and giggling voices. I push open my creaking bedroom door without saying hello to the others.

'What the hell!' I exclaim.

There are two people with limbs entangled lying on my bed, their clothes scattered on the worn carpet.

'What are you doing in here?' I screech.

Kayla stretches her arms lazily above her head, pushing away a woman I've never seen before. They're both stark naked. Kayla giggles and says, 'You need to get up, Dolls.'

Whoever Dolls is sits up, her pendulous breasts swinging as she twists her legs off the bed.

'What the hell are you doing in my room?' I ask Kayla, narrowing my eyes.

Dolls picks up her clothes and blows me a kiss before squeezing past me out of the room.

'Got a bit carried away,' Kayla says as she yawns. 'And this bed was the nearest.'

'Get the hell out of my room!' I say, grabbing one of her ankles.

'No need to get worked up.' She kicks her ankle free of my grip.

Something snaps inside me. How dare Kayla have sex with some random woman on my bed in my private space, a space I pay much too much to rent! This tiny room is all I have that is solely mine, and now she's desecrated it. Sparks flash in front of my eyes, and before I know what I'm doing, I'm grabbing her long hair and tugging her off the bed, kicking her bare limbs as she struggles to break free.

'What the hell are you doing!' Kayla screams. There's a thump as she bangs her head on the side of the bed, and I let go. She's right. What the hell am I doing?

She stands up, rubs the back of her head and glowers at me. 'Psycho,' she says before scuttling out of my room.

I slam the door behind her and sink onto the floor. *Shit.* My life is a mess. I'm going to have to look for somewhere else to live, because I can't risk Kayla reporting me to the police for assault, and that's exactly the sort of right-on thing that she would do. She calls herself an activist, a feminist and an all-round, anti-establishment, gender-neutral human being. She may not like the police, but I've little doubt she'd throw me to the wolves. I start packing up straight away, but after filling one suitcase, I start crying. Big, ugly tears flow down my face as I realise what a mess my life is. I have no home of my own, no car, no savings, no partner and no friends except my mates from Narcotics Anonymous, and it's not like they're the most reliable of friends. There's no point in storming out tonight, because I have absolutely nowhere else to go. I'll look for another flat share and get out of here as soon as I can.

I change the sheets on my bed and lie down, scrolling through my phone. An article pops up about a German heiress who pretended she was worth a fortune. She mingled in high society and racked up debts of millions, because, in fact, she was a nobody without a penny to her name. I can't help but admire people like that, with such gumption, so little fear, they actually get away with it. It makes me think. Perhaps that's what I should do: fake it until I make it. I sure as hell don't want to stay here all evening, listening to that headbanging music, trying not to gag from the stench of burned Indian food.

My only smart, little black dress lies on top of the open suitcase. I get off the bed, remove my work clothes and pull the dress on. It's got long sleeves and sits just below my knees, covering up all my scars and fitting like a glove. I stare at myself in the mirror attached to the wardrobe door. My long blonde hair tumbles over my shoulders, hiding the scars on my neck. I paste on some makeup, slip my feet into a pair of stilettos and smile at myself. I look good.

I sneak out of the flat without seeing any of the others and walk briskly towards the bus stop, careful not to wedge my thin heels into cracks in the pavement. It's my lucky day. The number 12 bus pulls up just as I arrive. I hop on it and climb to the upper deck. Covent Garden, here I come.

I choose the first smart hotel that I walk past. A uniformed doorman stands outside, and I nod at him as I walk through the revolving doors into a wood-panelled reception area. Piano music tinkles, and the air smells of roses, but I don't want to hang around here in case the staff ask me questions. I stride straight through the reception area and turn right onto a corridor. About halfway along, there's a blackboard on a stand:

Will and Martha's Engagement Party.

I glance through the open door, and there must be a couple of hundred people milling inside a room decorated with coffee-coloured and cream roses. They hang from the ceiling, around the window frames, off monstrous candelabras six feet tall, and the guests, mostly wearing cocktail dresses and open-necked shirts, are sipping champagne. If Will and Martha are spending this much on an engagement party, I can't begin to imagine what their wedding will be like.

'Good evening, ma'am,' a waitress says as she edges past me, holding a tray of champagne glasses.

'Thank you.' I lift off a glass and walk into the room. I tip back half the glass to give myself Dutch courage.

'Are you Will or Martha's guest?' It takes a moment to realise that the middle-aged man at my side is addressing me. His hair is thinning, and his belly protrudes over his black suit trousers.

'Martha's,' I say. 'And you?'

'I'm Will's boss. Hugo Pendlethorpe.' He extends his hand, and I shake it. His palm is clammy, and he squeezes my hand too tightly.

'Carrie White.' I tilt my head to one side and flutter my eyelids. 'They make such a stunning couple, don't you think?' I make sure that I speak in plum tones, rounding off my words, pronouncing every syllable.

'Absolutely,' he agrees.

'And Martha is so happy. It fills my heart with joy.'

'What a lovely sentiment. So what do you think of the champagne, or rather the sparkling white wine? Ridiculous that we can't call it champagne just because it's grown in the UK rather than France. I invested in a vineyard near Rheims, but I sold it last year and bought into a British winery in East Sussex. I'm expecting great things.'

'It's delicious,' I say, although as the last time I drank champagne was over a decade ago, I'm not sure I'm the best to judge.

'Are you here with your partner?' He licks his fleshy lips as he glances at my ringless fingers.

'No, I don't have a partner. And you?' I step a little closer to him, invading his personal space. I notice a slight shine of sweat bloom on his brow.

'Um, no. I'm divorced, and work gets in the way of relationships. You know what it's like!' His laugh is fake.

I can't say that I do, but I just smile at him, tilting my head slightly and blinking quickly. I take another sip of champagne and keep my eyes on his. 'Looks like we were meant to meet,' I say huskily.

'Would you... Would you be free to have dinner with me, Carrie? I'm a member of the Roundstone Club, and they serve fine cuisine up until midnight.'

'Well, thank you,' I say. 'That would be a pleasure.'

The truth is, I'm bloody starving. I can't remember the last time I had a decent meal, and although this man is unattractive and boorish, he's easy pickings. Lonely, rich and reckoning he's going to get lucky tonight. Who knows? He might, depending upon his level of wealth. Perhaps he'll be my ticket out of my current mess. And then I chastise myself: *Let's not run before we walk.*

'So what do you do, Carrie?' he asks as we walk side by

side out of the reception room and back to the main entrance.

'I have my own women's clothing brand. I'm a designer.'

'Wow,' Hugo says. 'I should have been able to tell that just by looking at you.'

I want to howl with laughter. The dress I'm wearing comes from Tesco! Yes, the supermarket. I wonder how shocked Hugo Pendlethorpe would be if he knew that. And better still, I stole it, so it didn't cost me a penny.

'Hold on one sec,' he says as we arrive at the hotel reception desk.

'Can you get my car for me?' he asks the concierge. 'It's Hugo Pendlethorpe, and I've got a black Porsche, registration HP 002.'

'Of course, sir. My colleague will drive it around to the front of the hotel.'

He turns towards me. 'I need the little boys' room. Won't be a tick,' he says and winks at me. *Yuk.*

A couple of minutes later, a black Porsche pulls up at the entrance. I walk towards it and hold my hand out to the concierge. To my surprise, he gives me the key. I hesitate for a moment. I could get in this car, drive it away and cash it in for serious money, and that would be the end of my problems. Except, of course, it wouldn't. This is central London; there are CCTV cameras everywhere. The car's probably got a tracker in it and an immobiliser. Instead, I walk around to the passenger side and climb into the car. A couple of moments later, Hugo is next to me in the driver's seat.

We drive in silence for a few minutes, me enjoying the comfortable leather seat and the warmth of the car.

'Change of plan,' he says as he weaves through the streets of Mayfair. 'I thought we could go back to mine, and we'll order in. You can try some of the wine from my vineyard. You don't mind, do you?'

'Of course not.' I can't decide if I do or don't mind. If he tries anything that I don't like, I've got a few self-defence tricks that should overpower him, especially as he looks like he hasn't been inside a gym in the past decade. We pull up into an underground garage, and he parks his car in between an Aston Martin and a convertible Mercedes. As we go up in the lift to the penthouse, I wonder if I've just got very lucky. If this is genuinely his home, this penthouse in this luxury building, then Hugo Pendlethorpe is undoubtedly loaded. We step straight into a vast living room with ceiling-to-floor windows looking over the rooftops of London.

'Wow,' I say as I stare at the lights.

'It's fabulous, isn't it?' Hugo steps next to me and places a hot hand on the small of my back. 'Not that my wife thought it was up to scratch. I'll open a bottle of bubbly, but what would you like to order in to eat? Chinese, Japanese, Thai?'

'You choose,' I say. 'But I've got a very healthy appetite.'

A flush creeps up his neck, and I realize he thinks that was a double entendre. It wasn't. I'm just starving.

Twenty minutes later, we're seated on his white leather sofa, drinking champagne, and Hugo is talking at me. I don't care. It means that I can zone out, enjoy the surroundings and tip back the booze. When the doorbell rings, he hurries towards it and returns with three large freezer bags. Takeaways don't come in white cardboard boxes with silver lids over here. Instead, everything is packed in ceramic dishes, and even the cutlery is provided. He places everything on a glass table, and we both dig in. I've absolutely no idea what I'm eating, but it's delicious, and I can't get enough of it.

'I love a woman with a healthy appetite.' Hugo grins at

me. His face swims in and out of view, and I realise I've drunk more than I thought. 'You're so beautiful,' he says.

'Thanks.' It's hard to keep up the posh accent with this amount of alcohol sloshing inside me. 'You must be very wealthy,' I say. I wonder if my bluntness will scare him off, but he just laughs.

'I do all right. My ex-wife kept the house in Hampshire, but I've still got the chalet in the Alps. Do you ski?'

I want to laugh hysterically. I guess he didn't notice my limp, but even if I could physically ski, where the hell would the money come from?

'I used to,' I say, 'but these days, I prefer to spend my summer yachting around Greece and Turkey.'

'You have a boat?' He looks impressed.

'Yes, but I haven't got a clue how to sail it. I have a crew for that.' It crosses my mind that I will have to sell the imaginary boat if Hugo and I become an item, because although he's not my type physically, I can push any of that to one side for the money.

'Can I kiss you, Carrie?' Hugo has edged his chair right next to mine.

'Of course you can, Hugo,' I say. I turn to him and squeeze my eyes shut. I haven't had this much luck in years. He puts a hand behind my head and pulls me towards him. Against all odds, Hugo knows how to kiss. Well, that's quite the surprise. And then he's holding my hand and pulling me towards the vast leather sofa, and although I'm not the sort of girl to sleep with a man on the first date, my body is craving touch.

He pushes me down onto the sofa and kneels next to me, kissing me again, and then his hands are everywhere, and he's pulling the tight black dress over my head, and I'm just going to enjoy the sensations and keep my eyes squeezed shut and pretend that he's George Clooney.

And then he stops. I feel a chill on my bare skin, and I open my eyes. Hugo is standing next to the sofa, his shirt open and his fat hairy stomach exposed, staring at me, a look of disgust on his face.

'I'm sorry. I shouldn't have. I made a mistake. You see, I'm still married, and my wife… I shouldn't be doing this. I'm really sorry, Carrie, but it's best that you leave.' He picks up my dress and shoves it towards me; then he turns away and walks towards the windows.

The bastard.

The complete and utter bastard.

Neither of us say a word. I dress quickly and hurry out of his flat. I let his front door close gently behind me and then jab the lift button. This isn't the first time I've been rejected like that, and no doubt won't be the last.

My body disgusts. My misshapen, scarred body, rough and rubbery to the touch, is revolting. Dressed in a figure-hugging black dress, the wrapper promises so much, but what you see on the outside is an illusion. I am broken. Physically, mentally and emotionally.

As I stumble out into the cold London night, I let out a screech. Hugo fucking Pendlethorpe, with his thinning hair and piggy eyes and sagging body, has rejected me. I'm more revolting than he is. Worthless. And very, very angry.

4

LEONIE

'Markus Klausen rang, and he's picking you up from the office at 5 pm this evening,' Denise says. 'Which is in precisely fifteen minutes.'

'What?' I push my chair backwards from my glass desk. 'Which property does he want to see?'

'Mmm,' Denise says, with a wide grin on her face, her chin balanced on her fingers with her index finger pointing upwards. 'No property. Just you.'

'Bloody hell, Denise. What have you done?'

'It was Zac, actually. He and your mum decided it was about time you had a date. Markus rang to talk to you when you were out, and, well, the conversation just went in the right way.'

'I can't believe you all did that!' I exclaim, standing up and pacing the office. 'I don't even have nice clothes on.'

Denise tips her head to one side. 'You look great. You always look great, Leonie. A swipe of mascara and lippy and you're ready to go.'

'I'm not in the mood. I'm really tired and was going to flake in front of the telly tonight.'

Denise gives me one of her looks, and I sigh. 'Okay, I'll get ready.'

OUR OFFICE IS OPEN-PLAN, although we have one small meeting room off to the side where I can talk to clients in private. Mum, who works here part time, mans the reception desk and the phones. Zac and Denise sit at large kidney-shaped desks facing the entrance, and I sit behind them at my glass desk, directly under the window that looks onto busy Knightsbridge. Erin, the newest of my recruits, has the desk next to me, although she's rarely in the office. On the whole, we go to meet our clients rather than them coming here. It's not like we have a shopfront on a shopping street, advertising the properties we've got for sale. Our service is discreet and upmarket, and we pride ourselves on working quietly and efficiently behind the scenes, helping our clients acquire the house of their dreams.

We share the bathroom facilities with the office next door, which is some financial services holding company that probably does some dodgy dealings, because it's rare there's anybody there. I try to make myself look passable and wish I'd washed my hair this morning and put on a dress rather than the ill-fitting trousers I wear when I'm doing site visits to unfinished properties. But this will have to do. As Denise suggested, the lipstick helps. As I stride back into the office, I hear his deep, honey-coated voice, and my limbs freeze.

'There she is,' Denise says. She winks at me as Markus turns around. He's wearing a navy blue suit and a white shirt with an open collar, and he's clutching a bouquet of hand-tied flowers – my favourite, tulips, even though it's out of season, and I've no idea where he's found them.

'For you,' he says, blinking almost bashfully.

'How did you know?' I say, accepting the bouquet.

'Know what?' he asks.

'That tulips are my favourite.'

'I didn't know, but they're my favourite, too. I love their promise of spring, despite it now being autumn. I'm glad we have similar taste.' There's an awkward pause before he asks, 'Are you ready to go out?'

Markus takes me to a wine bar in a mews tucked behind Knightsbridge. They serve champagne cocktails, and nibbles are canapés of gravlax and sushi. We sit in plush velvet chairs with a small glass-and-bronze coffee table wedged between us.

'I hope you didn't think this was too forward of me,' Markus says. 'I just really wanted to see you again, and as I was in the area this afternoon, I thought I'd see if you were free.'

'My colleagues took the decision out of my hands.'

'I hope I haven't inconvenienced you,' he says.

'Not at all.' I can't stop the blush rising into my cheeks.

We sit awkwardly for a moment and then both speak at the same time. 'You first,' he says.

'I haven't had the chance to find you any properties yet,' I say.

He shuffles forwards so his right knee is almost touching mine. 'Let's not talk about work. So tell me, Leonie, what do you do in your spare time?'

'I know it makes me sound boring, but not much. The business is all-consuming, and by the time I get home, I tend to flop in front of the television. Or if I have the energy, put on loud music and bake a cake. I like brisk country walks, not that I do those often enough.'

'Me too. I used to have a dog, and the best weekends were spent walking along the Downs, lunching in a pub and then getting back home to a hot bath. I miss that.'

'I'd love to have a dog, but working and living in central London, it's not really possible.'

Conversation flows easily, and we discover that we have distant but mutual friends from my days at Oxford. After our third round of drinks, Markus glances at his watch.

'I'm so sorry, Leonie, but I'm going to have to go. I promised to meet up with a colleague who is back in the UK for one night only.'

I can't help but feel a wave of disappointment. The past two hours have sped past, and I rather hoped our drinks might lead on to dinner and perhaps more.

'Of course,' I say awkwardly. 'I need to get home to finish off some work.'

'I was wondering whether you might join me for dinner tomorrow night?'

'Tomorrow?' I'm taken aback.

'Is that too soon? Too forward?'

'No, no. Not at all. I'd love to.' It's such a relief that he must feel the same way, that he's not going to play games and keep me guessing or waiting.

Markus beams at me, and as he helps me into my coat, he places a quick kiss on my cheek that sends electric sparks throughout my body.

The next twenty-four hours pass painfully slowly. All I can think about is handsome Markus Klausen, and I spend the day hunting down suitable properties for him in Kensington and Chelsea, my other clients forgotten. Eventually, it's time to meet Markus for dinner, and this time I've brought in a change of clothes, and I'm dressed up in a short black dress with long over-the-knee suede boots that show off my slender legs. Denise whistles as I leave the office, and I throw her a filthy look. She tips her head back and guffaws.

Markus is already at the restaurant, and he jumps up the moment he sees me, pulling back my chair, pouring me a glass of champagne from a bottle of Laurent-Perrier standing in an ice bucket.

'I've made something for you,' he says. 'I hope you don't think it's naff or old-fashioned.' He reaches into his jacket pocket and produces a pen drive.

'What's on this?' I ask as he slides it across the table.

'A playlist of some of my favourite songs.'

'That's really kind.' No one has ever done that for me.

We make small talk about the weather and a hike Markus took along the Sussex seafront last weekend.

'How did you get into the property business?' he asks, taking a sip of champagne.

'Dad has a property business, Wilding International, and they do large domestic and commercial developments. Mum helps out in my business, too.'

'So Castaway Property Search is a family business?'

'Um, no. Not really. It's mine.' I'm not going to go into the ownership details and the fact that Dad expects me to report into him on a fortnightly basis and that ultimately he controls the purse strings.

'Do you have any siblings?' he asks.

'My brother, Sam, but he's not in the business.'

'And your parents, do they live in London?'

'Sam and I were brought up in Horsham in West Sussex, and my parents still have a house there, although they mostly live in London during the week.'

We're interrupted by the server. 'What can I get you both to eat?' he asks.

I flip open the leather-backed menu, but Markus leans forwards and places his hand on it. 'Do you have any dietary requirements?'

'No,' I say.

'In which case, let's get the tasting menu.'

'Two tasting menus?' the server asks.

'Yes, please,' Markus says before I can even question what that means. 'I've eaten it here before, and it's amazing. You'll love it,' Markus reassures me. 'And if you don't, I'll eat yours!'

I'm a little taken aback by his forcefulness, because I like to choose my own food, but Markus seems so earnest, I decide to let it go.

'And your brother? Does he work in the property sector, too?' Markus asks.

I smile. 'No, Sam lives in South Africa.'

'Older or younger?'

'Older, and he's not interested in property.'

What I don't tell Markus is that Sam walked away from everything. He couldn't cope with the heavy expectations that Dad laid on his shoulders: the expectation that he would forgo all his own interests to take over the family business, the incessant arguments that Sam wasn't bright enough, didn't work hard enough, lacked focus and drive. He travelled for a year after school, but then gave in to Dad's nagging and went to university. Halfway through his second year, he quit. I know he had a massive argument with Dad when they were discussing Sam's future, but Sam has refused to share the details. But it must have been bad for my brother to take a flight to Cape Town and then send a message to Mum and Dad saying he had emigrated. I have never seen Dad so angry and Mum so disappointed. For a time, they cut him off altogether, and I wired him money from my healthy allowance. Of course I did; he was penniless and alone on the other side of the world.

These days he returns to the UK once or occasionally twice a year, and relations between him and our parents are still frosty. Our parents, Gus and Brenda, think he's a failure. They're forever disparaging about his work as a sometimes surfing instructor, other times historical tour guide. They don't understand his love of military history and his forever increasing library of books; they can't see that their son is truly happy with his simple life, that a modest income doesn't equal failure.

I respect Sam and just wish I had his strength of character. But I can't ever walk away from Wilding International. Unlike my brother, I owe Dad too much. Sam, of course, doesn't understand why I'm willing to remain under Dad's thumb. Whenever he questions it, I just say that I love the property business. And I do, on the whole.

The first dish arrives, and it's a medley of beetroot cooked in several different ways. The flavours burst onto my tongue.

'What about you and your family?' I ask Markus. I can't stop wondering about his personal circumstances; what made him leave that beautiful coastal home?

'I'm the only child of parents who are now sadly deceased. I grew up in squalor on a fabulous estate in Scotland, living in a draughty castle with a moat and several thousand acres of Scottish wilderness. Typically asset rich and cash poor. I was sent off to boarding school at a young age and then, much to my parents' dismay, ditched university and went straight to work in the city. I was a trader for many years and now am involved in investments and private equity.' He pauses and then locks his eyes onto mine. 'My long working hours weren't conducive to relationships.'

'Have you ever been married?' I ask.

He shakes his head. 'I've never met the right woman.' He holds my eyes for too long, and I feel a flush creep up my neck. 'But I haven't been a monk. I've had a couple of long-term relationships, hence the big house in Angmering. Honestly, Leonie, I've had enough of games. I want to settle down, start a family. Grow up, I suppose.'

'And why the move to London?'

'I'm after a simpler, easier life. No commuting, nearer to my friends. Being able to go out for dinner in places like this without having to worry about who's driving home.'

'I've found you a few potential properties,' I say.

'I'd love to look at them. Can we talk tomorrow?'

The rest of the evening passes in a blur of scrumptious food and non-stop conversation. When, eventually, Markus asks for the bill, we realize we're the last couple in the restaurant. We hurry outside, where the air is damp and cold, and I do an involuntary shiver. Markus pulls me to him and wraps his arms around me, he then gently lowers his lips to mine, and we kiss. It's long, passionate, and as the sensations begin to thaw my out-of-practice body, I know that I am lost. Every fibre of my being craves this man, so when he eventually pulls away and gently strokes the hair from my face and says, 'Can I call you a taxi to take you home?' disappointment courses through me.

A black cab with its orange sign lit up approaches, and Markus steps forwards, his arm outstretched. To my frustration, the taxi pulls over and comes to a halt in front of us.

'I want it, too,' Markus whispers into my ear. 'But I've got to get up at the crack of dawn tomorrow.'

I'm glad of the darkness as I feel my face redden.

'Are you free in the afternoon, to show me some of those properties?' he asks.

'I'll check my diary and let you know,' I promise. 'And thank you for a wonderful evening.'

'It's me who needs to thank you, Leonie. It was a glorious evening.'

The next day, I'm buzzing. I'm in the office, trying and failing to concentrate. Zac scrunches up his eyes at me. 'There's something different about you.'

'The date!' Denise squeals. 'How did it go?'

Erin stops what she's doing and stares at me, as if she's waiting for a debrief. She's only worked here for just over a fortnight, and I'm conscious of behaving unprofessionally in front of her.

'Really well,' I say. I turn my attention to my computer. When I glance up again, all three of them are staring at me.

'You can't leave it at that!' Zac says.

'I'm showing him some properties this afternoon.'

Denise does a whoop-whoop noise, and I try to ignore my coworkers.

I meet Markus outside a portered block of flats off Sloane Avenue. He's looking more casual today in a smart pair of black jeans and a pale blue open-necked shirt with a black wool coat over his arm. The apartment has three good-sized bedrooms and a view over the wide street below, but Markus doesn't seem enamoured.

'I hope you don't mind me saying, but I find this a bit soulless. I'd like something modern, but it also needs some character.' He reaches to me and squeezes my hand.

'All right,' I say, because I agree with him. 'I've got a mews house to show you off the King's Road.'

Markus seems more impressed with it, but I can tell this isn't the one for him. I've shown enough properties to clients to know immediately if it's property love at first sight. There's a spark in the viewers' eyes, a slight breathlessness as they pace around, looking once, twice, three times throughout the property. And Markus seems more interested in me than whether the marble in the kitchen is from Italy, or if the outside space is large enough for a BBQ. The third property is a maisonette near South Kensington. It's empty of furniture except a large king-size bed that has been left in the master bedroom. Markus does a swizzle, as if he's taking in a 360-degree view, and then suddenly his hands are around my waist and he's kissing me so hard my lips feel as if they're being bruised. And then he's pushing me gently onto the bed, and I want this more than I've ever wanted anything.

'We shouldn't,' I say breathlessly. 'I shouldn't.'

'You're too beautiful, Leonie. I can't control myself around you.' And then he pauses, raising himself up on his elbows to stare into my eyes. 'You want it too, don't you? Because if you don't...' His words drift away, and I lift my hands up, my fingers in his hair, and bring his head back down to meet mine.

We make love right here in this empty apartment, and the excitement, the very naughtiness of it makes my body scream for more. Markus is both passionate and caring, without a doubt the best lover I have ever had. And when it's all over, I find myself simultaneously crying and laughing, because I've never done anything like this before, and I don't want this moment to ever end.

'Have we just christened your new home?' I ask as I lie on the bed, tracing my fingers around Markus' lips, both appalled and slightly impressed at my unprofessionalism.

'No, I'm sorry. I'm afraid I'm falling in love with the agent and not the property.'

I'm startled for a moment because Markus has just used the *love* word, and we barely know each other. The attraction is undeniable, but falling in love? And then, as if he realises he's spoken out of turn, he's up off the bed, throwing my clothes at me and getting dressed himself. 'Race you to it!' he says.

Afterwards, we go to a bistro near South Kensington tube station, and then suddenly, Markus glances at his watch. 'I've got to go if I'm going to get the last train home.' He groans.

'You could stay with me,' I suggest.

He stares at me, those blue eyes making my insides melt all over again.

'Really? Are you sure?'

I bite the side of my lip. 'Only if you're up for a repeat.' I grin.

'I'm up for a repeat all night long,' he says, trailing a finger across my lips.

And so, after our meal, which he insists on paying for once again, we walk hurriedly towards my mews house, just a few hundred metres away.

My home is tucked away on a cobbled street between South Kensington and Earl's Court. Dad acquired the property as part of a larger development, and he gifted it to me for my twenty-fifth birthday. I have every intention of paying him back, because it's not right that someone of my age is living in such a prestigious London address mortgage- or rent-free. Every month, I've been putting aside money into an interest-bearing account. Eventually, I intend to pay him the full lump sum.

I have two bedrooms, both with en-suites, and a large living room with a vaulted ceiling with skylights that flood the room with daylight. The kitchen is open-plan, and it's sleek and modern. But Markus doesn't seem to notice my home with its neutral decoration and the occasional pop of bright colour. Markus is just interested in me.

That first night sets the tone for the coming weeks. Four out of five weekday nights, Markus stays with me. I give him a key, and in return, he couldn't be more caring. At the weekends, he brings me breakfast in bed; after long workdays, I return to him cooking in my kitchen, producing stews and pies and roasts with a flourish. Flowers arrive for me at work, just because, and on my birthday, he whisks me away for a weekend staying at a luxury spa hotel in the North Downs.

In the early days, I was terrified of my dreams; terrified I'd have my recurring nightmare of being stuck in the wreckage of a car, unable to get out; terrified that I might say something I regret in my sleep. But sleeping in Markus' arms seems to keep the dreams at bay, and when I asked him if I ever spoke in my sleep, he frowned at me and said I was the quietest, least wriggly sleeper he'd ever met.

It's not long before Mum says that I should introduce her to my boyfriend. Zac and Denise say the same, but for now, Markus and I are so wrapped up in each other, I just want to keep him for myself. These early days seem so precious. It isn't until much, much later that I wonder whether subconsciously I knew my world was going to fall apart, and that's why I savoured every single moment with my new love.

5

CARRIE

'How was your week, Carrie?' Melanie Pleat leans forwards in her chair. She has a kind, open face and hair cropped short that changes in colour from black to silvery grey depending upon the season. Her therapy room has bright white walls and pictures of the sea. She sits on a brown seat that swivels, and she faces me, where I sit on the cream sofa. I've sat here for so many hours over the past years, it's a wonder the seat hasn't moulded to my backside.

'Not the best week,' I say.

'Why's that?' Melanie has an everlasting pot of patience. Sometimes she's so kind I just want to thump her.

'I had a bad date.'

'What's a bad date?'

I sigh. 'He took me back to his place, gave me food and drink, and then we started to make out. When he saw my body, he couldn't get me out of there fast enough.'

'What do you mean, when he saw your body?'

'I was in my bra and pants, and he saw all my scars, and then it was 'I've made a mistake, I'm still in a relationship, I think you should leave'. It was pretty bloody obvious, the disgust on his face. And who can blame him? I am disgusting. Disfigured, revolting.'

'Oh, Carrie,' Melanie says, disappointment in her voice. 'Could you perhaps be wrong, and he really was overcome by guilt?'

'Nope. He wasn't even subtle about it.'

'If someone loves you, he won't care about your scars. How many dates had you been on with this man?'

I scoff. 'Dates? No. This was a hookup.'

'Which really isn't what you need, is it? You've said yourself that you'd like a loving, mutually respectful relationship.'

'There's a difference between what I want and what I can get. Who wants me?' I wave my hands around. 'I'm second-hand goods, gross.'

'We've talked about this many times before, Carrie. You are so much more than your physical body. It's you as a whole person that someone will fall in love with. It clearly wasn't meant to be with this man.'

I chew at the side of my fingernail. Melanie is sounding like a worn record.

'Look, I've decided that today is my last session. Therapy isn't helping me.'

Melanie frowns. 'You've come such a long way in the last few years.'

'And that's the problem, isn't it? It's been years, yet I still don't have a decent job, a lover or a proper home. You're the only friend I really open up to, Melanie, except you're not even a real friend. You're my bloody therapist. I can only talk to you between 5.30 pm and 6.30 pm on a Tuesday evening. I'm sorry, but I'm done.'

'What do you mean, you're done?' I can see the worry in her eyes. Whenever I say anything too negative, she's concerned I might take my own life. At least, I think that's what she means. Perhaps she's just worried about losing a long-standing client.

'I don't mean done, done,' I explain. 'I'm just going to do something else to make my life better. Perhaps I'll move house, get a new job out of London, abroad even.'

'You're so brave, Carrie.'

'Yeah, well, what choice do I have?'

'You can do whatever you set your mind to. A change of job or home may be very good for you, but I don't think you're ready to quit therapy yet.'

I cross my arms.

Melanie leans forwards again. 'You're strong, Carrie. Look at everything you've achieved. You're fully mobile, you're holding down a full-time job, and you've come off all the painkillers. I don't think you give yourself enough credit for everything you've achieved.'

'But it's not about what you think, though, is it?' I know enough therapy-speak to realise Melanie is giving me her personal opinion as opposed to acting as the objective therapist. That's another reason why I need to end things. We're in danger of crossing over into the familiar.

I glance at my watch. I've got fifteen minutes to go until the end of my session, but the time has come. I gather up my bag and coat and stand up.

'Thanks for everything, Melanie,' I say, and I hurry out of her office before she can stop me.

The problem is everything in my life is second best, and

Melanie just doesn't get that. How can she know what it's like to have the perfect life and then lose it all? How can she know what it's like to look in the mirror and see a revolting, deformed body? And to see that look of disgust mirrored on other people's faces. I saw a man in hospital who was literally missing half his face. There was no right eye, no nose and a misshapen mouth. People cringed away from him; children cried. He was a freak. Only I understood, and I stared straight at his eye and smiled at him. He would understand how it is to be undesirable.

I walk dejectedly through the streets of London. It was easier when I was taking the painkillers. There's a reason why they're called painkillers, and it's not just because they numb the pain. They numb everything, and it's so much easier to feel nothing. The trouble was, I became addicted, and that was a particularly horrible place to be.

It was Melanie who encouraged me to attend Narcotics Anonymous. It was the last place I wanted to go, to be surrounded by other broken souls like myself, the forgotten. I couldn't deal with my own pain, let alone other people's. Yet it was my salvation, eventually. I made a handful of friends, people from all walks of life, and we helped each other. It took several years, but now the strongest painkiller I take is ibuprofen. Although I know I could return to the doctor's and demand oxycodone or morphine, I won't. I have an addictive personality, and if I sink that low again, I will never rise up.

It's not the physical pain that keeps me from sleeping. Oh, I have that, all right – the searing, burning nerve pain and the horrible muscle spasms and tightness around my worst scars. No. It's the emotional pain that is slowly ripping me apart. Every time I have an encounter such as the one with Hugo Pendlethorpe, I break a little bit more. I need purpose in my life. Perhaps I should work with people who are worse off than me, but charity isn't really in my nature. I'm not sure I was a nice person before, so how the hell can I be nice now? No. I just have to hope that something comes along that will propel me to change.

I'm on the bus, flicking through all the new listings on SpareRoom on my phone. I'm too bloody old to be doing a flat share. I select one bedroom and studio flats. Right at the top of the list is a place in Paddington. There's something about the picture of the living room that reminds me of my old home. Perhaps it's the pot plants in the window or the colour of the curtains, but before I realise what I'm doing, I'm clicking on the 'call the advertiser' button. Briefly, I glance at the eye-watering deposit required and the monthly rent, which I can't possibly afford. But I deserve somewhere like this, somewhere that is my own home.

An hour later, I'm viewing it. The space is much smaller than the photograph suggests, with a bed that's hinged up to the wall and a little kitchen with two electric rings and an oven that wouldn't be big enough to cook a chicken for four. But I don't have any friends, so it's not like I'll be cooking for anyone except me.

'I'll take it,' I say to the agent, who looks like he's nineteen years old and trying to give off Elvis vibes.

'We'll need to run the credit checks and stuff.' He locks the apartment up behind me. 'I'll be in touch.'

I let myself dream. It might be small, but the space would be mine to do whatever I like with it. Perhaps I'll do what Melanie suggests and sign up to a dating app. I'll actually get to know someone before showing them my revolting body. Maybe it really will make a difference. But when I get back to Peckham, and Kayla is prancing around the living room with her girlfriend and the music is loud enough to cause the building to crack, I know it's just that. A dream. I don't have the money to go anywhere else.

6

LEONIE

Markus and I have been dating for three months today. It has been a whirlwind of a romance. The most intense, intimate relationship I've ever had; I've fallen for him hard. He told me that he loved me one month after we met (I don't count that very early reference to love), and I told him I loved him four weeks later. We rarely spend a night apart.

When we returned home from that romantic weekend away for my birthday, he gave me a Tiffany box, and inside was a beautiful silver necklace with pave diamonds set into a circle. I wear it every day. Since then, he's forever buying me gifts, expensive jewellery in boxes that come from Cartier or Harrods. We eat out a couple of times a week, always the best restaurants, the ones with awesome reviews. And I've given up trying to find Markus a new home. It's as if we now have some sort of tacit agreement. What's the point in him buying somewhere new when we're spending practically all of our time together? I haven't articulated my thoughts, but the obvious next steps would be for us to buy somewhere together. Or am I being too presumptuous?

I still haven't introduced him properly to Mum and Dad. Mum met him very briefly when he turned up to collect me from work one evening. With big eyes, I thought she was going to swoon. It was embarrassing. But now she's invited us both for Sunday lunch, and if our relationship is to progress, I know this is something I can't avoid.

Mum and Dad live in London during the week, in a four-storey house near Marylebone, but during the weekends, they decamp to their sprawling place near Horsham in Sussex.

It's there Markus and I are headed this morning. Markus sold his Tesla a few weeks ago, saying that now he is living in London most of the time, a car was an unnecessary burden, so it's me who is driving. In contrast to Markus, who is leaning his head back against the seat, his eyes closed and singing along out of tune to Radio Two's greatest hits, I'm feeling uptight. My parents are so judgemental, and I'm worried that they won't approve of Markus: the fact he's a decade older than me, that he isn't a doctor, a lawyer or an entrepreneur, that right now he doesn't even own his own home, because Sandcastle House was sold. At the same time, I know I shouldn't care. This is my life, not my parents'. So what if they don't like him? Yet I can't ever seem to fully banish that insidious little voice that says, *You owe your dad. You owe Gus. You mustn't disappoint him.*

'Whoa!' Markus says as we pull into the driveway. 'Quite a house.'

I don't say anything as we get out of the car and walk up the steps to the front door. It's a mock Tudor house with black beams and white walls, and there's something inherently ugly about it, especially as it's the home of a leading property developer who should have better taste. The black front door swings open, and Mum is there, her arms wide-stretched, as if she hasn't seen me in weeks rather than twenty-four hours.

'Darling,' she says overexuberantly, and then stands on tiptoes to kiss Markus on the cheek. He hands her a bouquet of flowers that we picked up from the flower stall by South Kensington tube station. I'm glad that they're red and green, Christmassy, and there are none of my and Markus' favourite tulips.

'Come in, come in,' she says. I notice she's wearing a dress I haven't seen before. Mum is conscious of her expanded waistline and the horrendous side effects of menopause with which she seems to enjoy regaling me.

Dad is in the living room. A capacious room with patio doors that open up to the sprawling garden. He strides over to Markus and shakes his hand, doing that thing where he puts his other hand over the top of Markus' to show that he's the one in charge. He produces a can of beer from the fridge underneath his bar on the far side of the living room and hands it to Markus.

'Take a seat,' he commands. Markus squeezes my hand, and we sit together on the sofa opposite Dad.

'So tell me, what is it that you do?'

And so the interview begins. Markus talks about what he does in the city, and after a while I zone out. I excuse myself and go to see Mum, who is busying in the kitchen.

'Such a nice-looking man,' Mum says.

During lunch, Dad asks Markus about his family and where he went to school, not even being subtle as he tries to work out where Markus sits in the social class system. What

Dad conveniently forgets is that his father was a manual labourer, and that it's his new-found wealth that has propelled him up the social scale. Who the hell cares where Markus went to school? When my boyfriend talks about the Scottish castle where he grew up, Dad's eyes grow wider. *Bingo.* Dad is impressed. There's some talk about the possibility that Mum and Dad met Markus' parents one year when they were up in Scotland staying with old friends. Somehow I doubt it.

After lunch, Dad wants to watch rugby on the television, and Mum suggests I take Markus for a walk through the woods. It's a relief to get out of the oppressive house. We wrap up warmly, and I lead him through the garden to the footpath beyond. Fallen leaves have cushioned the muddy path, and we stroll hand in hand through the dense, bare-leaved trees until we emerge, blinking, into a big field with low grass. We follow the footpath upwards until we're at the brow of the field, a beautiful oak tree sitting high on the horizon.

'Leonie, there's something I want to say.' There's a formality to Markus' voice, and for a horrible moment I think he's going to dump me. Then he's let go of my hand and is fumbling in his pocket. To my bemusement, he goes down onto one knee and holds out a hand.

'Leonie Wilding, will you marry me?'

I'm totally caught off guard. There's a ring glinting in the low sunlight in the palm of Markus' hand. I open and close my mouth. Markus is asking me to marry him! I can see the confusion and doubt start to cloud his face, but he's got no reason to worry.

'Yes!' I shout. 'Yes!'

And then he's pushing the ring onto the fourth finger of

my left hand, and I'm staring at the square-cut diamond, and Markus is picking me up under my arms and swinging me around and around until we're both so dizzy we collapse in a heap on the wet, muddy grass with me laughing and crying all at the same time.

I don't notice anything on our walk back home. The sky could be falling down for all I care. I'm getting married to the love of my life, and I couldn't be happier. I push the door open and shout, 'Mum! Dad!'

Mum appears, and her eyes widen as she stares at us with a look of horror. I realise that we're both covered in mud, our coats damp, our hair mussed up, my lips swollen from kissing.

'We've got something to tell you!' I exclaim as Dad appears in the hall. 'Markus has asked me to marry him, and I've said yes!' I hold my hand up so they can see the ring.

There's a beat of silence during which I will my parents to react in the right way, and then suddenly they do. Mum claps her hands together, and tears spring to her eyes. Dad says, 'I think this calls for a bottle of bubbly.'

The afternoon passes in a whirl. Mum goes straight into wedding-planning mode, asking question after question.

'We'll pay for the wedding, won't we, Gus?'

'No,' Markus interrupts, but Dad bats him away.

'Of course we'll pay for it. That's what the parents of the bride do.'

'That's terribly kind of you,' Markus says. He shuffles awkwardly on the sofa.

'What time of year do you want to get married?' Mum asks. 'I think March. No point in hanging around. And let's have it here. The daffodils look so lovely in the spring. We can have a marquee in the garden. How many people, do you think, Gus? Three hundred? We can lay on buses and get people to leave their cars on Jim's field.'

'Mum!' I interrupt. 'We've only just got engaged, like, twenty minutes ago. Can you slow down?'

Dad throws me one of his dagger stares. 'Your mother has been looking forward to this moment for the past thirty years. Don't deprive her.'

'I'd always imagined having a small wedding, something intimate,' I say. 'We could do family-only on an exotic beach somewhere.' Although the truth is I never really imagined getting married at all.

Mum's face drops.

'Well, you'd better talk her out of that notion, Markus.' Dad laughs. 'We'll want to invite everyone we know.'

I stand up suddenly. 'Thank you for lunch, but we need to get back to London.'

Markus looks at me quizzically. 'You haven't even finished your glass of champagne, darling,' he says.

'Another time. If you don't mind, I really need to get back.' I have a sudden realisation that by marrying Markus, I can escape the clutches of my parents. Or at least share the load with him. Dad never listens to me. He just steamrollers ahead regardless of whom he hurts along the way. Well, that is over now. I am determined that my marriage will represent freedom. I've served my time, been subservient to Dad for long enough. It's over now. It doesn't mean my conscience is clear, it never will be, but I'm over Dad's control.

'Your parents aren't so bad,' Markus says.

'Believe me, they are. Or at least Dad is. This is our wedding, and I want it to be for us, not them.'

'Yes, but you're lucky to have family.'

I glance at him, and he's staring out of the side window of the car. 'I'm sorry.' I squeeze his hand. Markus is right; at least I have family.

'I'm going to call Sam,' I say, using the car's voice command system to dial his number.

'Hello?' My brother sounds sleepy through the car's loudspeakers. 'Everything all right?' His slight twang of a South African accent always startles me.

'You're on loudspeaker. I'd like you to say hello to Markus. Your future brother-in-law.'

'Hi, Sam,' Markus interjects.

'Hello, Markus,' Sam replies, and then there's a beat of silence. 'Oh my God, sis! You got engaged?'

'Yes!'

'Congratulations! Congratulations to you both!'

'We've just been to see Mum and Dad. Mum wants three hundred people in a marquee in the garden. You will come, won't you?'

'I wouldn't miss it for the world. But don't let them steamroller you into anything, Leonie. You know what they're like. Don't let them take control.'

'I won't.' Although, I'm thinking, perhaps I will. Perhaps this can be the final swan song, the very last time I'm in their clutches, because wedding planning is a big deal, and I've got a business to run.

'Let me know the date. Sending you both loads of love.'

'Your brother sounds lovely,' Markus says. 'I'm looking forward to meeting him.'

The next morning I walk into the office, unable to keep the grin off my face. I don't say anything, but the four of us (minus Mum, who doesn't work on a Monday) are having our weekly Monday meeting, and then suddenly Denise's eyes fall on my ring finger.

'Bloody hell, Leonie. Is that what I think it is?' She grabs my hand and holds it up in the air.

I let a smile creep across my face. 'Oh my God! You're engaged!' she shrieks.

I catch Zac's eye, and he looks away. I feel bad, regretting not warning him. He tries very hard to pretend he doesn't care, but I know he still holds a torch for me, and that split-second look of hurt reminds me that I need to be gentle towards him.

'Congrats,' he says, but his smile doesn't quite meet his eyes.

'How exciting!' Erin says. 'Beautiful ring.' It is beautiful. It's a simple cut solitaire that glistens in the light, and despite its size, it feels light and comfortable.

'Have you talked about what sort of wedding you'll have?' Denise asks.

'It seems like my parents will be taking over. A big one, apparently.'

'If you like, I can introduce you to my good friend Margot,' Erin suggests. 'She's a wedding planner, and she's brilliant at her job. She's had to deal with plenty of bridezillas in her time. Not that you'll be a bridezilla, of course.' Erin reddens.

The phone rings, and Denise reaches across to answer it.

'Yes, of course, Brenda,' she says and then hangs up.

'What does Mum want?' I ask.

'Just to say that she's placed an engagement notice in both the *Times* and the *Telegraph* newspapers.'

I groan.

7

CARRIE

I'm at the dentist. It's taken me thirty-eight days to get an appointment, during which time I've gone through six bottles of clove oil and back-to-back packs of paracetamol and ibuprofen. It's been so hard, because I know that one stronger painkiller would ease the agony in my jaw, yet I force myself to endure the pain. It's strange, too, how significant pain in one area of your body diminishes or removes the pain elsewhere. It's as if my brain can't cope with multiple areas of agony and focuses on the one that screams the loudest. I suppose if I had the money to pay for a dentist's appointment, I would have been fixed weeks ago, but I don't have the money, so I have to wait for the NHS.

There are nine people in the waiting room, and none of us look at each other. I pick up the last remaining magazine from the table in the middle of the room and flick through it, stopping at the property pages. I didn't get that studio apartment in Paddington. Of course I didn't. My credit rating is crap, and I'd only be able to afford the deposit if I robbed a bank. My eyes rest on the photo of a woman. Her face is so familiar, yet I can't place her. The name means nothing either. Leonie Wilding. She's the director of a company that finds new houses for the rich and famous. Chance would be a fine thing. My eyes are drawn back to that face. Where have I seen her before? She has hazel eyes, widely set, and mid-brown hair pinned up in a messy bun. She's wearing a navy jacket with sharp shoulders, and there's something about her expression that grips me. Perhaps I went to school with her or knew her from before.

Before.

I drop the magazine. The woman directly opposite me looks up and scowls.

It comes to me in a horrifying flash.

It's not before. It's *during.* I gasp and cover my mouth with my hand. I saw that face when I had my accident.

I saw those eyes peer at me in the dark before unconsciousness claimed me. I saw that face when I flickered between life and death.

My heart starts racing so quickly, it feels as if it's pumping right out of my chest. I'm trembling from head to toe, my body temperature veering between freezing cold and burning up. I can't breathe. Without thinking, I shove the magazine in my canvas tote bag and stand up. The air in the waiting room is dry and lacking oxygen. I move towards the exit, but dizziness is making the room spin, and it feels like I'm weaving towards the door. I fumble with the handle, my breathing so shallow, I think I'm going to pass out. Someone opens the door, and I tumble out into the damp, cold day. I try to run, but my feet catch on the pavement, and I stumble again, finding myself sitting on the wet paving stones, my back up against a brick wall.

'Are you all right?' A woman, maybe my age, is peering at me, an umbrella keeping both of us dry.

I shake my head, because I'm not all right, yet at the same time, I know this feeling will pass. I've had too many panic attacks, and even though it feels like I'm dying, deep down I know I'm not.

A woman in a dark blue tunic bends down in front of me. She's wearing a badge, and the words swim. *Mary. Dental Nurse.*

'Here. Breathe slowly into this paper bag,' she says, crouching and gently placing the bag over my nose and mouth. 'Breathe in, one, two; out, one, two. And again, in, one, two; out, one, two. You're going to be just fine. You're not the first person to have a panic attack in a dentist's waiting room, and you won't be the last.'

I swallow hard and almost smile. I couldn't care less about having a tooth filled or extracted. I couldn't care less about having my mouth prodded and my jaw fixed wide apart. Instead, I think about the article, the magazine that is shoved inside my bag, and what happened nearly a decade ago.

'I'm sorry,' I say eventually. 'I'm prone to these. You are really kind.'

I lever myself upwards and lean against the brick wall. 'Would you like to come back inside? Gilly will make you a warm cup of tea.'

'No. No, sorry, but I think I'll give the appointment a miss today. I'll pop into the surgery to get a valium before my next appointment.'

She smiles at me sadly. 'All right. You take care, and come back and see us soon.'

I haven't moved out of the flat share in Peckham yet. I

will do as soon as I find somewhere else, because the atmosphere between me and Kayla is worse than horrible now. I lie down on the lumpy bed and try to grapple with the memory I've spent a decade trying to forget. The recollections are shards and fragments, things that might be memories or simply my imagination playing tricks. I take the magazine out of my bag and flick to page thirty-one. Leonie Wilding. Her eyes stare out of the page, and I know viscerally that she is the woman. The woman I have been seeking all these years.

She's attractive, clever and rich, if this article is telling the truth. She runs her own business called Castaway Property Search, finding luxury homes for the rich and famous, people too busy to do their own dirty work. Of course she does. I let the magazine slip onto the floor, and I close my eyes.

Life was so good then. I was happy, pregnant, engaged to be married, and I had a high-flying job running a small advertising agency, coming up with clever campaigns, presenting my brilliant ideas to clients. I suppose I was a bit like Leonie. But back then, I was the person before.

I lay in that ditch for two whole days and two whole nights. The police told me that's how long it took for them to find me. The doctors told me it was a miracle that I was still alive. So when was it that Leonie Wilding peered at me? Was it shortly after my car careered off the road, or was it sometime later, in the forty-eight-hour period before I was rescued? Did she cause the accident, or did I hit a tree, which is what the police think? Perhaps she took one look at me and thought I was so mangled, had so many life-changing injuries, I wasn't worth rescuing? Because it wasn't her who found me in the end. It was a local farmer. He and his lovely wife visited me in hospital a couple of times, bringing me home-made jam and pickles. Did Leonie Wilding leave me there to die?

The police said that if I had been found straight away, I may not have lost my baby. I may not have had so many injuries, injuries that left me with life-changing scars, a limp and infertility. Injuries that destroyed my confidence and ended my engagement. Injuries that resulted in years of painkiller addiction and even more years of therapy. Perhaps the accident didn't go the way the police said. Perhaps it wasn't my fault at all.

What if. What if. What if. The most futile two words ever. It's not as if I can go back and change anything. If she did nothing else, Melanie Pleat made me realise the futility of *what if.*

I may remember little about the accident itself, but my memories of the hours running up to it are in vivid technicolour. I'd had a rough day at work, lost a big client because they felt my brief wasn't on point, that I'd got a bit stale with my ideas. I was livid. I went home and poured myself a glass of white wine. God, I needed that drink. But unfortunately for me, Reece came home early from work and found me slumped on the sofa with the big glass of wine in my hand. He went ballistic.

'You're so irresponsible, drinking when you're pregnant! Don't you care that you're harming our baby? What sort of crap mother are you going to be?' He threw his arms up in the air and glowered at me. 'You know what, Carrie, I can't do this. I can't be with you, a baby murderer.'

'For heaven's sake, stop being so melodramatic,' I said. 'It's one glass of wine, which won't do the slightest bit of harm.'

'You're wrong. This is just the thin end of the wedge. You don't deserve to be a mother, Carrie.' He clenched and unclenched his fists. And then Reece, the father of my unborn child, and the man I thought I'd be spending the rest of my life with, stormed out of our apartment.

I sat there on the dark grey reclining sofa that Reece and I had chosen together, expecting him to return after ten minutes, twenty perhaps. But he didn't. And he didn't pick up when I called him. I knew where he'd gone: to Corbridge, the delightful market town where his twin brother lived, where they would be drowning their sorrows in the posh pub, because Reece wasn't like me. He came from money, had the privilege of education – and occasionally, that air of entitlement that wound me up so very much. I'm not proud of the fact that I finished the very large glass of wine, then raced out to my car, intending to drive to Corbridge. But I didn't make it that far.

I open my eyes and stare at the damp patch on the ceiling. There were no damp patches in our stunning duplex penthouse that had views over the river Tyne. Although as it turns out, the apartment was never mine, and when all those months later I was turfed out of hospital, I had no home. Reece had installed a new woman in our penthouse.

I sit up and pull my laptop out from under the bed. After firing it up, I type Leonie Wilding into the search engine. Surprisingly, lots pop up. I grab a notebook and pen that I stole from the stationery cupboard, and start jotting down notes. Leonie would have been sixteen or seventeen at the time of the accident. So young. What was she doing peering at me? Had she been in the car that hit me, or was she just randomly wandering through the woods? As I dig deeper, I find out more about her parents, Gus and Brenda Wilding.

Self-made millionaires, the Wildings have a property empire; even a decade ago, they were building luxury residential blocks all over the southeast. But they're a southern-based family, so what was Leonie doing in Northumberland? Or has my memory played tricks on me, and it wasn't Leonie who peered at me? How can I trust a memory that shimmers and disappears like shadows?

It takes a lot of digging, but eventually I find it. Brenda's family come from County Durham, and she and her husband owned a house on the edge of Northumberland National Park. I look on Zoopla and see that it was quite the modern mansion, yet they sold it just six months after the accident. That's strange, isn't it? Was the Wilding family running away? The more I think about it, the less of a coincidence this seems. I am convinced that Leonie Wilding was there, those eyes peering at me. And if I'm right, she needs to be brought to justice.

I no longer have a number for the police officer assigned to my case, so I call the central police station and ask to speak to Michael Ryan. It's no surprise that he's been promoted during the past decade; now he's a chief inspector. Michael Ryan is one of the good guys, and although he should probably fob me off onto someone lower down the scale, he doesn't.

'Do you remember me?' I ask as he comes onto the phone.

'Of course I do. You had a rough deal.'

Unexpectedly, tears well up in my eyes. 'I always said another car was involved, and now I know one of the people in the car. She's Leonie Wilding, and she's a posh estate agent in London. I'm positive she was at the scene of the crime.'

Michael Ryan is silent for a moment before eventually saying, 'I'm sorry, Carrie, but there was no case to answer. There was no evidence to suggest that it was anything but an accident just involving your car. Unless you have any evidence to the contrary…' He lets his words fade out.

'But she was there. My memory has come back.'

'I'm afraid that we need more than a memory. We need evidence to place her there, marks on a car, a tracker device, CCTV.'

'So you can't help me?'

'I'm sorry, Carrie, but no. There's nothing to suggest any crime took place.'

I hang up. I know it's rude, and Michael Ryan is only doing his job, but it feels like I've been let down all over again. I'd felt guilty back then, as if I was to blame for the death of my baby, and I got what I deserved when my body was smashed to smithereens. Except now, I am positive that I wasn't alone during the whole of those forty-eight hours, and if I had been rescued earlier, then I might now have a ten-year-old daughter and a life that is fulfilled and happy.

I chuck my phone across the room, and it bounces off the wall. It doesn't make me feel any better. Now I'm just angry. No. I'm furious. I'm through with the poor-me attitude. Once again, no one cares.

And once again, I have only myself to rely on.

8

LEONIE

'Are you okay?' Denise makes me snap out of my reverie. I realise I've been staring out of the window for the past ten minutes. Another bouquet of unseasonal tulips was delivered ten minutes ago, and as much as I love them, the weekly arrival – to mark the day of the week we had our first kiss – is getting a little ridiculous. Markus loves his romantic gestures, and yes, they're sweet, but they are beginning to feel a bit claustrophobic.

The office phone rings. As Mum isn't here today, Denise answers. She puts her hand over the receiver. 'It's Markus, for you.'

As much as I love my fiancé, and yes, I really do, the interruptions to my work are irritating me. Before, he used to call on my mobile, but now he knows I won't answer it during the day, so he calls on the main office line.

'Tell him I'm on another call, and I'll see him later.' The thing that I don't understand is how Markus can take time out of his busy working day to call me so frequently. And it's not like he's got anything important to say. He just wants to know how I am, what new properties I'm showing, what I'd like for supper. Sometimes I wonder how he's able to interrupt his own work so frequently.

Denise frowns at me, and when she ends the call, she asks, 'Are you sure everything is alright?'

'Yes, yes. I'm just really busy.'

'I wish I had someone who loved me as much as Markus adores you,' Denise says softly. It makes me feel guilty.

'Denise is right,' Zac interjects. I thought he was on another call, but he must have been listening in. 'You're lucky to have him.'

'Okay, I get the message.' I laugh, but it sounds a little strangled. 'It's just all gone so fast, and it feels like I'm playing catch-up.'

'The course of true love,' Zac says, surprisingly without any irony in his voice.

'You still going to meet Margot, the wedding planner, this afternoon?' Erin asks. For a moment, I wonder if she's on commission; then I hate myself for the thought. Erin has been nothing but friendly since she's joined our team.

'Yes. Meeting Mum there at 3 pm.'

It never crossed my mind to farm out my wedding planning to a professional, but on reflection, it seemed like a good idea. After all, I'm working full time, and every evening Markus has something planned: a visit to the theatre, to see my favourite band, a meal in a new up-and-coming restaurant. I'm not sure I've ever been so busy. Then I remembered Erin's contact, and I gave Margot's details to Mum.

The wedding planner has an office in Mayfair, although when I step inside, it's more like being in someone's posh front room, with comfy sofas and vases of flowers on sideboards. Margot Beaumont is early forties, with almost-white blonde hair swept up into a chignon, wearing what looks like a pale pink Chanel suit and matching shoes. She and Mum are already deep in conversation when I arrive. Mum gives me a quick peck on the cheek, and we settle down on satinwood chairs around an inlaid satinwood table. Margot has several leather-bound binders in front of her, along with a lined notepad and a burgundy Montblanc pen.

'Congratulations on your engagement,' Margot says. 'Who's the lucky man?'

I try not to roll my eyes over her cliched opening remark. 'Markus Klausen.'

'Klausen?' She frowns. 'Of the Klausen family of North Hampstead?'

'I'm not sure,' I say, because I still haven't met a single member of Markus' family, and Markus told me he was from Scotland.

'What date are we looking at?' Margot asks.

'March,' Mum says.

'The year after next?' Margot asks.

'Good heavens, no. This coming March, next year. Four months is quite enough time to plan a wedding, isn't it? Leonie and her fiancé aren't getting any younger, and Gus and I can't wait to be grandparents.'

It seems that everyone wants this wedding to happen as soon as possible. Everyone except me, perhaps, for it feels like I'm being swept up in a tsunami of white froth and love hearts.

'That's very quick, but we pride ourselves on fulfilling the wedding of your dreams within your dream timescale.' She opens a big diary and suggests the third Saturday in

March. 'So what sort of wedding do you have in mind, Leonie?'

Before I can open my mouth, Mum answers for me. 'There'll be three hundred guests, and we'd like a marquee in the garden of our Sussex house. We'll want a full orchestra, white peacocks and flowers to match the red-and-white theme.'

'What?' I scrunch up my forehead. 'This isn't what I want!'

'No, it's what Dad and I have always dreamed of. A bigger, brighter version of our wedding, and that will be perfect for you, darling, because you're a bigger and brighter version of me.'

I open and close my mouth, because I doubt very much that what Mum has just said is a compliment. 'But this is my wedding, not yours,' I say softly, glancing at Margot, who is busying herself flipping through the pages of one of her binders.

'Yes, it's your wedding, but Dad is paying for it.'

'I'd like white and peach, full of delicate roses and tulips,' I say, biting the side of my mouth. I knew that Mum and I might have a different vision, but I did expect her to at least listen to what I want.

'We didn't have any money when your Dad and I got married, so we've dreamed of going all out for your wedding.' She turns to Margot. 'Leonie is our only daughter. And fortunately, money is no object when it comes to our girl.'

'Planning a wedding is very stressful, and we often find that mums and brides have different visions,' Margot says diplomatically. 'Perhaps we can combine both of your wishes. How about a theme of white and peach as Leonie wants, and white peacocks?'

'I suppose so,' Mum mutters, but I know what's going through her head. The red-and-white theme will be Dad's idea, and she won't want to disappoint him. And that's the thing. Both Mum and I feel we owe Dad so much, though for different reasons. If it weren't for Dad, I'd have spent the last few years in prison, and I certainly wouldn't be living in London in luxury. He may be domineering and strong-willed, but Dad gives us a good life.

We discuss other elements of the wedding: the shape and decorations in the marquee, the shapes and sizes of the tables, the menu and drinks, the floral arrangements, and the timings of the day, hair and makeup. And then, when my head feels like it's going to burst, Margot says, 'Shall we go next door and look at dresses? The Dress Boutique is owned by my friend. I have no affiliation, but you might like to try on a few and decide what style you like. There's no obligation to buy from her, of course, although as time is short, you'll probably have to choose an off-the-shelf dress and get it altered to fit.'

As we walk into the shop that smells of violets, Mum and I are each handed a glass of champagne. I can feel a headache thrumming in my temples, and I'm not at all sure I'm in the mood for wedding dress shopping, but Mum is buzzing with excitement. Margot introduces us to Jemima, the shop owner, and after promising to email us her proposal for the wedding of my dreams, she leaves us in the dress shop.

'How about something like this?' Mum suggests, fingering the tulle on a fairy-princess-style dress.

'I don't think so,' I mutter. Just because Mum looked like

a white Christmas tree when she got married doesn't mean I intend to.

'I'd like something simple and slinky,' I say to Jemima.

She appraises me, looking me up and down, and then smiles. 'I have just the dress.'

A couple of minutes later, she is holding up a long satin dress with simple spaghetti straps.

'It's lovely,' I murmur.

'A bit stark, isn't it?' Mum says. 'Plain Jane.'

'How about you try it on?' Jemima leads me to a changing room with plush rose velvet curtains. As I pull the dress on, I stare at myself in the mirror. I was never one of those girls who planned her wedding and kept a Pinterest board of her favourite dresses. In fact, I never thought I'd actually get married, that I didn't deserve such happiness. Yet here I am, gazing at myself wearing the most beautiful, sleek dress I've ever seen, which fits me like a glove and makes me look almost model-like.

'How are you getting on in there?' Jemima asks.

I pull the curtains back, and she inhales sharply as she looks at me. 'Wow. Just wow.'

'Let me see,' Mum says, sloshing her champagne as she stands up.

'It's a bit ordinary, isn't it? More like a nightdress than a wedding dress.'

'I disagree,' I say. 'It's perfect.'

'Just occasionally, the first dress a bride tries on is the one, and I think this is such an occasion. All it needs is a little taking in around the waist, and perhaps the hem could come up a couple of centimetres. It's a one-off dress made by the designer Harriet Hardcastle. She dropped it off this morning, and I just knew it would fly out of the shop.'

'I love it,' I say quietly.

When Jemima tells Mum the price, my knees almost give way. It's the cost of a car, ridiculous.

'If you love it that much, then we'll take it,' Mum says, although I hear the hint of begrudging in her voice.

'It's a crazy price,' I whisper to Mum. 'I'll find something else.'

She stares at me as if I've said something insane. 'We'll take it.'

Jemima smiles tightly, as if she hasn't just heard our little exchange. She pins the dress and then helps me slip it off. 'It'll be ready for collection in three weeks, but of course, we can hang onto it until nearer your wedding. We'll just need to take fifty percent as a deposit today.'

I wish I could pay for the dress, but I simply don't have the cash. Mum steps in front of me and hands Jemima her American Express card.

The next day, I have an early appointment to view a property in Surrey, and decide to take Erin with me. She used to work in a leading estate agency, but wanted a change. When I advertised for a new agent, she was by far the best candidate. Erin is in her mid-forties, a single mum with a sixteen-year-old daughter. It's a bit weird employing someone so much older than me.

We chat a bit about some of our clients, but unlike with Zac and Denise, our conversation is strictly work-related. I don't feel one hundred percent comfortable with Erin, but I remind myself that she is a colleague and only a colleague. It's not like she needs to be a friend.

I might feel a little uneasy around her, but my client clearly doesn't. Erin has all the facts at her fingertips; I marvel at how efficient she is. On the way back to the office, her phone rings.

'Do you mind if I take it? It's my daughter.'

'Of course,' I say.

'No. Out of the question. It's a school night. See you later.' She groans as she ends the call. 'Sixteen-year-olds. They're so irresponsible at that age, thinking they're all grown up. You'll discover that when you have your own family.'

I already know, I think to myself. *I already know.*

We don't make it back to the office until gone 11 am. Mum is at her desk, regaling Denise and Zac with all the details of my wedding.

'Hey, it's meant to be a surprise,' I say, dumping my bag and turning my laptop on.

'It's only us,' Zac says. 'We won't tell, will we, Denise?'

She pretends to zip up her lips and throws a wink at me when Mum isn't looking. 'Oh, Leonie, would you mind double-checking these invoices?' She passes me a couple of sheets of paper. Often, I wonder how we managed without Denise. She's uber-efficient; our diaries are always up to date and invoices issued on time. She's officially our office manager, and she's fast made herself indispensable.

Mum only works mornings, so she's gone by lunchtime. At 1 pm, Denise leaves too, but returns with sandwiches for Zac, Erin and me. We sit eating at our desks.

'What are you doing about a hen party?' Zac asks.

'I don't want one.'

'You can't not have a hen do,' Denise says. 'We'll organise one for you, won't we, Zac?'

I think I see Zac flinch ever so slightly. He's being very magnanimous and supportive.

'You can be an honorary girl for the evening,' I suggest, and then I wonder if I'm being horribly thoughtless. But I can't imagine a hen party without my best friend Zac being there.

A few weeks pass, and the wedding plans race ahead, largely without my input. Work keeps me busy, and Markus and I slip into a relaxed routine. Markus has officially moved in with me, and most evenings he's home before me. We go out less these days, which is just as well, as it was exhausting. Instead, Markus has taken to cooking every night, and I'm regularly assaulted by delicious scents and treated to an excellent meal. I tell Markus to stop cooking so much; otherwise I'll never fit in my wedding dress.

And then it's Christmas. We haven't been back to my parents' Sussex house since the afternoon Markus asked me to marry him, but the expectation is for me to spend Christmas with them.

'What do you normally do for Christmas?' I ask Markus one evening in mid-December.

'Forget about it. Not having siblings or parents is hard. The last few years, I've gone away on holiday, haven't bothered with a tree and the like. Christmas is for families, but next year, perhaps we will be a family. Maybe we'll be three.'

'Mmm,' I say. It's the first time Markus has suggested he wants children sooner rather than later. 'My parents have invited us to join them for Christmas lunch.'

'That's great!' he exclaims before I can say that I was rather hoping we could wriggle out of it. 'I'm so happy to be part of a family again. You'll have to tell me what I can buy your parents as gifts.' And Markus seems genuinely excited, like a little boy, and I don't have the heart to say I'd much rather go away just the two of us.

Although they invite us to stay the night, I tell my parents we'll come down for the day only. I'm feeling a flicker of nerves, because I've a horrible feeling I know what Dad intends to discuss. As we pull up in front of the house, Dad opens the front door. He's looking bigger than ever, and I worry about his health. He's clutching a cut-glass tumbler filled halfway up with whiskey.

'What can I get you to drink, young man?' he says to Markus, putting his arm around Markus' shoulders and propelling him inside.

'Whatever you're having, Gus,' he replies.

We follow Dad into the living room, where Mum has put a seven-foot Christmas tree decorated with all the gaudy gold and red baubles that she's had forever.

'Merry Christmas,' she says, kissing Markus enthusiastically on the cheek.

Dad doesn't ask me what I want to drink, and just pours me an orange juice. Perhaps one day I'll shock him and demand a triple gin and tonic. We perch uncomfortably on the sofa, facing Mum and Dad in their armchairs.

'We haven't done wrapped presents this year,' Mum says. 'Your father had a better idea.'

I hold my breath, wondering what excessive display of generosity he has come up with, and then immediately feel guilty for being ungrateful. Mum hands me an envelope addressed to Leonie and Markus.

I open it. Inside, there's a photo of a house. I turn the photograph over, and on the rear it says:

Dear Leonie and Markus, We have bought you this house near Dorking. You'll need a proper-sized family home after your marriage.

Love, Mum and Dad.

I'm speechless and not in a good way. Yes, I know it makes me sound so ungrateful, but it's up to Markus and me to decide where we want to live, and what kind of house. I want us to buy our future home, choose it together. Yet my parents have once again taken control and made the decisions for me.

'Wow!' Markus says. 'This is so incredibly kind of you. We're bowled over, aren't we, darling?' He places a kiss on my cheek.

I stand up because I need to take a moment, work out how I'm going to respond to this, because I haven't fully explained to Markus how my parents control me with money. And there is no way that I want to live in that house. I'm quite happy staying put in my mews house in London.

'Thanks, Mum, Dad,' I say, and disappear into the bathroom. I let out a little screech of frustration. Will Markus understand if I turn down the gift? Doesn't it make me seem like a spoiled rich bitch? After a while, Mum knocks on the door.

'You all right in there, Leonie? The turkey is ready.'

Christmas lunch is delicious, because Mum's food always is, and the dishes she doesn't like to cook, she orders in, but I'm quiet during the meal and let Dad and Markus do most of the talking. After the Christmas pudding with brandy butter, I struggle to move, I've eaten so much.

And then there's the moment I've feared.

'Got a few things to discuss with your future husband,' Dad says to me. 'Why don't you go and join your mum in the kitchen?'

'I'd rather stay here.'

Dad gives me one of his death stares, but I don't budge. Markus shuffles uneasily and puts his hand over mine.

'Right. If you insist. Brenda and I would like you to sign a prenup,' Dad says.

This is exactly what I was worried about. 'Absolutely not,' I say vehemently.

'I completely understand your fears, sir.' Markus surprises me with his warm tone. 'But I can assure you that I have extremely successful investments in leisure complexes all across the globe. I'm financially independent and will be able to keep your daughter in the manner to which she has become accustomed.'

'Indeed. But we can't look around corners, and I would feel much happier if you would sign this thing.' He leans back towards the sideboard behind the dining table and lifts up a large white envelope.

'Dad. No. Just no.'

Markus squeezes my shoulder. 'If your father would like me to sign this, then I will.' He takes the envelope. 'I'll have a read through over the next few days. Now, is there anything I can do to help Brenda?'

9

LEONIE

It's a month before our wedding, and Mum stopped coming into work ten days ago. She said she needed the next few weeks off to concentrate on the wedding plans. Considering it's my wedding and we have a wedding planner who is doing all of the hard work, I think that's ridiculous. Not that I say anything. I'm rather glad that Mum isn't in the office, spying on me and reporting back to Dad.

Meanwhile, Dad is going on and on about the prenup, which Markus still hasn't signed. He would have signed it if I insisted, but somehow it just seems wrong. It's as if we're expecting our marriage to fail before it's even started. If I had the slightest inkling that Markus wasn't the love of my life, then I wouldn't be going through with this wedding. But I am sure. Markus is a good man. Kind, attentive, funny and did I mention that he's good looking? He still makes me weak at the knees, and sex, well, it's amazing. My only niggle of doubt is that we're doing all of this so quickly. But as Markus says, he's a decade older than me, and when you know, you just know.

This morning I'm expecting the florist. Neither Margot nor Mum know that I've been in touch with her directly, but I've asked for a sample bouquet so I can confirm I'm happy with all the flowers. I'm on the phone when she arrives, so Denise offers her a cup of coffee whilst she waits. But I can't concentrate on the call because I can see the flowers the woman is holding.

'Would you mind if I call you back in half an hour?' I ask the estate agent I'm speaking to.

'No problem.'

I take a deep breath as I put the phone down, push my chair back and walk to the front of the office. The florist extends the bouquet towards me. It is large and circular, full of dark red roses and white spray.

'I hope you like it,' she says, her face open and expectant.

'This isn't what I ordered.'

She scrunches her eyebrows together. 'I'm sorry?'

'My wedding is going to be peach and white, with pale roses and tulips and white hydrangea heads. It was all written down, and the brief was given to you by Margot Beaumont, our wedding planner.'

She looks confused for a moment. 'Oh yes. That was the original brief, but it got changed a fortnight ago. The new brief is for red and white.'

Tears spring to my eyes, which I know is pathetic, but this is what it feels like to be constantly undermined by your own parents.

'Who gave you the new brief?' I ask tightly.

'Um, I'd have to look at the job sheet. Isn't this what you want?'

'No. My wedding is going to be peach and white, and I want flowers to match.'

'Well, it's just as well we've had a dummy run, isn't it?' She laughs awkwardly. 'Leave it with me, and I'll get it all swapped back to the original instructions.'

As soon as the woman has left, I pick up the phone and call Mum.

'Why did you change the floristry brief?'

'And good morning to you, too,' Mum says. 'What are you talking about?'

'The wedding florist came over with a sample bouquet, and the brief was changed to red and white.'

There's silence on the other end of the phone.

'Why would you do that to me when you know I want peach and white?' I insist.

'I didn't,' she says. 'I haven't ever spoken to the florist. It's all been done through Margot.'

'So you changed the brief with Margot, did you? Is the marquee going to be red and white, too? Do you know that red and white signifies bad luck? Is that what you want for me, Mum?' I'm shouting now, pacing the small area between my desk and the window.

'You need to calm down, Leonie. There clearly has been some mix-up, but it's nothing to do with me or your dad. We want what you want. And for heaven's sake, relax. There's nothing worse than a bridezilla.'

I slam the phone down. I know I shouldn't, but Mum knows exactly which buttons to press, and I'm livid. What else has she changed behind my back? Is this wedding going to be a disaster?

'Are you all right?' Denise asks quietly. I'm embarrassed that she heard every word of that conversation. At least Zac and Erin are out of the office.

'Not really. I don't want bloody red and white flowers. I

need to speak to the wedding planner and double-check everything else is how I want it.'

Fifteen minutes later, Margot has reassured me that nothing in my original instructions has changed. The colour of the flowers must have been a mix-up on the florist's end. An unfortunate mistake that can easily be corrected.

Later that afternoon, I decide to collect my wedding dress. I take a taxi to the shop in Mayfair, and I'm excited to try the dress on again. After putting on weight before Christmas thanks to Markus' cooking, I've made an effort to lose a little weight over the past few weeks. It wasn't difficult: too much work and too little sleep have made me perpetually weary. Jemima isn't there, and I'm greeted by a younger woman who doesn't introduce herself.

'I'm here to try on my dress and take it with me,' I say.

'And your name is?'

'Leonie Wilding.'

She pulls up a database on her laptop and squints as she looks through it. She's taking a very long time, and my stomach starts knotting. 'Is there a problem?'

'Mmm,' she says, screwing up her nose. 'I can't find you in the system. Do you remember when you purchased the dress?'

I look at my phone and find the date I was first here with Mum.

'Ah, yes,' she says eventually. 'The order was cancelled a week later.'

'What?'

'It's here. Customer no longer wants the dress. It was sold to someone else the next day.'

'That can't be possible.' I'm gripping the edge of the table. 'But it was my dress. We paid a fifty percent deposit.'

'Yes, I see that. It says here that the customer will come in to choose a new dress.'

'But I don't want a new dress! I want that one. It was perfect.'

'I'm very sorry, but it was a one-off. We haven't got anything exactly like it. I can find you something similar, but depending upon the alterations, it'll take about six weeks to fix. We're very busy at the moment.'

'I haven't got six weeks!' I exclaim. 'I'm getting married in less than a month.'

There's a sharp intake of breath. 'I'm very sorry, Ms Wilding, but unless we can find something that fits you perfectly, I'm not sure we'll be able to help.'

'Can you tell me who cancelled my dress order?' I ask.

'One moment.' She chews the inside of her cheek. 'Ah yes. A Mrs Brenda Wilding.'

'Mum!' I exclaim. My blood feels like it's going to boil over. Why the hell is Mum doing this to me? It doesn't make sense.

'Would you like to look at some other dresses?' the saleswoman asks.

'No,' I say. 'No.' And I storm out of the shop.

By the time I'm home, I'm even angrier. I turn the key in the lock and hope that Markus will be out. He's not.

'Hello, darling!' he shouts from the kitchen. 'Good day?'

'Bloody awful day,' I say as I stride towards him.

'Hey.' He pads towards me with bare feet. He's wearing jeans and a polo shirt that has the creases of a newly unpacked item of clothing. He engulfs me in his arms, and I bury my face into his chest. 'What happened?'

'My parents are trying to sabotage our wedding.'

'What? I thought the big wedding was all of their idea. I thought they were paying for it.'

'Yes, and it looks like they've taken complete control. Mum cancelled my dress.'

'What!' He lets go of me and steps backwards. 'What do you mean she cancelled your dress?'

'She rang the dress shop and said I'd changed my mind. I knew she didn't like it, thought it looked like a nightie, but how could she do that behind my back?'

'Are you sure she'd do something like that? Your mum just seems so… I don't know, nice.'

'We're about to find out.' I pull my mobile phone from my bag and jab in Mum's number.

She answers on the first ring. 'Why did you cancel my dress?' I snap.

'What?'

'My dress has been sold to someone else because Brenda Wilding rang up the shop and said I didn't want it anymore.'

'Darling, I would never do something like that. You know I wouldn't. Whilst it wasn't my first choice for you, I knew how much you loved it. Love at first sight, it was, like when you met Markus. The shop must have screwed up.'

'It seems a bit of a coincidence that both the florist and the dress shop had cancelled orders, both apparently cancelled by you.'

'Darling! Leonie, it wasn't me. I promise it wasn't.'

'Then who the hell did it?'

We're both silent, so eventually I mumble a half-hearted goodbye and end the call.

Markus tries his best to distract me for the rest of the evening, but I'm in a foul mood. If Mum didn't cancel the orders, then who did? I even wonder if it was Markus.

Perhaps he's getting cold feet, but I quickly discount that. He's too loving towards me, promising me that I'm the best thing that ever happened to him, doing everything he can to make me fall deeper and deeper in love with him.

The one person I can talk to who truly understands our parents is my brother, Sam. Yet Sam doesn't know anything about the guilt I've been carrying for the past decade, or the horrific secret that Dad insisted I keep. Sometimes I wonder whether Sam and Dad have their own secret, and that's the real reason he bolted to South Africa. When Markus is installed in front of the television, watching the World Cup, I call my brother.

'I genuinely don't think it was Mum,' Sam says after I explain the events of the day. 'I spoke to her only last week, and she told me how lovely you looked in the dress you'd chosen.'

'Really?' I'm surprised. I thought Sam only spoke to our parents a couple of times a year.

'She wanted to make sure I was coming to your wedding, that I'd remembered to buy you a present.'

'And have you?' I laugh.

'Well, not yet, obviously. I've still got three weeks to go.'

'Do you think Dad might have done it, if Mum didn't?'

'Come on, Leonie. That doesn't make any sense. He's shelling out tens of thousands on a fairy-tale wedding for you, to which he's invited all his business contacts. He's going to want you to look like a princess, for it to be the loveliest wedding anyone has ever attended.'

'I suppose you're right,' I say eventually. 'Maybe it's just all a horrible coincidence. Now I've got to find an off-the-peg dress.'

'Just as well Harvey Nichols and Harrods are your local stores, and that Dad has deep pockets.'

'I think I might get something from Monsoon or Whistles and be done with it.'

'You'll look stunning whatever you choose.'

'Can't wait to see you.'

'You too, little sis.'

When I explain to Denise and Zac about the wedding dress debacle, they're both shocked. Denise asks Zac if he can hold the fort for a few hours while she offers to go with me to find another dress. I'm thankful for her support, because I'm not sure I'm up to doing it alone. After trying on a handful, I select a dress I find in Harvey Nichols. It's not as perfect as the one in the wedding dress shop, but it fits me well enough, and most importantly, I pay for it myself. Just because Dad said he'd fund the whole wedding doesn't mean I want him to.

'The planning for your hen party is going well,' Denise says as we walk back to the office, a huge shopping bag holding my dress hung over my shoulder.

'No strippers. Promise?'

She laughs. 'No strippers.'

My hen party is being held at the Marlborough Hotel in Mayfair. Zac and Denise have invited Mum, Gran – my mother's mum – my aunt Chrissie, my cousin Sheryl and three girlfriends from my uni days, and Erin, because it would have been awkward not to have invited her. When we were compiling the list, I realised with some shock that other than Denise, I haven't made any new friends since I left Oxford. I've been so focused on work, my social life has been, well, pretty much non-existent. I've been to friends' parties, engagement parties and the occasional wedding, but my world has become surprisingly small. The upside of that was it made choosing who to invite to my hen party rather easy. The huge number of guests coming to our wedding comprise largely Mum and Dad's friends and contacts. I know that sounds old-fashioned in today's day and age, but the truth is, the big wedding is for them.

'Don't do anything I wouldn't do,' Markus says as he waves me off.

'I'll be home by 10 pm,' I predict.

The hotel is grand. All brass and velvets and glistening lights with tinkling piano music and people talking in hushed voices. I'm relieved, because the last thing I want is some raucous party.

'Leonie!' I swivel around and see Zac wearing a much-too-tight T-shirt with the words *Leonie's Hens* on the back. I do a double take, because I haven't seen Zac wear anything tight, and he's surprisingly well-toned.

'Denise forgot to order a man's size.' He laughs. 'Very tasteful, don't you think? Come with me, we've got a room upstairs.'

We take the lift to the fifth floor, and I follow Zac along a plush corridor. He uses a key card to open the door.

'Happy hen party!' nine female voices yell.

It's a big room with a stucco ceiling, and there are eleven high-backed armchairs positioned around the walls of the room. In the centre is a wooden floor, which looks like a dance floor. Peach and white balloons line the ceiling, their curvy ribbons bouncing just above everyone's heads. All my hens, including Gran, are wearing a T-shirt.

'This one is for you,' Denise says, handing me a T-shirt, which unlike the others is bright pink and says *My Name is Leonie and I'm a Hen!* A server appears from nowhere and hands me a full glass of champagne. I notice then that everyone else is also clutching glasses, mainly half drunk. 'First up is chill time,' Denise says. 'Take a seat.' She points to one of the highjack chairs, and I settle myself in.

Five women arrive, dressed in white tunics and black trousers. We're all offered the choice of a manicure, pedicure or facial. I choose a manicure, which makes drinking the copious amount of champagne tricky. Most of the time Mum or Zac are feeding it to me. And then the door opens, and a man in a suit strides in.

'I'm sorry, ladies, but I have to ask you to leave.'

'What!' Denise exclaims.

'You haven't paid the deposit, and regrettably, you'll need to leave.'

'But this is my daughter's hen party!' Mum says, her voice indignant. 'We always pay our bills.'

'Which one of you is getting married?'

Everyone points at me. The man strides towards me, and my beautician moves to one side. He stands so close, he's in my personal space.

'What's your name?' he asks rather aggressively.

'Leonie Wilding.'

'Well, you can save the day, Leonie.' He undoes his tie, and then music starts playing, and before I fully realise what's going on, this supposed manager is shedding his clothes just inches from my face. He strips down quickly so he's bare chested, without a hair to be seen, and his tight underwear leaves nothing to the imagination. Now he's gyrating to 'Dirty Dancing', and I just want to squeeze my eyes shut with embarrassment. Mum is laughing, but Gran looks horrified.

'Come on, guys, I specifically said no stripper.' There's a

lot of laughter and whooping, and then the stripper grabs my hand and makes as if he's going to place my hand on his groin. I pull away quickly, smudging my newly applied nail varnish. I'm not a prude; far from it, when I think about what Markus and I get up to in the bedroom, but this is too much. My friends are doubled up with laughter, and from the corner of my eye, I see a couple of them are videoing. Gran just looks bemused.

Eventually, and none too soon, the stripper leaves.

'Next game,' Denise says excitedly. 'How well do you know your fiancé? We've recorded Markus asking some questions and then answering them, and we'll see how well your answers match up.'

'Really?' I ask, my voice heavy with dismay.

'What a good idea,' Gran says. 'Better that you find out about him warts and all before actually tying the knot.'

'All right,' I say, finishing off my glass of champagne. I'm already feeling woozy and have lost count of how much I've drunk. Markus' voice booms through the speaker in the ceiling. 'Hello, my darling, and I hope you're having a fabulous hen party. We'll start off with an easy one. What's my favourite food?'

'Chocolate,' I say.

'If you get the answer wrong, you have to down a glass in one,' Zac says. My hens clap in unison as we wait for Markus to speak again.

'Chocolate,' he says. I grin.

'How old was I when I lost my virginity?'

I glance at Gran, who is frowning at Aunt Chrissie. I'm surprised that Markus has gone along with this.

'Do we have to do this?' I ask.

My hens all squeal, 'Yes!'

'Seventeen,' I say, guessing, as I've no idea how old he was.

'Fifteen,' Markus' disembodied voice says.

'Drink, drink, drink!' the girls shout. I tip back another glass of champagne, all the while thinking fifteen is quite young. I wonder how many women he's actually slept with.

'Where's the weirdest place I've ever had sex?' This is getting too much. I wouldn't mind if Gran, Mum and Aunt Chrissie weren't here, but they are, and it's embarrassing.

'I don't know,' I say quietly.

'Guess!' someone shouts.

'In the back of a car.'

'Hardly weird,' Zac says. I glance up at him, and he blushes fiercely. Mum is staring at him with wide eyes. Embarrassing.

'A cold room in a butcher's shop. Brrr,' his voice says. I shiver involuntarily.

'I think that's enough now,' I say, but the others ignore me.

'Drink, drink, drink!'

I'm feeling really tipsy now. This is exactly what I didn't want to happen.

'What's my favourite sex toy?'

Aunt Chrissie looks like she's going to explode. My cousin Sheryl is in stitches. Chrissie stands up and whispers into Gran's ear. They both walk out of the room, followed quite swiftly by Mum. This is not what I wanted, not at all. I get up and follow them out, with Zac on my heels.

'Come back!' someone shouts.

'I'm sorry,' I say as I open the door to the corridor, shouting after them. 'This isn't the sort of hen party I wanted.'

I hurry down the hallway to catch up with Mum, Zac a couple of steps behind me.

'You don't have a very good choice of friends, do you?' Gran says acerbically. 'Nought we can do about that now. You go back, and we'll make our own way home, won't we, Brenda?'

'I'm sorry,' I say again, although this situation is not of my making.

'Go back, love,' Mum says. Zac stands next to Mum, wringing his hands, looking awkward. I guess he feels guilty because he helped organise my hen party.

'Go back, both of you,' Mum repeats. I watch Mum, Gran and Aunt Chrissie walk slowly down the corridor towards the lift. Zac puts his arm in mine, and we traipse back into the room, me leaning on him heavily as the effects of the alcohol make the corridor sway.

'Sorry,' he says.

I smile at him and step away, gesturing at one of the servers. 'Please can you fill my glass with sparkling water rather than champagne, please?' I whisper. I think my words are beginning to drawl. I've had quite enough to drink.

My girlfriends sweep me back up in the fun. There are more questions, some deeply personal and embarrassing, others banal, but I quickly lose track of everything. It isn't until the next day that I wonder whether the server really was giving me sparkling water.

The next morning, I awake with a throbbing head and aching limbs. I force my eyes open and quickly shut them again. The sunlight hurts. And then I open them again. Where the hell am I? The memories of last night return in fragments. Am I still in the hotel? I can't be, because this place has a familiarity to it.

'Need a sick bucket?'

I turn towards the male voice. His face swims in and out. What is Zac doing here? I rub my eyes and haul myself up in bed. I'm relieved to see that I'm wearing my underwear, but how did I get here, and why am I in Zac's bed?

Oh no.

Please no.

My face flushes with shame, and I clutch the duvet, pulling it up to my neck. Surely I didn't end up in bed with Zac?

He must be able to read my mind because he says, 'Don't worry. Nothing happened, but you were so wasted I brought you back here.'

'Did I say anything, do anything?'

He frowns at me. 'Other than throwing up in the hallway and mumbling complete nonsense, no. There's nothing bad to report back to Markus.'

I close my eyes. I'm not worried about my bad behaviour being reported back to my husband-to-be. No. The reason I don't drink is I'm terrified that I might inadvertently share my secret, because drink loosens one's tongue, doesn't it? It makes you lose control. And I never, ever can afford to lose control.

10

CARRIE

Today is the day that my life is going to change for the better. I don't know that for sure, but I have a good feeling. I'm interviewing for a new job, and it's a job that I really, really want. The first job that I feel excited about since before the accident. I am wary, though, because I know all too well that the more you want something, the greater the disappointment is when it fails to materialise. I've done my homework, but I'm still nervous. No. More than nervous, terrified that I might blow a once-in-a-lifetime opportunity. If I get this job, I'll be able to realise so many of my dreams, not least having proper money in my bank account and being able to get out of this hideous flat.

I'm wearing a suit. It's new, from Marks and Spencer, a dark burgundy colour and office-smart. I stand in front of the bathroom mirror and practice my smile. That's what Melanie Pleat told me to do. To smile until you feel warmth in your gut and the smile becomes genuine. It hasn't worked for me before, but today I'm feeling a flicker of excitement and the realisation that I might actually be within grasping reach of joy. I rehearse some of the potential interview questions in my head.

'Why do you want this job?'

'What can you bring to this company?'

'How relevant is your previous experience?'

I know what I need to say; I just hope that my brain doesn't freeze on me in the moment. Or even worse, what if I have a panic attack? I could take a tranquilliser beforehand, but that might make me too spaced out. My mind relapses into all of the negative what-ifs, so I ping the elastic band around my wrist so hard, I let out a little yelp.

I need to go.

For a change, my bus connections all work, and I find myself in the poshest part of London half an hour too early. Not that it matters, I'd rather be early than late. I find a Costa Coffee and queue up.

'An Americano,' I ask. I stand back and wait for my drink to be ready. When I've paid for it, an exorbitant price, I pick up the cup and walk towards a table near the window. There's a middle-aged man on his phone pacing towards me. I move to the left, but he does too, and then the next thing I know is that burning hot coffee has spilled on my suit trousers, leaving a dark brown stain down my groin and left leg.

'What the fuck!' I yell at him.

He looks completely startled and wedges his phone in his pocket. 'I'm very sorry.'

'Sorry! I'm about to go to the most important interview of my life and you do this to me!'

'I'm sorry, it was an accident. I'll get you some paper towels.'

I put the coffee cup on the nearest table and pause for a

second. I'm seeing red. Literally red, and if we weren't in a public place where everyone is staring at us, I would strangle him. The anger boils and spits, and I know I need to get out of here this very instant.

I race for the door, striding along the street, muttering *bastard* under my breath. I glance down at myself. Shit, I look a total mess, and my leg burns. What the hell am I going to do? I have twenty minutes to sort this, and even if I rinse my trousers with water, they won't be dry in time. There's only one solution: a change of clothes.

It helps that I'm walking along one of London's smartest streets with clothes shops either side. Holding my bag in front of the hideous stain, I stride into a fancy boutique, the sort of shop I've steered clear of for the past decade.

'Good morning, ma'am, how can I help you?' The saleswoman steps forwards.

'Just looking,' I say. I walk quickly around the rails and grab two trouser suits. One in navy, the other in impractical cream, both in a size ten and size twelve.

'Can I try these on?'

'Of course.'

The navy suit in a size ten fits like a glove, but when I look at the price tag, I nearly choke. It's priced at over a thousand pounds. Who the hell spends that sort of money on a suit? I glance at my watch. Time is running out, but then I get lucky. Another customer enters the shop. I peek around the side of the curtain, and she's asking to try on a size fourteen in a hideous pink dress. The shop assistant explains she'll have to look in the stockroom to see if they have the correct size. I watch as she disappears behind a door. Now is my time.

I tug the labels off the jacket and trousers, leave my

Marks and Spencer suit in a pile on the floor, and I literally run. I race through the shop, feeling the staring eyes of the customer on me. I run as fast as I can along the pavement, my slight limp forgotten, pushing past dawdling tourists and bumbling shoppers until I'm absolutely sure that I'm not being chased by some security guard. I stop to catch my breath and lean against a wall next to a construction site. I glance at my watch. *Shit*. It's 11 am, and I should be at my interview right now. With trembling fingers, I find my phone and pull up the address and a map. I'm only a couple of hundred yards away, but I'm sure I look a mess with a bright red face and hair out of place. I walk briskly to the office block and ring the bell. The door clicks open.

My heart is hammering now. I'm about as far away from being calm and collected as I could be. That bloody man in Costa Coffee. If I don't get this job, it'll be his fault.

I call the lift, get in it and study myself in the mirror. Nothing much I can do now except run my fingers through my hair. The lift pings open. I push my shoulders back, smile widely and walk forwards.

'Hello, I'm late for my interview. I'm really sorry, but my bus had an accident, and we had to wait for a replacement.'

'Goodness, I hope you're all right.' The woman at the front desk must be late fifties or early sixties, but she's definitely had work done to her face, because her skin is stretched unnaturally tightly over her high cheekbones, and her lips are a little too plump.

'Yes, yes. I'm fine, just a bit overheated and very apologetic for being late.'

'Why don't I get you a glass of water?'

'Thank you. That's kind of you.'

She walks over to one of those water machines and pours a glass before handing it to me. I drink it in one long swig.

'Are you ready for your interview now?' she asks.

I smile and smooth down my designer trousers. They feel good. 'Yes, I say. Yes. I'm very ready.' I follow her across the small open-plan office, and she opens a door, holding it back for me as I walk inside.

'Good morning,' I say with my hand outstretched. 'My name is Denise White, and it's a pleasure to meet you.'

'Good morning, Denise. I'm Leonie Wilding. Please take a seat.'

11

LEONIE

I lied to Markus. I know it's stupid, because I shouldn't feel the need to, but I didn't tell him that I awoke in Zac's bed. I told him that I'd had too much to drink and stayed the night over with my cousin Sheryl. He was so lovely about it, cooking me a fry-up, making me a virgin Mary, nipping out to the pharmacy to buy me Alka-Seltzer and insisting I go back to bed and sleep off my hangover. And then later in the day, he slipped into bed beside me, and we lost ourselves in each other for another couple of hours.

Sometimes I have to pinch myself that I got so lucky. Markus seems to know what I need before I need it, and then there are the presents. He buys me thoughtful gifts, just because. Sometimes they're useful, such as when he brought me a new umbrella because the spokes were broken in my battered old one, and he dropped it off at the office because the forecast was for rain. Other times, he buys me jewellery, expensive and beautiful pieces in blue Tiffany boxes or in dark olive and gold bags from Harrods. Our relationship is definitely intense, and he likes to keep me all to himself, as he explains it, so we've rarely been out with our respective friends. Markus has only met Zac a couple of times, and that was in passing. In fact, the only one of his friends whom I've met is Wayne, his closest and oldest friend, who will be the best man at our wedding. Wayne surprised me a bit. He's rather rough and ready, unlike Markus, who is debonair and charming. I can't see Wayne schmoozing up Mum and Dad in the way Markus does. They've been best friends since they were kids, apparently, Wayne being the son of the tenant farmer who farmed Markus' parents' estate in Scotland. I find it hard to imagine them wading through rivers and picking up dead pheasants after a successful shoot, but apparently that was what they did.

I'm sad I will never get to meet Markus' parents, both of whom passed away nearly a decade ago. An only child, it must be hard for him having no immediate family. I suppose it's one of the reasons Markus seems so fond of my parents; we're an instant family for him. Even the prenup doesn't seem to faze Markus or make him think less of them.

We've talked about past relationships, although there are no significant ones in my case, but I haven't shared information on the fling that Zac and I had all of those years ago. Markus has had two long-term relationships, but apparently I'm the first person he has proposed to. I'm rather relieved about that.

Wednesday nights are the only nights of the week Markus and I spend apart. He explained that he has a regular evening in the pub with Wayne and a couple of other mates, followed by a round of poker. I was a bit taken aback by that, but Markus laughed at me and said they played with pennies, and the most he's ever lost is five pounds. I don't want to be one of those wives who stop their husband from having friendships, so I choose Wednesday nights to meet up with my friends, which, due to a lack of them, normally involves a drink in a wine bar with Zac and Denise.

Markus and I have had an early supper, a ready-made meal from the freezer, and now he's going out to meet his mates. I'm staying at home. It's less than a week to the wedding, and I want to be rested, especially after the raucous hen party.

'I won't be late,' Markus says, placing a quick kiss on my lips as I lie on the sofa in front of the television.

'Enjoy,' I say. 'It's your last boys' night out as a single man!'

Markus does a mock shiver and then hurries out. I swing my feet onto the ground and pad into the kitchen to fetch a glass of water. And there on the table is Markus' wallet. He's not going to get very far in the pub without any money.

I grab my phone and punch in his number, but it rings out. I look out of the window and see that he's climbing into an Uber. Without thinking, I grab my house and car keys and run downstairs, but just as I arrive outside into the cold night, the Uber pulls away from the kerb. I'm not sure why I think this is a good idea, or perhaps I'm not really thinking, but I jump into my car, and I follow him. I wish I'd ask him which pub they meet up in, but I didn't. The traffic is light, and it's easy enough to keep up with the slow-driving silver Prius, although I almost run a red light at one point. I flash my headlights a couple of times, but the Uber driver just isn't noticing me. The car takes various back roads, and then suddenly it indicates to the left and comes to a halt in front of a dingy brick building somewhere between West Kensington and Hammersmith. I wonder for a moment if Markus is collecting Wayne, because there is no pub on this road, and there aren't even any obvious residential properties. It's strange.

Markus gets out of his car and heads across the road. The Uber leaves. I could easily wind my window down and shout out to him, but something makes me hold back. I watch as he opens a blue door with paint peeling off it and disappears inside the run-down building. I wait for a few minutes, just in case he's collecting a friend, but deep down I know he's not. What is Markus doing, and why has he lied to me?

I lock up my car and follow my fiancé's footsteps. I expect the blue door to be locked, but it isn't, and it opens with a squeak. Inside, there is cheap lino on the floor and a wall with a large noticeboard. It's filled with notices about Narcotics Anonymous, how to seek help if you're feeling suicidal, how to manage if you're on benefits. There's a door just beyond it, and I can hear voices from within.

Footsteps behind me make me jump. A woman with matted grey hair and a limp hobbles past me.

'Are you coming in?'

'Um, I'm not sure.'

'It's always hard the first time, but you need to remember we've all been newbies once upon a time.'

'Yes, thank you,' I say, although I've no idea what she's talking about. She opens the door, and I notice a piece of paper sellotaped to it that says 'NA – please don't disturb'. As she walks inside, I catch a glimpse of the room and see people seated in a circle. Markus is there with his back to the door.

And then it hits me. NA. Narcotics Anonymous.

The woman glances back at me, but I turn away and stride to the front door. What the hell is Markus doing at a

Narcotics Anonymous group? My initial thoughts are perhaps he's a volunteer here. Maybe one of his parents was an addict, and he's doing this as a way to give back. But why not tell me the truth?

As I slide into my car, I realise that there's only one obvious reason as to why Markus is here. That's because he's an ex-addict himself. My sophisticated, handsome fiancé has, or had, a drugs problem.

I drive home slowly, my mind in turmoil. Has he kept this from me because he's ashamed? Does he think I might not want to marry someone with an addictive personality? But actually what hurts is that he's kept it a secret. I try to rationalise with myself. Better a secret like this than him having another woman stashed away somewhere. But it stings that he hasn't felt able to open up to me.

I think back over the past whirlwind few months. Even though we've lain in bed and shared some of our deepest secrets, I realise there must be so much that we don't know about each other. I've never told Markus about the accident, and I never will. I have kept the promise that I made to Dad a lifetime ago. It has crossed my mind that Dad might say something to me, just a little reminder not to mention anything to Markus, but he hasn't. Dad may not trust my judgement on many things, but he surely knows that I would never talk about what happened on that terrible night. Instead, I just let it eat away at me, condemning me to a lifetime of guilt, a lifetime of knowing that I don't really deserve happiness or success. And as I haven't told my truths to Markus, I suppose he may well be hiding some of his own.

Back at home, I don't know what to do with myself. I try to read a book, but the words swim, and I can't concentrate. The television isn't much better. Eventually I take the vacuum out and hoover the house. Not that it needs doing, because I have a cleaner who comes twice a week, also courtesy of my parents.

My heart plummets when I hear Markus' key in the door just before 10 pm.

'You still up, darling? Thought you were having an early night?'

'We need to talk.'

'Oh dear. I don't like the sound of that,' he says, joviality in his voice. He walks into the kitchen, and I follow him. He pulls out a chair and sits down.

'What's up?'

'You left your wallet at home.'

He bashes his forehead with the palm of his right hand. 'I know. Such an idiot. The lads had to pay for my drinks.'

'But you didn't go to the pub,' I say. His eyes lock onto mine, and for the first time since we met, I feel a frisson of fear.

'What are you saying?' His voice is expressionless.

'I followed you because I wanted to catch up with you to give you your wallet. If you'd checked your phone, you'd have seen a missed call from me.'

He takes his phone from his pocket and switches it back on. It beeps with a message. Mine.

'You bloody followed me, Leonie? Don't you trust me?'

'You're not listening. I followed you to give you your wallet. There was no ulterior motive, but why were you attending a Narcotics Anonymous meeting?'

There's an expression on Markus' face that I haven't seen before, and it makes me step away from him. In the months we've known each other, I've never seen him lose his temper, but his eyes are flashing, and a vein is throbbing on the side of his temple. And then it's as if the air has been released from him, and he lets out a loud sigh.

'I attend NA meetings because I used to be addicted to prescription drugs.'

'You never told me,' I say in a small voice.

'I didn't tell you because I'm not proud of it. It's a part of my past, and it's not relevant to my present or my future.'

'But you're still attending.'

'I go along every so often before stressful events.'

'Our wedding.'

He nods.

I scoot a chair over so I'm sitting right next to him. 'I wish you'd felt you could tell me.'

'Hardly a great chat-up line, is it? Hello, my name is Markus Klausen, and I'm addicted to oxycodone.'

'Is that what you were addicted to?'

He nods. 'I've been clean for nearly two years.'

'What happened?' I ask, holding his hand.

'I was in a car accident and had bad whiplash. I was given painkillers, just co-codomol at first, but the pain didn't go away, and before long I was on oxycodone. It's a horrible drug, Leonie. It plays with your brain. You don't want to be on it, but you can't live without it. And then I was working too hard, which is why I changed jobs and chose a more balanced life. But the main thing is I'm clean now.'

'I wish you had told me,' I say.

'I should have done. I don't want us to have any secrets, yet I'm the one who kept this from you. Can you forgive me?' he asks as he takes my hands and stares into my eyes.

I think then of my secret, which is so much bigger, so much worse than a prescription drugs habit. I think of how I can never be truly honest with my future husband.

'Do you want to call off the wedding?' he asks, but I'm not really listening. I'm thinking of how my life is truly wonderful, whereas the man who died will never again experience love. Will never experience anything.

I realise then that I haven't answered him. 'Of course not. I love you, Markus, and I totally agree – no secrets.' I don't even bother to cross my fingers behind my back.

12

CARRIE

'Hey, stranger, how are you doing?' I elbow Markus as I sit down next to him.

'Yeah, good. And you?' he asks.

'Loads to tell you, but coffee first.'

We're in a little diner in the posh part of Peckham, the part that has become a hub for trendy creatives. The diner now calls itself a coffee shop, because that's the way of gentrification, but it still smells of oily breakfasts and burned coffee, and the tables are still sticky. This might now be a desirable area, but one thing is for sure, Castaway Property Search doesn't venture over this way, so the chances of running into Leonie here are about zero. It's becoming increasingly difficult for Markus and me to meet up, something that I hadn't really factored in when I first conceived my plan. I can't even call him, so I've had to buy a burner phone, from which I send him the occasional carefully worded text.

'What are you drinking? An Americano?' Markus asks. That's what I like about him. He might be a grifter and a chancer, but he's a gentleman about it. He remembers the details: your favourite coffee, your birthstone, the name of your first pet. And I owe Markus a lot. Quite possibly even my life.

We met a few years ago at Narcotics Anonymous. If you haven't been to one of those meetings before, you might be surprised. Every single walk of life is seated in that circle. The super-wealthy toffs like Leonie; the upper-class chancers now down on their luck, like Markus; the complete down-and-outs sleeping rough; and people like me, who had it all and then lost it. We're all seeking to break free of the disease that is addiction, and we're all committed to the Twelve Steps and the Twelve Traditions. Markus became my sponsor. We just clicked; not in a physical way. No, Markus made that very clear early on, but our journeys have been vaguely similar, and the truth is, for all his faults, and he has many, I like the guy.

'One Americano with a fine biscuit on the side.' Markus places it on the table with a flourish. 'So how have you been?' he asks as he sits down opposite me.

'Good, good.'

'You look totally different,' he says. 'Totally fabulous, actually.'

'That's what having a purpose and a decent pay cheque does to you.' I laugh. 'Oh, and an expensive haircut and new clothes.' I take a sip of my coffee. 'How's the relationship going?'

'Well, as you know, we're engaged to be married. I think it might be luuv.' He drawls out the word.

'From her side only, I hope,' I add.

'And how could she fail to fall in love with me?' He puffs his chest out.

'Ha, ha,' I say, but secretly I'm thrilled. My plan is going exactly as I'd hoped. When I discovered who Leonie Wilding was, I made it my mission to find out everything about her, and what I found sickened me. Leonie is rich, beautiful, well educated. She's a somebody in a world where 99.9% of people are nobodies. She's swimming along in her gilded life without the slightest thought or hint of remorse for the devastation she wreaked on my life. The more I thought about it, the more I think about it, the more I am convinced that she *was* there when I was lying in agony in that ditch, half in and half out of the broken car. She should be made to pay for what she did through the justice system, but let's face it, that's broken. Instead, it's up to me to organise retribution, and that's exactly what I'm doing. I have a number of objectives, which I've written down in my diary.

1. *To lose out in love and have her heart broken*
2. *To suffer humiliation in her personal life*
3. *To never have children*
4. *To fail in business, preferably losing her business in a humiliating fashion*
5. *To have a short life filled with pain and misery*

When I found out about Leonie, it gave my life the purpose it's been missing for so long. My first step was to recruit Markus. He's always looking for the next adventure or scam, and he's very good at it. I told him all about Leonie, how she deserved to be brought down, but I didn't share the details of my accident, and that's because I don't trust Markus. If he's scamming someone else, the chances are he might try to scam me. I don't even think he'd do it on purpose because we're genuine friends, but the man just can't help himself. He likes the good life, and he doesn't like to work. Go figure. Anyway, I had the genius idea of Markus trying to get Leonie to fall in love with him. Obviously, there were a lot of variables over which I had no control, the biggest being would Leonie even fancy him? Markus is exceptionally good looking, and he certainly knows how to turn on the charm, so I thought the chances were high. But one never knows how chemistry works. But the plan has gone far better than I'd dared hope, and now they're engaged.

'A week to go,' he says.

'I can't wait.' The grin won't leave my face. 'There's she'll be, all dressed up in her finery, waiting at the bottom of the aisle for the groom, who will never turn up. It's just genius, and I'll be at the church, able to enjoy every moment of her devastation. I'll record it on my phone so you can see it afterwards.'

'Okay,' Markus says, but his eyes are drifting off towards the door.

I've adored every moment of Leonie's grand love affair, and it's gone better than in my wildest dreams. It's Markus this and Markus that in the office; it would be nauseating if I didn't know how Leonie's heart is going to be broken.

'I still don't know how you managed to get a job at Castaway,' Markus says.

'I've had quite a bit of luck in this journey,' I muse, and goodness, do I deserve it. 'She advertised for an office manager, and it's genuinely within my skill set. Don't forget you've only known the down-and-out me, the angry addict.'

'I suppose so. So when will I get my money?' Markus asks.

Ah, here we go. The wheeler dealer. Markus might have

given up the drugs, but he still needs his fix, and these days he gets that from dodgy deals and scams. I've promised him ten thousand pounds for stitching up Leonie. I've absolutely no idea where I'm going to get that kind of money from, but I'll face that problem when I have to.

'When you've held up your side of the bargain. After the wedding. So what are you going to do next? Have you got another project lined up?' I air quote around the word *project*.

'Actually, no. I'll just go with the flow.'

'But no drugs?'

'Come on, Carrie. I even went to an NA meeting last week. Leonie found out.'

'What do you mean?'

'She followed me there.'

'Does she think you're not trustworthy?'

'No, nothing like that. I left my wallet at home, and she followed me to give it back to me, but it didn't feel great admitting the addiction to her.'

'Probably made you seem more human, less perfect.'

'But I am perfect,' Markus says, without even the faintest hint of irony.

13

LEONIE

Today is the day. Today I'm getting married and committing myself to the love of my life. I'm full of conflicting emotions: excitement, love, terror. Until now, I've been sure about Markus, but today I woke up at 5 am and lay in bed wondering if I'm doing the right thing. We haven't even known each other for seven months, and he failed to tell me he was an ex-addict. Yet he is the most loving, attentive, kind man I've ever met. I know I can't walk away from him.

Tonight is the first night Markus and I have slept apart in months. I'm in my old bedroom, the room in my parents' Horsham house, which is exactly the same as when I left home for university. There are posters on the wall and a dressing table crammed full of outdated perfumes and nail varnishes that won't open. Hanging on the far wall in front of the huge built-in wardrobe is my wedding dress. The second-best wedding dress.

As the sunlight pours through the cracks in the curtains, I think how charmed my life has been. And inevitably, my thoughts linger on the man in the car. If my father hadn't chased me that day, the trajectory of my life would have been totally different. The police would have arrived; I would have been arrested; I wouldn't have gone to university. Dad's business would have been brought into disrepute, and perhaps he wouldn't be the successful man that he is today. And it's because of him that I live this life of luxury. I hate myself for taking from him, but what choice do I have? I'm not as resourceful or brave as Sam. Besides, I owe Dad so much more. He saved me, and he's continued to save me, giving me a wonderful life, a business that I find fulfilling, a future where I won't have to worry about money, and today. The perfect wedding.

And yes, I'm consumed with guilt. For every milestone in my life, I think how I was responsible for that poor man never experiencing the same thing. What I did was horrific. I killed a person and left them there, and yes, it has burned my conscience for a decade, and it will continue to do so for the rest of my life. And that's why I'm struggling with today, because deep down, I don't think I deserve happiness.

I'm not in the slightest bit sleepy now, so I get out of bed and throw on some old clothes. I slip out of the house and walk into the massive marquee that takes up a large part of the garden. Its ceiling is almost black and studded with twinkling lights that look like stars. The sides are lined with gentle swathes of fabric in white and peach, my chosen colours. I smile to myself as I try to imagine what this place would look like in my parents chosen colours of red and white. A bordello, perhaps. The tables for ten people are in place, and soon the marquee will be bustling with people, laying the tables with white linen cloths, silver cutlery and sparkling glasses. And the florist will arrive and fill this place up with romantic roses, while drooping tulips in the softest shades will lean over circular glass vases in the centre of every table.

I think of the three hundred guests arriving later today, many of whom I don't know, and for a moment I consider running away, finding Markus and getting on the next flight to the Caribbean, where we can have a romantic wedding just for the two of us. But I shake that thought away. Today is as much for my parents as it is for me and Markus.

I walk for an hour, enjoying the low mist and the cacophony of birds, and when I eventually return, Mum is up making coffee, fluttering around the kitchen, a bundle of nervous energy.

'An hour to go before the caterers and florist arrives,' Mum says, handing me a cup of tea.

'I'd prefer coffee,' I say.

'You don't want to have coffee breath today of all days.'

I try not to snigger. I can see what Mum is doing here, trying to control every element, trying to make today completely perfect.

Two hours later, the place is a hive of activity. Margot, our wedding planner, has taken control, acting like a general with her pages of lists and the barking of instructions. I'm glad I don't have to get involved. Mum has turned one of her spare rooms into a dressing room just for the wedding, and in here, the three makeup artists are setting up their equipment, ready to make me, Mum and my bridesmaids beautiful. Meanwhile, I'm seated in front of a large mirror with a hairdresser drying my hair into luxuriant curls.

'You're looking beautiful,' my cousin Sheryl says as she sits down next to me. She's holding a bottle of champagne, which she expertly uncorks. 'Where are the glasses, Aunty Brenda?' she asks Mum, who perches on a stool.

'I'll get them.' Mum leaps up.

'A bit early in the day, isn't it?' I suggest.

'Dutch courage.'

The photographer takes a photograph of me, and I jump, the hair iron burning the back of my ear. 'Ouch,' I say, and everyone is immediately apologetic and overly concerned. It's not only Mum's nerves that are frazzled. Tension is getting to me, too.

'Knock, knock.' Dad puts his head around the door. 'Everyone decent?' he asks, although it would be too late if we weren't. 'A parcel just arrived for you.'

He hands me a flat box wrapped in white tissue paper and tied with a white bow. We've had a stack of wedding presents already, which I intend to open when we're back from our honeymoon. I lift the small envelope from the box and tear it open. Inside is a card showing two hearts intertwined.

> *To the love of my life on our wedding day. I never knew it was possible to love someone as much as I love you. My heart. My soul. My life. My wife. I adore you. I can't wait to be your husband. Markus xxx.*

Tears well in my eyes. I definitely don't deserve this much love and adoration. Carefully, I remove the tissue paper. I'm holding a navy box lined with white satin. I lift up the lid and gasp. Inside is a beautiful diamond necklace. The chain is simple, platinum I assume, and the pendant comprises one very large circular diamond, another one slightly smaller underneath it, with five more smaller diamonds decreasing in size. It's about an inch long, and the stones sparkle and glisten.

'Wow, that's beautiful,' Sheryl says, peering at it.

'Yes, it is,' I say as I carefully lift the necklace out of the box. 'It's from Markus. A wedding present.'

'You are so lucky,' Sheryl says.

The hairdresser fastens the necklace around my neck, and it sits perfectly in the hollow between my clavicles. It feels surprisingly light for such a beautiful piece of jewellery, but it will look stunning with my wedding dress. Everyone in the room oohs and aahs.

Forty-five minutes later, my hair and makeup are done. I barely recognise myself. The excitement is palpable, but there's one person missing. Sam should have arrived last night, but his flight was delayed by several hours. I haven't seen my brother in nine months, and I miss him. I wonder what he'll think of Markus. While my parents love my future husband, I have a niggle of doubt regarding Sam. I can't quite put my finger on it, but I'm not sure that Markus is Sam's type. Then I remind myself that it's me who's marrying him, not my brother.

Back in my bedroom, I lift the wedding dress off the hanger and lay it on my bed. Mum bustles into the room. 'Nearly forgot,' she says, holding out a pale blue strip of fabric that looks like a large scrunchie.

'What's this?'

'Something borrowed and something blue. An old garter that your gran gave me. It brought me luck on my wedding day. You need to wear it.'

Laughing, I slide it up my leg. Mum helps me into the dress, and she carefully, and painfully slowly, does up every single one of the little buttons on the back of the dress.

'I've dreamed of today since you were a little girl,' she says. 'You make such a beautiful couple, you and Markus. I just wish you were wearing a veil.'

I didn't feel the need for a veil. I want to be able to see Markus and all my guests clearly as I walk up the aisle, and veils feel somehow old-fashioned.

'Right, the cars are here, so I'd better go,' Mum says as she opens the bedroom door and walks straight into Sam.

'My boy!' She throws her arms around him. I feel for Mum. I know how much she misses her son, but for the sake of marital harmony, she's had to side with Dad.

'Wow, you look stunning, both of you,' Sam says, leaning in to give me a kiss on the cheek. I note that he's wearing a suit but no tie. I don't suppose Dad will be happy about that.

'Are you exhausted?' I ask.

'Nothing a couple of glasses of champagne won't cure. Mum, the bossy wedding planner woman says that you and I need to leave for the church.'

And then they're gone, and I'm left all alone standing on the landing at the top of the stairs. Dad appears at the bottom. 'You look beautiful, Leonie,' he says, and for a moment I wonder if his eyes are welling up a little. I walk carefully down the stairs, hanging onto the handrail tightly, careful not to step on my long dress.

At the bottom, Dad puts his arm out, and I thread mine through it. 'I am so proud of you, Leonie,' he says.

I'm startled. That's quite possibly the first time my father has ever paid me a compliment. Even when I graduated from Oxford with a first – because all I did during my time there was work – I only got a cursory 'well done'.

'We've never talked about it.' His voice is low. 'But I'm so relieved that the terrible thing you did as a teenager hasn't affected your life.'

I flinch. Why did Dad have to mention this now, just as I'm about to step into the vintage Rolls-Royce that is taking me to the church? And how wrong he is, I think. Outwardly perhaps it seems that way, that I'm functioning at a high level, yet it is seared in my conscience. I'm careful as to how much alcohol I drink, for fear that it might loosen my lips. I feel the need to stay in control all the time. I regret the accident and walking away every single day.

The chauffeur helps me into the car while Dad walks around to the other side and gets in next to me. For the first ten minutes of the journey, we don't say a word, and I realise that the only conversations I ever have with Dad are about work. Most of the time, he's criticising me for something I have or haven't done. At least I know that my children will have a better relationship with their dad. Markus is the polar opposite of Dad. He's open, warm, and thoughtful, and work is definitely not the most important thing in his life. Markus has explained to me on more than one occasion that it's taken him years to achieve the perfect work-life balance.

Dad interrupts my thoughts. 'I still wish he'd signed the prenup.' I clench my jaw. I'm not going to get into an argument about that when I'm just a few minutes away from getting married. God, he chooses his moments.

The church spire comes into view. It's an ancient church with a beautiful slate roof and imposing stained-glass windows. The first thing I notice are the flowers: a fabulous archway of pale roses fully enclosing the porch to the large wooden door. It looks stunning. The second thing I notice is Wayne pacing up and down the path, his phone attached to his ear. He glances up at the car, his eyebrows knotted together. Dad's snide remark has sown a seed of anger, and it increases as I wonder what's so important that Wayne has to leave the church, to step away from his duties as best man. Some dodgy business deal, I suppose.

As Dad and the chauffeur help me out of the car, a couple of other of Markus' friends appear, men I have only been cursorily introduced to when I collected Markus from the pub. They're dressed in suits, a rose in their lapels. The three of them have their heads close together, but I'm too far away to hear what they're saying. Shouldn't they all be inside the church, supporting Markus, waiting for Dad and me to walk down the aisle to the wedding march?

Something tightens inside my stomach as I look at their faces, and then Wayne walks towards me. I can't fully read his expression, except I know that something is very, very wrong.

14

CARRIE

This is the moment I've been waiting for. My foot is jiggling up and down with excitement, but it's a different excitement to what most of the guests are experiencing. Of that, I'm sure. I'm seated midway back on Markus' side of the church. Although I'm officially Leonie's guest, Markus has so few people to support him, the groomsmen suggested all the guests sit anywhere they wish. I'm on the aisle, and I refused to budge up, even when some stuck-up elderly guests tried to shovel me along. I want a good view, and from here, I've got one. The church looks beautiful, if churches are your thing. There are huge arrangements of roses up near the altar and sprays of peach-coloured flowers attached to the ends of every pew. Rose petals are scattered along the aisle, which seems a bit premature to me, as I thought they were scattered after the marriage ceremony.

Every single pew is taken, and the guests are dressed up to the nines. Many of the women are wearing hats, some much too big. It's selfish, I reckon, to wear a hat that will obscure the view of the people behind you. Some of the men are in dinner suits, but mostly they're wearing dark suits or blazers with ties. There's a lot of braying and fake laughter. Now an organ is playing quietly, background music for the moment. The groomsmen are standing up at the front of the church, three men in their thirties, each with a rose in their lapels. The one with the shaggy blond hair and the air of a rascal seems particularly worried. He's forever checking his phone and tapping the pocket of his jacket, checking he's got the rings, I assume. I snort to myself. He won't be needing those.

The whispers start about fifteen minutes before the official start of the wedding. *Where is Markus? Why isn't the groom here?* The three men pace out of the church, but the rumours have already started. People are whispering behind their hands, looks of concern: *What's happened to Markus? Has he had a change of mind?* The panic of a few swiftly spreads to the masses, and now Brenda is here with the bridesmaids, and the best man has reappeared in the church. He's talking in a low whisper to Brenda. Leonie's mother looks like she's about to burst into tears. I expect she will, very soon.

I get up, leaving the order-of-service pamphlet and a pashmina on my seat so no one nabs my place. I walk quickly and determinedly towards the exit. I want to have the best view in the house for when Leonie arrives.

And then a maroon and cream Rolls-Royce with a cream ribbon in a V across the bonnet pulls up in front of the church. This is the moment. I stand back until Leonie is out of the car. I have to admit that she looks beautiful with those tumbling locks and big blue eyes and a dress that skims her curves. Her pompous father walks around to her side and takes her arm, but then the best man is striding over to talk to her, and I watch as if in slow motion, the utter shock settles on her face. How her eyes widen and her mouth becomes a perfect O, and the blood drains from her skin. Now it's my time.

I rush up to Leonie, ignoring the small group of people who are hovering.

'You look stunning,' I say, blowing her an air kiss. And then I frown, an exaggerated look of concern on my face. 'Is everything all right?'

She shakes her head, tears pooling in her lower lids. That perfect makeup won't be perfect for much longer.

'The bloody bastard hasn't turned up!' Gus spits out the words. 'All of this, all the money spent, all the guests and he's humiliated us, the total bastard.'

For a moment, I feel sorry for Leonie. Her father's only worried about the wasted money and how he's going to look in front of his guests. He hasn't given a second's thought to his daughter's shattered heart.

I pass Leonie a handkerchief, but she seems frozen, the shock of being jilted too great.

'Perhaps he's had an accident,' she murmurs.

'Or perhaps he isn't the man you thought he was,' I say, but Leonie ignores me. She's looking straight over my shoulder, and her expression changes, her eyes crease, and she lets out a little moan. There's the slamming of a car door, heavy footsteps.

'Markus!' she cries.

I turn around, and there the bastard is, dressed in a pale grey morning suit, a peach bow tie and his hair just slightly messy. What the hell is Markus playing at?

He grabs Leonie's hand and kisses it. 'I'm so sorry for

keeping you waiting, darling.' He is breathless. 'And on the most important day of our lives.'

'What the hell happened?' Gus barks.

'I'm sorry, sir.'

I have to look away. It's unbearable to watch and listen to this sycophant, to realise that my puppet has gone off-piste.

'I was on my way to get a taxi when an old woman fell into the road. It was shocking how everyone else just walked straight past her. I called an ambulance, but the paramedic dispatchers asked me to stay with the woman until they arrived. She had no one else, you see. That took about half an hour, and then she asked if I would accompany her to the hospital. I could hardly say no. But then I realised I couldn't even call you or Wayne. I'd left my phone in the hotel room, because I knew I wouldn't need it today. I'm so sorry I'm late, my darling. You look utterly gorgeous, by the way.' He leans in and places a quick kiss on her lips.

'Okay, everyone,' Wayne says, clapping his hands. 'We all need to get back inside the church.'

I try to catch Markus' eye, but he's carefully avoiding looking at me. I walk back in with the other groomsmen.

'He's here now!' Wayne shouts, and all the guests break into applause. I sit down heavily on the hard wooden pew, anger churning my guts. Markus literally runs up the aisle, up to the altar, where he shakes hands with the vicar.

'Sorry!' he says loudly so that everyone can hear. 'So sorry I'm late. I'll explain it all later.'

And then silence falls, and the wedding march starts up. Everyone turns to look at the door, and Leonie enters with her father, her face one of radiance. What is Markus playing at? Is he going to come up with a reason why he can't marry her, or perhaps he's planted someone in the congregation who is going to do that? The hymns and the sermon and the prayers are interminable. I find it difficult to sit still, my foot jiggling up and down, and the woman sitting next to me throws me dagger stares. To hell with her. Finally, it's time for the vows. *Don't screw it up now, Markus.*

It's so quiet in the church you could hear a pin drop. Leonie and Markus face each other as the vicar stands in front of them. Here we go.

'First, I am required to ask anyone present who knows a reason why these persons may not lawfully marry, to declare it now.'

I wait, my breath bated. *Someone say something now.* There is a long silence, and I wonder if I should jump up and speak, tell everyone that Markus is a fraudster, that he doesn't really love Leonie, that this is all part of my plan for revenge. But I don't. I just stare straight ahead, anger pooling in my chest.

The vicar smiles at them. 'The vows you are about to take are to be made in the presence of God, who is judge of all and knows all the secrets of our hearts; therefore, if either of you knows a reason why you may not lawfully marry, you must declare it now.'

Come on, Markus. Now is the time. Except he's smiling at Leonie, holding her hands, gazing into her eyes. What the hell is he playing at? And I realise with dismay that Markus has played me. He's going to marry Leonie.

The vicar carries on. 'Markus Edwin Klausen, will you take Leonie Jayne Wilding to be your wife? Will you love her, comfort her, honour and protect her, and, forsaking all others, be faithful to her as long as you both shall live?'

Markus smiles. 'I will.'

The bastard. The complete and utter bastard. Why has

he changed our plans? What the hell is he doing? I completely tune out the rest of the service, trying and rather failing to swallow my increasing fury. I'm seriously considering disappearing back home after the service and not attending the reception, but what if Markus pulls a stunt there? If I'm going to move forwards with my plan, then I have no choice but to grin and bear it, get through the rest of the nauseating day.

Leonie's parents definitely have more money than taste. It's the first time I've been to their house, not that I have the chance to actually go in it, as the reception is being held in an opulent marquee in their huge garden. It's a mock Tudor house, ugly in all its fakeness, edged with pink and blue hydrangea bushes. Everyone pours into the marquee, searching for their places on the two massive boards that list all the guests' names. I'm relieved to see that I'm on the same table as Zac. At least I'll know someone. For some reason, he seems as out of sorts as I am, unusually quiet, almost as if he doesn't want to be here. And then it strikes me. His eyes are fixed permanently on the top table, where Leonie and Markus are seated with her parents and other members of their family. Zac is in love with Leonie. He probably has been for all the years they've known each other, and today his dream of disappearing off into the sunset with her has been completely destroyed. Poor Zac. I know too well what rejection feels like.

The meal seems to take forever. The food looks better than it tastes. A smoked salmon and salmon mousse starter followed by quail as a main course. I've never eaten quail before, and frankly, I'm not sure what's so great about it. It tastes like dried-out chicken. Conversation has been stilted because I'm not in the mood to make carefree chat with the two guys either side of me. One is some business partner of Gus'. After dropping unsubtle hints that Gus maybe not the honourable businessman he portrays himself to be, I turn to the other side. Andy is a friend of Leonie's from university days, a rather earnest and dour-looking fellow in his late twenties who works in insurance and shared a house with Leonie in their third year. I suspect that Leonie was trying a bit of matchmaking by sitting us together because Andy is quick to tell me that he's single and eagerly searching for a life partner. A life partner who won't be me.

And then the toastmaster hits the side of a glass with a knife, and everyone falls silent. Markus stands up.

'First of all, an apology. I'm sorry for being late to the church and giving my beautiful wife palpitations. As those of you who know me are aware, I'm never late, so being so to the most important event of my life was disappointing. Suffice to say, I had to accompany an elderly lady to hospital who had fallen in the road, and because I was on my way to my wedding, I'd left my phone in the hotel in my suitcase, so I couldn't warn anyone what had happened.'

I almost choke on my lemon sorbet. What a load of absolute bullshit; just another one of Markus' yarns to suggest that he's the hero of the hour. The man should start writing fiction; he's that good at it.

'And now, to Leonie. The love of my life. The most beautiful, intelligent, caring woman in the whole world. I will be pinching myself for years to come, unable to believe that she has chosen me to be her husband. Aren't I the luckiest guy alive!'

That elicits a gentle chuckle. *Yeah, right.*

'Some of you may know that we met at a house viewing. Love at first sight for Leonie was the house; for me, it was her. I had a few million in my pocket ready to buy the home of my dreams, but what I didn't count on was meeting this princess. I knew straight away that any future house had to be chosen by her, not me. So how did I get her to say yes, I'm sure you're all asking? Honestly, I don't know.

'So today is the proudest day of my life. Actually, second proudest. The proudest was when I won the egg and spoon race at primary school.'

There's half-hearted laughter, because it's obvious he lifted that joke from a 'how to write a wedding speech' website. I bet Markus is pissed about that, but he recovers quickly.

'As some of you will know, my parents have sadly passed on. I'm confident they're looking down on us with pride and joy, but I'm very blessed to have wonderful parents-in-law.' He turns towards Brenda and Gus. 'Mum, Dad, thank you for giving Leonie and me the most special day ever. Thank you for producing this amazing woman and for letting me marry her. Although I have to say, you didn't get much of a choice in that one.'

Oh my God, this is nauseating. He's calling Leonie's parents Mum and Dad! I'm not sure I can listen to any more of this, yet I can't leave the table without drawing attention to myself.

'It feels like I've waited a lifetime to marry the woman of my dreams, and I'm pretty sure there are a few people here who also feel Leonie is the woman of their dreams–' Markus glances at our table, and a flush creeps up Zac's neck. That wasn't kind, but then Markus has a steely core, and I'm pretty sure his kind behaviour is learned and, when he chooses, displayed simply to get his own way. 'I asked a good mate what's the key to a happy marriage. He told me to find a woman who's good at cooking and cleaning. A woman who's a beast in bed. A woman who is really wealthy. And then he said, just be sure these three women never meet.'

This elicits a bit more of a laugh.

'But I didn't need to find three women. I've got all of that in one amazing package, my Leonie.'

Oh, Markus. Is it really a good thing to tell your wedding guests that you married her for her money?

'Fortunately, I'm also good at keeping house, I'm also rather good in bed and have plenty of money myself, so we make a great match.'

Modesty was never Markus' strong point.

'Please will you raise a glass with me, to my wonderful wife, Leonie!'

Everyone gets to their feet and toasts the bride. I have to sit through another forty minutes of speeches. Warren, whose speech has definitely been lifted from a speech-writing book, and then the father of the bride. Gus' speech is literally all about himself and his business, how his company builds the best homes in the UK, how he's made squillions and is so happy that he could invite all his clients and prospects. He only makes one reference to Leonie: how pretty she looks today. If I didn't loathe her so much, I might even feel an iota of pity. What a shit of a father.

It seems like hours until the happy couple cut their cake. It's a huge thing with five tiers covered in white icing and numerous little flowers in a peach colour. I don't know why Leonie has chosen that as her colour theme, because it's insipid. As they hold the big knife together, it plunges deeply into the cake, and I shock myself with violent thoughts as to what I might do with that blade.

Afterwards, as the cake is being cut by the serving staff,

Leonie and Markus meander between their tables of guests, chatting politely, accepting congratulations. At one point, I see Markus whisper something into Leonie's ear, and then he makes his way alone to the back of the marquee. Quickly I get up and weave my way through seated and standing guests, many of them bellowing, thanks to all the alcohol consumed. I catch a glimpse of Markus disappearing into the gentlemen's toilets. No cheap portable restrooms here. There are two rows of fancy toilets with proper flushing mechanisms and gold-plated sink taps.

'Markus!' I say in a whisper as he reappears.

He glances around shiftily. 'Denise, how lovely to see you here. Are you enjoying yourself?'

'Cut the crap,' I say in a low voice.

'Around the back,' he whispers. I follow him outside and to the rear of the row of toilets.

'What the hell are you playing at? You're not meant to have married her,' I exclaim, my voice wobbling slightly as I think of how he's betrayed me.

'Oh, come on, Carrie. You can't expect me to give all of this up. I'm going to make a fortune being married to Leonie.'

'If it was about the money, you could have asked me to pay you more.'

'You couldn't give me what I'm going to get from the Wildings in a million years. This is a fabulous lifestyle, and besides, I've grown to like Leonie. She's attractive, good in bed, a kind woman. I may never get another opportunity like this.'

I feel like I'm going to explode. I thought Markus was my friend, but he's played me.

'Look, I know you're pissed off with me, but you need to

see it from my perspective. My life is so much better with Leonie. Gus has really taken to me, and he's even talking about me joining the business, stepping into his shoes one day. It's like I'm a son to him. I'll make sure that you get money too, so don't worry.'

'You don't understand, Markus! It's not about the money.'

I can't believe this. It's the absolute opposite of what I wanted, and my plan has totally backfired. No, it's worse than that. Leonie is in a happy relationship. She's in love, and her world is perfect.

'I'll tell Leonie the truth,' I spit. 'I'll tell her this marriage is a con, that you're only with her for the money.'

'But I've just told you, that's not true,' he says. 'I'm in it for the duration. Besides, it's not me but you who are being the most deceitful, pretending to be Denise in the office, infiltrating yourself into her life for some petty revenge. If you say anything about me, I'll tell Leonie the truth about you, that your real name is Carrie, and your CV is completely fake. This conversation is over. I've got to get back to my beloved. The best day of my life.' He smirks at me, and if he hadn't moved away so quickly, I would have slapped him.

15

LEONIE

After the mix-up with the flowers and my wedding dress, I have to admit that I was nervous whether anything major would go wrong on the day itself. I needn't have worried. It was a dream wedding. I felt like a princess, and other than the fact I probably didn't know a third of the people there, it was perfect. I will never forget our first dance. The band played 'Endless Love', and Markus swept me around the dance floor, his strong arms around my shoulders and waist, his eyes never flickering away from mine. When the music stopped, he kissed me, such a long hard kiss that our guests started wolf-whistling and cheering. I didn't know it was possible to feel such love for another human being.

Now we're on holiday in Santorini. Dad and Markus had quite the run-in over our honeymoon. Dad wanted to pay for it as a wedding gift to us, but Markus was insistent that he should pay as the groom. Dad won, of course, because Dad always wins. We could have gone to the Maldives or somewhere more exotic, but Markus was so kind and said he didn't want to spend too much of Dad's money. So here we are, on this stunning volcanic island, walking hand in hand along Oia's narrow, winding, white-washed streets. There are so many tourists, thousands of them disgorged from the monster cruise liners docked far down below us, but even though the place is crowded, it doesn't detract from its beauty. The scent of olive oil mixes with citrus and the sugary sweetness of baclava. I push my sunglasses further onto my nose, the glare of the sun reflecting off the bright white of the buildings making me squint.

'Let's go down here,' Markus says, pulling me towards steps that descend steeply. Ahead of us, the bright blue dome of a church mimics the colour of the azure sea, and I think how lucky we are, how lucky I am, to be somewhere so beautiful.

It's quieter down this street, and as we pass yet another jewellery shop, I pause to look in the window. 'Those earrings are beautiful,' I say, pointing at a pair of drop earrings with stones that glisten as brightly as the sea.

'Try them on,' Markus suggests.

'No, I don't need any more earrings.'

'Surely you can never have too much jewellery?'

I finger the diamond necklace that Markus gave me as a wedding present and think of all the other pieces of jewellery that he's given me, beautifully wrapped in boxes from Tiffany and Cartier. Before I can stop him, he has opened the shop door and is tugging me inside.

'My wife would like to try on the earrings in the window,' he says.

I grin at him. I don't think I'll ever tire of being called Markus' wife. The shop assistant takes his time, removing the earrings from the window, carefully taking them off their little plastic stand and handing them to me.

'Beautiful,' Markus murmurs. 'So beautiful.'

I look in the mirror, and yes, they're pretty.

'I want to buy them for you,' Markus announces. 'A memento of our honeymoon.' He turns to the shop assistant. 'We'll take them.' Markus doesn't even ask how much they cost.

The shop assistant wraps them carefully in tissue paper and then puts them in a little bag. 'That's three hundred and fifty euros,' he says.

I frown slightly, as I'm not sure they're worth that much, but Markus doesn't hesitate. He reaches into his trouser pocket. A frown crosses his face. He tries the other pocket.

'My wallet. It's not here.'

My heart plummets. 'Was it stolen?'

He bites the side of his lip. 'I'm not sure. I might have left it in the hotel room. I don't know. God, I'm such an idiot. Would you mind paying, and I'll give you the money later?'

'Don't worry, darling,' I say, 'I don't need the earrings.'

'I insist,' Markus says. 'They look beautiful on you, and I'll pay you back.' So I fish in my handbag for my purse and pay for the earrings.

As we leave the shop, I say, 'We'd better go back to the hotel to see if your wallet is there; otherwise we'll have to report it to the police.'

'What a bore,' Markus says. He seems strangely relaxed about the possibility of it being stolen, whereas the thought gives me palpitations. Thieves could easily empty his bank account.

Back at the hotel, Markus walks straight towards the safe attached to the wall in the wardrobe. It pings open.

'It's here,' he says, slapping his forehead with the palm of his hand. 'I'm such an idiot.'

And then he kisses me, and we make love with the patio doors wide open and the warm sunlight bathing our bare limbs and the gentle wind blowing the white gauzy curtains in and out of the room.

We get talking to another couple, also on their honey-moon. They're American, living in Paris due to his job, and they suggest that we join them on a private tour of the island, but Markus says no. He is very polite about it, but he explains that he wants to keep me all to himself because once we return home, we will both be very busy with work, juggling our commitments, so this week is sacrosanct. I'm not sure if they think he is weird or extremely romantic. We spend the next few days doing touristy things. We take a private tour in a white Mercedes and visit a red sand beach, a black sand beach, a couple of lighthouses and more blue-domed churches. We lounge by the small white swimming pool, and on our last night, Markus announces he's booked us into the best restaurant on the island, with Michelin stars and a sunset view to die for.

I feel completely relaxed, my skin slightly burnished from the sun, love making me mellow and oh so happy. We walk hand in hand to the venue, where we're seated next to a glass wall. The views are exquisite, looking over to other islands dotted in the sea, the sun setting and turning the sky impossible shades of oranges, pinks and deep purple. Even-tually the moon appears, glinting on the surface of the sea.

'I never want to leave,' I say, sipping at a cocktail.

'Me neither. This has been the most perfect honeymoon. I was thinking though, maybe we should accept your parents' offer of that house.'

'What do you mean?' I've already explained to Markus that I don't want to move out of London, that I want us to pay for our own home. What I haven't yet done is tell Mum and Dad that we're going to decline their kind offer.

'It's lovely in your mews house, but we could do with somewhere bigger, a house. A garden. The pitter-patter of little feet.' He leans forwards and takes my hand. We've only skirted around the topic of children, which in hindsight is stupid, but this has been such a whirlwind romance, I've just been focusing on the day-to-day. 'You do want children, don't you?' Markus peers at me expectantly.

'Yes, of course. One day. Not yet, though.' And I think I do want children; it's just that I've never felt worthy of bringing another life into the world, as if my guilt might rub off on my child, or something might go horribly wrong with my pregnancy, because I'm not deserving of a perfect baby. I know the thoughts are stupid, but we can't control the direction our brains go in.

The food is sublime, every mouthful bursting with flavour, almost an onslaught to our senses, and when the final course has been cleared away and I'm slowly drinking a fresh mint tea, I smile. I am so lucky.

It's pitch black now and getting chilly despite the patio heaters dotted around us. 'I'll get the bill,' Markus says, waving at a server.

He barely glances at the invoice when it arrives, and pops his credit card inside the leather folder.

'Thank you,' I say. 'This has been the most romantic meal ever.'

'You're right, it has.' Markus smiles at me, his eyes locked onto mine. 'I'm so happy to be with you, Mrs Klausen.' He leans across the table to kiss me.

We're interrupted by the waiter. 'I'm sorry, sir, but your card didn't work. Would you try again?'

Markus frowns, removes the card from the card reader and reinserts it, punching in his pin code. The same thing happens again.

'Perhaps this card isn't working. Do you have another one?' the waiter suggests.

But the same thing happens again. The card is rejected.

'What's going on?' I ask.

'I've no idea,' Markus says, running his fingers through his hair. His face looks pale in the low light, and I see frown marks that weren't there earlier.

'It's fine. I'll pay,' I say, quickly taking my American Express card from my purse and handing it to the waiter. It goes through immediately. As we get up to leave, Markus seems distracted, worried.

'Hey, what's up?' I ask, squeezing his hand at the same time as shivering in the cold night air. I wrap my pashmina around my shoulders.

'I'm going to need to make a couple of calls.'

'Of course,' I say. What I don't expect is that he means he needs to make them right now.

'Can you get back to the hotel alone, and I'll join you there in a few minutes?'

'Yes, of course.'

But it isn't until I'm walking along the narrow street back to our luxurious hotel that it strikes me as odd that Markus couldn't have these phone calls in front of me. What is it that I don't know about my new husband?

I'm in the bath when he returns, soaking in a glorious rose bath oil, flicking the fragments of petals away from my body. Markus knocks on the door. 'Can I come in?'

I'm comfortable around him now, less self-conscious than I was in the early weeks of our relationship, helped by the fact that he never stops telling me how beautiful I am.

Markus drags a small stool into the bathroom and sits next to the sink. He places his elbows on his knees and his head in his hands.

'Something terrible has happened.'

I sit up too quickly in the bath, sloshing water over the sides. My initial thoughts are something has happened to Mum or Dad, or Sam perhaps, and my heart starts thumping.

Markus doesn't look at me as he speaks. 'I invested in a massive new leisure complex in Turkmenistan.'

I relax back into the bath when I realise he's talking about money.

'And the whole deal has fallen apart. I don't know exactly what has happened, but as soon as we're home, I'll need to fly out to Ashbagat and find out what's going on.'

'I don't understand,' I say. 'What does this mean?'

He looks at me with tears in his eyes. 'It means that I might have lost everything.'

'Everything?'

'These aren't the sort of guys you mess with, Leonie.' He stands up suddenly, paces to the edge of the bath, bends into his knees and grips the side of it. 'But we're still on our honeymoon, and you, my delicious wife, need some loving attention. For now, I'm going to remain positive and just focus on us. Forget everything I've said.'

16

CARRIE

The office is tranquil with Leonie away, and my days take a gentle rhythm. I leave my new one-bedroom flat in Clapham and meander into central London, striding down Knightsbridge as if I belong there. I'm in the office for 9 am. Brenda hasn't been in to work since the wedding, which makes me wonder whether she's only there to keep an eye on her daughter. Both Zac and Erin are in and out, doing viewings, caring for clients. It gives me the time and space to think about Markus.

I am still livid with him. He's out of control and has completely let me down. How am I going to make Leonie suffer if Markus is being the good husband? The only thing I can hope for is that he bores of Leonie, which he may well do, because he doesn't have a great attention span. But if the money is too good, then he'll be on his best behaviour for as long as it takes. That puts a massive damper on my plan. Frankly, I'm not sure what to do about it.

I work through my mountain of paperwork, and by mid-afternoon I've processed most of the invoices. Zac has returned to the office, and he's at his desk, leaning backwards on his chair, sighing.

'What's up?' I ask, not because I actually care, but that's what you're meant to ask colleagues, isn't it?

'I'm broke.'

'How can you be broke? You earn a good salary here, and the commission is great.' I'm not on commission because I don't find properties for clients, but Zac's commission is, in my opinion, too generous. As I'm responsible for the payroll, I know exactly how much everyone earns.

'I've got to pay for my mum to have a carer, and my lifestyle has got expensive. I hate that my girlfriend has to pay for everything.'

Now that makes my ears prick up. This is the first time Zac has mentioned a girlfriend.

'You're in a relationship?' I ask.

'Yes, but I'm keeping it quiet.'

'Does Leonie know?'

He shakes his head. It's been obvious to me that Zac holds a torch for Leonie. You only need to see how he hangs on her every word, how he stands up for her all the time, to realise that he's in love with her. But perhaps now she's married, lost to him forever, he's bagged himself a new woman. Good for him.

'So she's high-maintenance, your new girlfriend?'

He laughs. 'No, the opposite. I just hate that she pays for everything.'

I'd like to probe some more, but Zac's phone rings, and he returns to his computer.

I get an idea. Zac and Leonie are tight, best friends, and in a way, Zac is blocking me from becoming closer to Leonie. I need Leonie to slot me into the best-friend, closest-colleague position, which Zac currently holds. So I need to get rid of him. Don't get me wrong, I'm not thinking about doing anything dramatic, but I could get Leonie to doubt Zac's honesty. Now that would be a blow to her.

I wait until Zac has left the office, and then I log into his computer using his password: ManchesterU! He's never been careful to hide it; in fact once he asked me to log in to his computer when he was out of the office. I then go into our banking website and transfer five hundred pounds from the company account to Zac's personal account. I set up an automatic transfer to make two further payments on the next two days for the same amount. I've kept an eye on Zac. He may charm the pants off potential customers, but his eye for details, particularly when it comes to matters of finance, is poor. I doubt he'll notice the influx of cash.

Leonie returns the following Monday, as does Brenda. Our little office is full of excited voices as we beg her for details of the honeymoon. She shows us photos on her phone, and I have to admit Santorini looks stunning. Those sunsets are something else. When Zac and Brenda have returned to their desks, I walk over to Leonie and whisper, 'Could we have a chat in the meeting room?'

She frowns but follows me into the small room. I shut the door.

'This is really awkward,' I say, wringing my hands. 'I'm sure it's just some silly mistake, but I've found an accounting anomaly. Five hundred pounds has left the business account for three consecutive days and gone into Zac's personal account. I really don't want to get him into trouble because he's such a nice man, but he was talking about money problems, and well – unless you've authorised this without telling me – it's kind of odd.'

Leonie pales and sits down. 'Zac?' She shakes her head as if she can't absorb what I've just said.

'I didn't want to say anything to him directly; thought it was best if you deal with it. I mean, I'm not sure what your policy is, whether you want me to report this to the police.'

'The police!' she exclaims. 'No, no. There must have been a mistake. I've known Zac for years. He's the most honest person I know.' But her voice fades away as if she's suddenly unsure of her words.

'I'm really sorry to throw out an accusation like this. I know how fond you are of Zac. I can show you the transactions,' I say, 'but perhaps let's wait until Zac is out. I checked his diary, and he has a client appointment at 11 am.'

I can tell that Leonie is really shaken, and I find it hard to hide my grin. Hook, line and sinker. The second that Zac is out of the door, Leonie is at my desk. I bring up the accountancy software and show her the three transactions. 'I can see which computer these were actioned from. Zac's. That's his IP address.'

'What's happened?' Brenda pipes up.

'I can't believe it,' Leonie tells her Mum. 'Zac has transferred one and a half thousand pounds from the company account to his private account.'

'Zac?' Brenda exclaims. 'That can't be right. Zac is as white as snow.' She sounds really indignant.

I get that the Wildings have known Zac for years, but that doesn't mean they actually *know* him.

'He did mention that he was having some money troubles, so perhaps he's just borrowing the money and was hoping to return it before you noticed,' I suggest.

'I'm going to have to talk to him,' Leonie says. And I can tell that's the very last thing she wants to do.

A couple of hours later, Zac returns to the office. He's buzzing because a client has put an offer on a multi-million-pound property in Hampstead, and the fees for Castaway Properties will be substantial.

'Can I have a word?' Leonie says tightly and leads Zac into the office. She shuts the door, but frankly, I don't know why she bothers. There are raised voices within moments. Zac looks through the glass wall and points at me. Brenda goes into the office, and there is more shouting. I just sit at my computer and plaster on a neutral face, all the while loving the bedlam I've created.

17

LEONIE

I had no idea where Ashbagat is. I looked it up. It's the capital city of Turkmenistan, which itself is the second-largest state in Central Asia. Landlocked, it became independent of Russia in 1991. Ashbagat is located near the border of Iran in a desert valley. According to Markus, it's a surprisingly modern city, full of otherworldly, newly built white marble buildings, with over a million inhabitants and plenty of thriving industries. Markus said it was the perfect place for a new retail and leisure complex, and he personally invested a fortune. I can tell that he's sick with worry as to what has happened, so I give him my blessing to visit as soon as possible. I tell him not to worry, that I'm sure Dad will help him out if he's in financial trouble, but then I regret saying that. The last thing I want is for us to be indebted to Dad. I want to break free from my father.

I miss Markus when he is away. It's the longest we've been apart since we met, and the house feels empty without him. I had every intention of meeting up with the girlfriends I've ignored for so long, but I feel an apathy without my husband and end up staying at home every evening. The issue with Zac hasn't helped my mood. He completely denies transferring any money, accusing Denise of making a mistake or setting him up, yet that makes no sense. Why would she do that? He's transferred the money back to the business account, but our relationship seems fractured now; that deep layer of trust somehow ruptured. I can't even discuss it with Markus because we agreed that we'd make no international calls whilst he was in Turkmenistan unless it was an emergency, due to phones being frequently monitored over there. It makes me wonder why he chose to invest so much money in a country so different from our own.

Five days after he left, Markus is home. I've prepared his favourite roast chicken meal and laid the table with candles and my best cutlery. When his key turns in the door, I throw myself at him. I've genuinely missed my gorgeous husband.

'Oh, darling,' he says, gripping me hard, burying his face in my hair. I sense immediately that something is wrong. He feels tense, reluctant somehow.

'How did it go?' I ask as he releases me.

'Not good, I'm afraid. I've lost everything.'

'What do you mean, everything?'

'A few months ago, I was a rich man. Today, I barely have a pound to my name.' He drops his suitcase in the hallway and wanders into the living room, sinking onto the sofa. He buries his face in his hands. 'Oh God, Leonie. When we said our vows for richer or poorer, it never crossed my mind that I might be poorer. Never. I'm so ashamed.'

I sit down next to him and put a hand on his thigh. 'What's there to be ashamed about? You did a business deal that went sour. You were successful once, so you can be again.'

He shakes his head. 'I don't know what I did to deserve you.' Tears spring to his eyes, and he seems really broken.

Two weeks later, we have settled into the rhythm of married life, except it isn't at all how I'd imagined it. The soured business deal appears to have leeched all the energy out of Markus. From what I can tell, he spends all day at home playing video games. Yesterday I received a notification on our joint Amex card to say that he'd spent nearly a grand on a new console. I managed to bite my tongue and not say anything, but it's tough. It seems to me that the harder I'm working, the less my husband is doing. Perhaps I wouldn't mind so much if when I returned from work, the house was tidy and there was a meal on the table. But the place is always a tip, and if I make a snide comment about food, Markus just suggests we order in. Before our wedding, Markus was an avid chef, but that person seems to have vanished. This evening, he is sitting on a big chair that still has plastic around its legs. It's hideous and takes up much too much space in the living room.

'What's that chair?' I frown.

'It's gorgeous, isn't it? It's my new gaming chair; it will stop me from getting neck and shoulder ache.'

I feel a burn of resentment in my throat. He has just spent my hard-earned money on a bloody gaming chair. 'Look, I get that you're feeling down, but you can't sit here playing video games day in and day out. You're a grown man, Markus. When are you going back to work?'

He stills. 'For God's sake, Leonie. You've no idea what it's like to lose everything. I feel utterly broken, and I need some time to recover from the scar of the leisure deal. In fact, I feel bloody emasculated. There you are swanning in and out with your successful business deals, and I'm stuck here feeling like a complete failure. Sure, I'll go back to work tomorrow if that's what you really want. I'll get a job sweeping the damned streets!'

'Come on, Markus, that's not what I want and not what I'm saying. You don't need to take the first job that comes along.'

He huffs and crosses his arms over his chest. 'I need a breather to work out what I want to do with the rest of my life.'

'I get it, I really do,' I say, trying to appease him. 'But it's hard for me when I return from work and find the place in a mess.'

He squeezes his eyes shut. 'You're not used to living with anyone, that's all.' He opens his eyes, and his expression relaxes, but he's still clenching his fists. 'All right, I'll make more of an effort going forwards. This whole deal has really knocked my confidence. Can you imagine how I feel knowing I'm financially dependent on you for everything? It's horrible, Leonie. It dents a man's pride. I just need some time to regroup and plan my next business.'

'I don't really understand what you did before,' I mutter.

'Come on, love. We've discussed it numerous times.'

Except we haven't. Whenever I asked about his work, he said he invested in start-ups, had previously worked in the city, and then he changed the subject. I didn't let it bother me, because it was obvious Markus had money. I think of all the designer jewellery he gave me, the fancy places we ate out. He was busy and successful. Back then, I didn't need the details.

'I've told you that I was an angel investor and a management consultant to various businesses, but I went all in with the Ashbagat deal. I'll never make that mistake again.' He jumps up from the sofa now and walks over to me, placing his hands on my shoulders and kissing me on the forehead.

'I want you to sit down on the sofa, and I'm going to run you a bath.'

'It's fine,' I murmur, but Markus doesn't hang around. He disappears upstairs and calls me up about ten minutes later. The bathroom has been transformed. He has taken every candle in the house and placed them around the edge of the bath, poured me a glass of wine and placed that next to the book I'm reading. The bathroom looks romantic and inviting.

'You have a good soak, and when you're done, supper will be ready.'

I lie back in the bath and allow myself to relax. We didn't have the argument I was worried about, and I ponder that we've done rather well. Perhaps we've got this marital communication thing nailed. All I had to do was share my concerns with Markus and he's on it. Yes, I'm worried about him, but on the other hand, I feel so looked after.

Half an hour later, he has ordered in Chinese food and is spooning it out onto dishes.

'You're right,' he says. 'I shouldn't be lazing about all day. Tomorrow I'll cook, and every day thereafter until I work out my new job. I'll do the cleaning, too, so you can get rid of the cleaner.'

'That's not necessary, Markus,' I say.

For the next few days, my husband is true to his word. The house is tidy, and there is food on the table when I get home. He's attentive and loving, and I have absolutely no reason to doubt our marriage. Except for a tiny little niggle, but I can't quite pinpoint what the issue is. I just know it's there. The little prickle of concern that all is not what it seems.

Mum has invited us for Sunday lunch, the first time I've been home since our wedding, the first time I've seen Dad.

'Welcome, welcome!' Mum says as we climb out of my car. 'We got the official wedding photos last week and can't wait to go through them with you.'

What? I assumed they'd be sent to me, not to my parents. Surely, it's my decision which ones we choose? I feel a bubble of annoyance that my parents are still in control. It's not right.

Markus gives Mum a kiss and shakes hands with Dad, and we settle ourselves in the living room. I've never liked this room. Despite looking out onto the garden, it's too dark. The oak panelling around the whole room is art deco in style, faux of course, and it means there is no space for any pictures. The furniture is also brown – a mixture of leather armchairs and brown chenille sofas. When we were kids, Sam used to pretend that monsters lived behind the wooden walls, and that if you pressed the correct panel, you'd be transferred to a terrifying Narnia.

'What would you like to drink?' Dad asks Markus. He's standing at his built-in bar at the far end of the living room.

'A gin and tonic, please,' Markus says.

As normal, Dad doesn't ask me, but I'm through with being treated like a child. 'I'll have one, too,' I say to Dad, and then immediately leave the room and wander into the kitchen to see if Mum needs any help. She's prodding the roast beef with a thermometer gauge.

'Would you like me to lay the table?' I ask, noting the kitchen table where my parents normally eat is bare.

'Already done. We're eating in the dining room.'

'The dining room? Why?'

'It's the first meal with your new husband. I thought it was worth celebrating.'

'But he's family now. I thought we'd be relaxed.'

'It's what your father wants,' Mum says tightly.

What Gus wants, Gus gets! I feel like saying, but I bite my tongue. I always thought my parents had the perfect marriage, never arguing, always discussing the business at mealtimes, a marriage of equals. Yet now I see it differently. Dad is controlling. Whether he's coercive controlling, I'm not sure. Perhaps. And Mum is on the constant receiving end. I remember when Dad said Mum was going to work at Castaway, that she could do mornings there. I was livid. Why couldn't they leave me to get on with it? Until very recently, I thought she was Dad's spy, but now I wonder. Perhaps she chose to work with me because it takes her away from Dad for a few hours every day. I've let Dad control me because of the accident; perhaps Mum lets Dad control her because she loves him. Or perhaps she has no choice.

It's a sobering thought. Perhaps we don't really examine our parents' marriage until we experience our own. Mum breaks into my ruminations.

'I've been thinking about Zac,' she says.

'Zac?'

'The money. He would never do anything illegal. I just don't believe it. Either that Denise set him up for some unfathomable reason, or it was a genuine mistake.'

'I don't know,' I say. 'It doesn't make sense, but I do know he's been worried about money lately. Perhaps he's got himself into debt.'

'Zac?' she scoffs. 'Don't be ridiculous, Leonie. He's a good man.' And then the oven beeps, and Mum sends me off to the living room to tell the men that lunch is ready.

'So how are you enjoying married life?' Mum asks Markus as we're digging into our meal.

'It's as wonderful as I hoped it would be,' he says, grinning widely at me.

'Have you decided when you're moving into the house in Dorking?' Dad asks. 'It'll be ready in a fortnight.'

'We can't wait!' Markus says at exactly the same time as I say, 'We've decided to stay put.'

Mum and Dad stare at us both quizzically. I glower at Markus, who lifts a hand up in the air and says, 'We're so grateful for your generosity, but Leonie and I still have a bit of talking to do.'

I clench my fists because I've made it totally clear to Markus that I have no desire to move out of London and live in a gifted house. There's an awkward silence in which the only sound is the clattering of cutlery on plates.

Eventually, Markus speaks. 'I assume that Leonie has told you about my disastrous business deal in Turkmenistan.'

'No, what deal?' Dad jumps in.

I sigh. Of course I haven't told them, and I'm taken aback that Markus is admitting a failure quite so openly. I should have told him to keep quiet about it, because Dad is so mocking of anyone who fails in business.

'I lost a lot of money on a retail and leisure complex. A salutary lesson learned. Rule 101 of business: don't put all your eggs in one basket.'

'I'm sorry to hear that,' Mum says. Dad scowls.

'I just try to remind myself that all the most successful

businessmen have had a failure along the way. Think Richard Branson, Steve Jobs, Bill Gates.'

'I didn't,' Dad says.

Markus ignores him, and I grip my fork, wondering what Markus is about to say next.

'I've been doing a lot of thinking, and forgive me if this sounds presumptuous, but I feel I have a huge amount to give to Wilding Properties. I'm an excellent salesman and have managed and closed massive deals in the past. Would you consider me joining your business?' He directs the question to Dad, but I feel a surge of anger. Why didn't my husband discuss this with me first?

'That's certainly an interesting proposition,' Dad says. 'What role were you thinking?'

'Perhaps I could step in as a director to Castaway. My lovely wife works much too hard, and if I was a director, I could ease some of her load. Of course, I have plenty to learn about the property world, but I'm a quick learner with a healthy dose of common sense.'

Before I can formulate any words, Dad jumps in. 'I think it's a marvellous idea. It was such a blow when Sam decided not to join the family business. Such a blow. And I need another man about the place. I can see that working very well,' Dad says before raising his glass of red wine.

I push my chair back. 'I'm sorry, but–' I can't speak, and I can't stay here. I am stunned and not in a good way. I know that if I open my mouth now, I will deeply regret my words. How dare Markus be so presumptuous! And there I was thinking our relationship was one of equals.

'Need the bathroom,' I mutter before fleeing the dining room and running through the house to the downstairs toilet. I lock the door and sit down on the seat, swallowing a silent scream.

Once again, Gus has taken control, but this time it is so much worse, because my husband, the man I genuinely adore, is following suit. And the hypocrisy is mind-blowing. Just a fortnight ago, Markus accused me of emasculation, yet he is quite happy to dose out a massive dollop of chauvinism. The two most important men in my life have backed me into a corner, but I'm not going to stay there. If Markus wants to join Wilding Properties, then that's fine by me, but he's not joining Castaway. It's bad enough having Mum there. No. I set up that business by myself. I've made it the success it is today, and my husband and father can back off.

18

LEONIE

I wait until we're in the car on the way home, and then Markus and I have our first full-blown argument. 'Why didn't you ask me first whether it was okay with me for you to join my business?'

'I did.'

'You did not!' I exclaim.

'Last week when you were complaining about me lounging around the house doing nothing.'

'We didn't talk about Wilding Properties or Castaway. You said you were deciding what you wanted to do.'

'And I did decide. I'm sorry if your memory has betrayed you.' Markus is looking out of the passenger window, so I can't see his face. My knuckles whiten around the steering wheel. I'm not an idiot. I am absolutely sure we didn't have that conversation.

'I don't want you joining my business. I love you, but I don't think it's a good idea, us working together.'

He bangs the palm of his hand against the glass. It startles me, and I jerk the car. 'I knew you'd hold the Turkmenistan failure against me. I could have kept quiet about it, just pretended everything was all right, but I value honesty, and honesty in our relationship above all.'

'So do I! But you've railroaded me, just like Dad does.'

'I'm sorry you see it that way,' he says tightly. 'I believe I will be a great asset to the business, and clearly your father agrees with me.'

'Dad's controlling, and I'd appreciate it if you weren't, too.'

'For God's sake, Leonie, when have I ever been controlling of you?'

I think back over the past months, and to be fair to Markus, he hasn't. He's only been kind and considerate. 'I love you, but I don't want you in my business.'

I'm not completely sure why. Is it because I don't trust him in business now I know how he's lost so much money? Or is it because he likes to spend more than I do? Or am I worried that I'll lose control of the one thing I have plenty of control over, because although Dad is the majority shareholder, he still leaves the day-to-day running of the business to me?

'You're not thinking straight,' Markus says.

'Don't you dare tell me what I'm thinking!' I shout.

'Do you think I'm not good enough?' he asks. 'Is that what this is all about? I'm good enough to be in your bed but not your office, is that it?'

'No, it's just–'

'I don't want to discuss this anymore. I'm hurt, deeply hurt and disappointed, and I know your father will be, too.'

'You know nothing about my father!' I exclaim.

'Stop the car,' he says. His voice is low and tight now. 'Stop the bloody car!'

And so I indicate to the left and pull over onto the verge.

'What are you doing?' I ask as Markus wrenches the door open. 'We're miles from home.'

'I'll make my own way back,' he says, slamming the passenger door closed. I sit there with the engine turning over, the indicator beating and my eyes full of tears, and I watch my husband as he storms off along the pavement without a single backwards glance at the car.

I drive all the way home, expecting my phone to ring. It doesn't. I try calling Markus, but it goes straight to voicemail. I want to talk to someone, to try to work out whether I was unreasonable, or whether he overreacted. I think about calling Zac, my default best friend, but things are still awkward between us. Then I decide that this is an issue between my husband and me, and I need to keep it that way. I wonder whether our fledgling marriage might be over, or whether we're strong enough to work this out.

And I wonder where Markus is right now. He admitted he was a former drug addict. Could he be in some dingy alleyway, buying illegal oxy, slipping back into his old habits? My brain turns over every horrible scenario. I try to eat supper, distract myself with the television, but I fail. I am desperate to see Markus. His phone is off, and after leaving eight messages, I vow to stop. Eventually, I take a shower and go to bed, praying he'll be home soon.

Markus returns at midnight. He takes a shower in the spare bathroom and then slips into bed beside me. I pretend I'm asleep, because what else should I do, and he puts his arms around me and pulls me towards him. I smell alcohol on his breath. He murmurs into my neck, 'I'm sorry, Leonie. I'm really sorry.'

The next morning, I have to get up early, and Markus is

still asleep. I don't feel great, but I need to pull myself together, as I have a massive road trip, visiting three properties and meeting a new client. Denise has emailed me my itinerary, including the property addresses and the contact details for the new client. The first viewing is a house near Cambridge, then northeast to Norwich, followed by meeting a new client at a rural property somewhere near the lovely Suffolk coastal town of Southwold.

The morning goes well. The two houses are fabulous, and I have a couple of buyers who I'm sure will love them. Now it's midafternoon, and I'm en route to the final appointment, meeting a woman called Lucy Douglas, who, according to Denise, is seeking a new home somewhere along the Suffolk or Norfolk coast. I plug the postcode into my car's satnav and start driving. An hour or so later, the satnav announces that I've arrived at my destination, yet all I can see are fields and hedges without a house in sight. I try my phone, but frustratingly, I'm in the middle of nowhere and have no reception. I'm reasonably good at directions, and I've never actually been lost before, but that's probably because I always look on Google Maps before setting off in my car. This morning, though, I was too preoccupied with the argument Markus and I had. I'm not sure what to do.

I drive around at a snail's pace, looking for any sign saying Oyster Grove, but I see nothing. I don't pass pedestrians or a friendly farmer. It's like the place is desolate. After about half an hour of hopeless meandering, I find myself in a small hamlet, and my phone pings to life. It beeps with a text message. I pull the car over to the side of the road and check my phone. It's a message from Denise.

Sorry but your Southwold client has just cancelled. I hope you get this message in time. Denise x

I groan with frustration. I've just wasted the past couple of hours driving here, and then failing to find the property, all for nothing. I turn the car around and head for the A12 and the wearisome journey back to London. I telephone Markus, hopeful that yesterday's argument can be put behind us.

'Darling,' he says when he answers. It's a relief to hear the normalcy in his voice.

'I'll be home in just over two hours, traffic dependent.'

'Perfect. I'm cooking you something special tonight.'

'That's kind of you,' I say, wondering if it's because of our argument last night. 'I've had a mixed bag of a day.'

'Well, you can tell me all about it over supper. We've got lots to talk about, sweetheart. I love you.'

When I hang up, my heart feels lighter because, despite our differences, despite Markus trying to railroad me like Dad, we still love each other.

The traffic is dreadful, so it takes me nearer three hours to get home. I've tried calling Markus a couple of times to let him know I'm going to be late, but his phone rings out and goes to voicemail. He's probably got the music turned up loud and is busy cooking, using every implement in the kitchen, as he's prone to do. I smile and hope that the food won't be ruined because of my tardiness.

I park the car in the garage and walk up to the front door. It's unlocked and leaning against its latch. Normally, we keep the door locked and bolted. It's weird. As soon as I step inside, I can smell burning food, so I hurry through to the kitchen. The oven is on, but the door is open; there are two pans of water on the hob, neither switched on, and some uncut courgettes and carrots on the side. I hurry back to the front door. Has Markus nipped out for a moment or popped over to one of the neighbours'?

'Markus!' I shout, straining to see both left and right on our narrow mews street. There's no answer, so I hurry back indoors, into the kitchen. I switch the oven off and remove the dish, placing it on a pot stand next to the sink. The top is burned black, and I doubt it's edible. Why did Markus leave it to burn? There's something not right. Some of the food is burned, and the rest hasn't been cooked.

I hurry into the living room, where the lights are turned off. 'Markus!' I say again. There's a quivery edge to my voice and a prickling on the back of my neck. I turn all the lights on downstairs, but he's not here. I run upstairs. The stairs light is on, as is the hall light upstairs. Is he in the bathroom with an upset stomach, perhaps? I rush into our bedroom and en-suite bathroom, but both are empty, as are the spare room and bathroom. Where is he?

'Markus!' I yell this time, but the house is silent. He must have stepped outside. I open the front door and look left and right again, straining to see, noting that only a few lights are on in our neighbours' houses. The mews is deserted, as it so often is. I walk to the left, past our garage, and that's when I see it. Our blue-lidded bin has been knocked over, card-board boxes tipped onto the road. I hurry to the side of our house, where we keep the two big bins. The light is even lower here between the bins, a couple of planted pots and the brick wall of the house.

I freeze and take a step backwards.

'No!' My voice sounds strangled.

And then I'm down on my knees. 'Markus! Markus! Wake up!' I cradle his head, which is so heavy, his neck limp, my hands covered in a sticky warm fluid, my brain not able to compute what I'm seeing.

'Markus! Wake up!' There's a horrible wailing noise, and for a few seconds it's as if my brain switches off, and then I realise the animalistic screams are coming from me.

'Markus! No!' I'm rocking backwards and forwards, tears flooding down my cheeks. I don't need a qualification in nursing to know that my husband is dead. His eyes are staring upwards, glassy, unseeing in the low light. There's a heavy coldness to him, even though he's still warm. Unnatural. Terrifying. 'Help!' I scream over and over again.

It's my neighbour Mrs Quinter who takes control, emerging from her house wearing a tartan dressing gown. I seem to recall she was a midwife before she retired several decades ago. She calls the emergency services, eases me away from Markus, but I don't want to let go. How can I let go of him? He's only been my husband for less than a month. I'm hysterical. I know I am, but I can't control myself.

'Miss.' There's a man now standing next to me. His boots and black trousers swim into view.

'She's called Leonie Wilding. Not sure what her new married name is,' I hear Mrs Quinter say. 'So sad. Only married recently.'

'Leonie, you need to let go now.' The stranger kneels down so he's at eye level with me. I see then that he's a policeman. Did I even hear the sirens over my wailing?

'We'll take her.'

'I can't leave him,' I sob.

'Leonie, we need to look after him now. You need to let go.'

A man and a woman, paramedics, ease me up and steer me away from Markus, and all I can think of is, aren't they contaminating the crime scene? I know innately that Markus has been murdered. There isn't that much blood if you slip and hit your head, is there?

They steer me towards an ambulance, and I see that our mews street has been cordoned off, houses that only a few minutes ago I thought were empty disgorging neighbours in doorways, peering out of windows to see what the commotion is. Blue lights flashing everywhere, people in uniform issuing commands into walkie-talkies, moving around with purpose. They usher me into an ambulance, where the lights are too bright. I'm wrapped in a silver foil blanket for shock, because I'm trembling violently, my teeth clattering in my jaw. The paramedics check me, but I don't know why because there's nothing wrong with me. They need to help Markus. Save my husband.

I let out another involuntary wail. Is this my penance? Of course I don't deserve happiness, but why wasn't I killed? Why Markus? And just *why?* Was it a random knife attack, the sort that seems to happen every day in London? Was Markus in the wrong place at the wrong time, or was it more sinister? Was it a planned attack, something to do with his Turkmenistan business deal perhaps?

'Leonie, the police would like to talk to you. Are you up to that?' the female paramedic asks me. She has a kindly expression on her small face.

'No, I don't know.'

'They just need a quick word so they can work out what might have happened this evening.'

I nod, holding a wodge of tissues up against my face. She

opens the rear of the ambulance. I make as if to follow her, but a policeman is there, and he stops me.

'Please sit down again, Leonie. I know this has been a terrible shock, but I just need a few words.' He climbs up into the ambulance, and the space seems crowded now, oppressive even. He crouches down in front of me.

'Can I confirm that the deceased was your husband, Markus Klausen?'

Deceased. How can Markus be dead? He was the most vital man I've ever met. I think I nod, because the police officer smiles at me, a pitiful smile that shreds my insides.

'Can you talk me through what happened tonight?'

I struggle to speak; my words are jumbled and come out as sobs. 'I came back from work, and the supper was burning in the oven, and the front door was open. I went outside and found him–'

'Do you remember what time you got home?'

I shake my head because the events of today are all jumbled up. Suddenly I feel completely and utterly exhausted.

'What's going to happen?' I ask.

'Your husband will be taken to the hospital for a post-mortem. I'm afraid your home is now a crime scene, and we won't be able to let you back in. Have you got somewhere you can stay for the next few days?'

'I want to be with Markus!' I cry.

The paramedic squeezes my hand. I'd forgotten that she was here.

'Anywhere you can stay?' she repeats.

'My parents,' I murmur, but as soon as I say that, I know it's the last place I want to be. 'Actually, my best friend, Zac.'

'Can you give me Zac's number? We'll call him,' the police officer says.

I realise that my phone is still in my jacket pocket, that I'm wearing my work clothes, my smart black suit and pale pink silk blouse. I glance down at myself and see the blood encrusted everywhere. With trembling hands, I hold the phone up to my face, and it unlocks. 'Zac Robinson,' I say, handing the phone to the police officer. I can hear the phone ringing and Zac's voice saying, 'I can't get to the phone, so leave a message and I'll call you back. Maybe.' The officer ends the call.

'Is there anyone else we can ring?' he asks.

'Denise. She's a friend from work. Try Denise.'

She answers the phone, and the police officer steps out of the ambulance, leaving the vehicle's doors open. There are so many lights now: glaring, blinding white and blue lights turning the exterior of my home from night to day. And so many people, some dressed in white overalls, others in uniform. Is this really happening? It's as if I've stepped straight onto the set of a crime programme.

The police officer returns and hands me back my phone. 'Leonie, we are treating this as murder. It looks very much like your husband was hit on the back of the head with something hard. Obviously, we'll know more after the forensic examinations. I just need to ask you, where were you between 5 and 7.30 pm this evening?'

I stare at him, unable to process the question. Why is he asking me that?

'Leonie?' he prompts.

'I was driving. I was out at meetings all day, in East Anglia. Markus was at home, cooking us supper. The oven was left open.'

'Thank you,' he says kindly. 'And is there anyone you can think of who might have wanted to harm Markus?'

I shake my head. 'He's a good man, my husband. A really good man.' And then I break down again into a sobbing mess.

Denise arrives sometime later. Her face is ghostly pale, and she's wearing jeans and a thick white jumper. When she sees me, she launches herself at me, throwing her arms around my shaking body, squeezing me so tight it almost hurts. It isn't until later that I realise the blood on my clothes has dried, and little flecks have transferred onto her.

'It's such a shock. I'm so sorry,' she says. 'So terribly sorry. The officer says you're to stay with me tonight, and they'll be in touch in the morning. Is that what you want?'

I nod, because I've no idea what I want. Actually, no, that's not true. I want to wake up from this nightmare and lie in Markus' strong arms. I want to feel his lips on mine and hear the words *I love you, Leonie.* Except I won't. Never again. And then I remember. I don't deserve love. I don't deserve happiness. I've taken a life, and now a life has been taken from me. Somehow this must be retribution, and I was so stupid to think that I might be able to dodge it.

19

LEONIE

Denise's flat is small. A one-bed apartment on the fifth floor of a concrete tower block. For some reason, I'd imagined she'd be living in a place more modern, more salubrious. Somewhere in keeping with the image she portrays at work: sleek, efficient, together. It explains why whenever we have met socially, it's been in a bar or restaurant. She mentioned a while back that after a failed relationship, she had fallen upon hard times, and this place is clearly evidence of that.

From the front door, you walk straight into the living room, which has a simple open-plan kitchen at the rear. There is a small black leather sofa with a matching chair and a glass coffee table. The walls are painted a pale yellow, and they're completely bare of pictures. Denise insists that I sleep on her bed and says she will take the sofa. I feel bad, because the sofa doesn't look long enough for her to stretch out on. She strips the sheets and then takes a set of linen out of her wardrobe that's still in its packaging. Shaking it out, she remakes the bed. I stand in the corner of the room, looking out of the window onto adjacent tower blocks. Although I have a good view of what the neighbours are doing, my eyes are unseeing, my brain unable to process that other people's lives are continuing totally normally.

Denise leads me back into the living room and gestures for me to sit on the sofa. She boils the kettle and then hands me a drink of hot, milky tea with two lumps of sugar. I think I'll be sick if I drink it. My hands are shaking too much to hold the mug, so I place it on the glass coffee table.

'Would you like a shower?' she asks. I glance down at myself. Of course I need a shower, but once I do, Markus' blood will be washed off me, and he will be gone forever. The thought sends sobs racking through me once again.

'There, there,' Denise says, patting my arm, handing me a piece of kitchen towel and then edging away from me. I feel bad because it's obvious I'm making Denise feel uncomfortable. She sits opposite me with her arms around her torso, her face in a frown. There's no guidebook for how to react in a situation such as this.

'I'm sorry,' I say eventually, wiping my face on the rough kitchen paper.

'Goodness, you have no reason to be sorry. I'm sorry for you.'

I'm just relieved that Denise doesn't ask for any detail. I don't think I could manage that.

A few minutes later, I've had a burning hot shower and cried as I watched the blood pour off my skin and disappear in pink puddles down the plug hole. Worried about using too much of Denise's hot water, I finish my shower, dry myself with a brand-new towel and tug on a pair of her pyjamas. They're from Primark and feel well used. She's given me a new toothbrush and toothpaste, so I brush my teeth and emerge from the bathroom. Whilst I've been in the shower, Denise must have been doing some clearing up, because she has a box of belongings that she's tugging from the bedroom through to the living room.

I look at her quizzically.

'Just making a bit of space in the bedroom; otherwise you'll bash your feet on all the clutter I've got under the bed.'

'Oh, you didn't need to do that for me,' I say.

'I've got some sleeping pills. Would you like to take one?' Denise asks.

'Yes. Yes, please,' I say.

I'm awoken to the banging on a door and Denise's voice saying, 'I'm coming.' It takes me a moment to remember where I am and why I'm here, and as soon as the memories come crashing back into my mind, the tears well up in my eyes, my chest choked with sorrow. Markus. My beloved husband is gone.

There are lower voices now and then footsteps. A gentle rapping on my bedroom door and Denise pops her head around it. 'The police are here. They want to talk to you. Help yourself to some clothes from my wardrobe.' I notice that she's already fully dressed, makeup on, ready for the day, even though it's only 7.10 am. The sleeping pill must have knocked me for six, because I didn't even hear the shower running.

Everything aches as I climb out of bed. I feel nauseous and have to swallow hard to settle myself. Selecting a pair of jeans and an old sweatshirt from Denise's wardrobe, which are both on the small side, I get dressed hurriedly and then emerge into the living room.

'Good morning, Leonie. My name is Detective Sergeant Matthew Ryan, and this is Detective Constable Lloyd

Chandry. We would be very grateful if you could help us with our enquiries.'

'Yes, yes, of course. Anything,' I say. Denise throws me a strange glance, which I can't decipher.

'If it's all right with you, it would be easier to have this conversation at the police station.'

'Oh,' I say, because I've never been inside a police station before. 'Do you want me to come now?'

'Yes, please. You can come with us.'

'Is she under arrest?' Denise asks, and my jaw drops open. It never crossed my mind that the police could suspect me.

'No,' DS Matthew Ryan says. 'As the next of kin and the person to find Mr Klausen, we need to ask Mrs Klausen further questions.'

'She hasn't even had any breakfast,' Denise says, a hard edge to her voice, which makes me think she isn't the greatest fan of the police. I wonder why.

'It's fine,' I say. 'I'm not hungry.'

I follow the two police officers out of Denise's building and to a black saloon car. I sit on the back seat and wonder how many actual criminals have sat where I am now. There's a strong scent of artificial vanilla, probably from one of those car air fresheners, and it's making my stomach curdle. 'Can I open the window a bit?' I ask. DC Chandry presses a button, and it descends by two inches.

The police station is in a modern building, all darkened glass and steel; it looks just like all the other office blocks along this street. The two officers walk quickly, and I have to take big strides to keep up with them. They lead me along several corridors, our shoes squeaking on the vinyl floor, and then we go into a small room with a table and four chairs.

There are no windows, and the fluorescent light above is too strong.

'Have a seat, Leonie.' DC Chandry gestures for me to sit opposite them. I shiver. It's very cold in here, but still the room smells of sweat, detergent and fear. 'Would you like a tea or coffee?'

'A coffee, please.'

He returns a minute later with a steaming cup of coffee in a disposable paper cup.

'Right, thank you for coming here this morning, at what must be a very difficult time for you. This is an informal interview; however, we are recording it. For the sake of the tape, the people present are Leonie Klausen, myself – DS Matthew Ryan – and DC Lloyd Chandry. You are here because you found your deceased husband, whom we believe to be the victim of murder. During this interview, I will talk to you about how and when you found him and what you had been doing earlier in the day. I'll also ask you about your husband and the relationships he had. The purpose of this interview is to glean any further information that might lead to a conviction for the murder of Markus Klausen. You may choose to end this interview at any time, and you do not have to say anything; however, anything you do say can be used against you in a court of law. You also have the right to legal representation.'

'A solicitor?' I ask. 'But you said this was voluntary, and I'm not under arrest or anything?'

'Exactly right,' DC Chandry says. 'Are you happy for us to begin?'

'Yes,' I say in a quiet voice, although the word *happy* seems so very wrong.

'Okay. Please tell us in your own words what happened

when you returned home yesterday evening,' DC Chandry says.

I take a deep breath and briefly close my eyes. I talk them through those horrendous minutes when I realised something was terribly wrong. My voice cracks when I explain how I found Markus, and DC Chandry pushes a box of tissues across the table.

'Do you know what happened?' I ask eventually.

There's a beat of silence. 'We believe that Mr Klausen was hit over the head with one of your cast-iron frying pans. It was found at the scene.'

'My frying pan?' I ask.

DS Ryan leans towards me. 'The problem we have is that the only fingerprints on the pan were your husband's and your own.'

'But that's obvious,' I say, my voice rising in pitch. 'It was only Markus and me who cooked with it.'

The police officers glance at each other before DS Ryan asks, 'Did you use that frying pan to hit your husband over the head?'

'No!' I exclaim. 'Of course I didn't. I love my husband!' I pause, shock ricocheting through me. 'I loved my husband.'

DC Chandry scribbles something in a notebook.

'How was your relationship with your husband?' DS Ryan asks.

'It was wonderful. We only got married a month ago. We were happy. The last few months have been the best few months of my life, by far.' I can't stop the tears, and DC Chandry asks if I'd like to take a break. I shake my head. Whatever this interview is, I want to get it over and done with as quickly as possible.

'Did you have money problems?'

'No, of course not. I'm very lucky. My family has plenty of money.'

'And your husband?'

I pause. 'Yes, Markus had money problems. Oh my God, that's probably why he was killed. He invested in a big retail and leisure project in Turkmenistan, and it went horribly wrong. He lost everything. Do you think they hired a hitman?'

'And who is they?'

'I don't know! His business partners.'

'And why would they do that?'

'I don't know. But Markus lost all his money.'

'Perhaps it was the other way around, and your husband owed them money?'

'No, he was a good and honest man.'

We sit there in an awkward silence, and I realise I don't know if Markus was genuinely an honest man. He seemed that way around me, but I never did business with him. And it's not exactly normal to be investing in somewhere as remote as Turkmenistan, is it?

'You see, Leonie, you have told us that you were at an appointment yesterday, driving around Suffolk, and for a period of that time you were lost without mobile phone reception. That's rather convenient, isn't it?'

'But it's the truth! I put the addresses in my car's satnav. It's got a tracker, so you'll be able to see where I was and when.'

'That might be the case, but anyone could have been driving your car. How do we know it was you?'

My heart plummets now. They really think I might have murdered Markus. 'What about CCTV?'

'What about it?'

'It will show me driving my car at the times I said I was. That's proof, isn't it?'

'Yes.' DS Ryan draws the syllable out. 'But if you were in a remote part of the country, there wouldn't have been any CCTV.'

Without a shadow of a doubt, I now know they think I did it. I am completely and utterly out of my depth. 'I'd like a solicitor. You said I could have one, didn't you?'

DC Chandry nods.

'In which case, I'd like one now.' There's an edge of panic to my voice.

'Interview suspended at 8.43 am.'

I'm left in this little room for another two hours, waiting for David O'Byrne to arrive. I keep on thinking how I'm being interviewed for the wrong murder, that if they ask me enough questions, I'll confess to what happened a decade ago. And then I think of Markus and how terrified he must have been, even more terrified than I am right now. What happened in the past just needs to stay in the past.

David O'Byrne is Dad's solicitor. He didn't seem keen to help me, but I sobbed that I was desperate, that I needed someone I could trust. And now he looks thoroughly unamused to be here, but I am very aware that Dad pays him a fortune for his services every year and that if I put in a bad word about him, well, that might be a serious blow to his practice. Besides, he was at our wedding, so he owes me, too. It's not like I wanted him there. Briefly, I explain what has happened, and a look of shock passes over his face. He tells me to say no comment to everything the police officers ask me.

The interview restarts, and once again, they go through the rigmarole of saying the names of the people in this small, oppressive room and that the interview will be recorded.

'Leonie Klausen,' DS Ryan says, 'we are arresting you on suspicion of the murder of your husband, Markus Klausen. You do not have to say anything. But it may harm your defence if you do not mention when questioned something which you later rely on in court. Anything you do say may be given in evidence.'

I think I see the flash of a smirk on his face, and I dig my fingernails into my palms, trying to swallow my gasp.

'But I didn't do it!' I exclaim.

David puts a damp palm on my forearm.

'No comment, but it's not true!' I exclaim.

'We have a witness who places you at your home at the time of your husband's murder,' DS Ryan says.

'No! That can't be possible.

'Leonie.' David scowls at me.

'And we don't believe the story about Turkmenistan and think that it's a convenient cover story to blame your husband's murder on some shadowy businessmen,' the police officer says.

I think I'm going to throw up. I should never have mentioned the Turkmenistan connection, as it's obvious it's only made things worse for me, and I do admit that it sounds dodgy. But I haven't made it up.

'We're going to be holding you in custody whilst we continue with our investigations.'

'What? You mean I'm going to be in prison?' It feels like my windpipe is seizing up, as if I can't breathe. They've got this all wrong. Completely wrong.

'You'll be held in a custody cell in the police station for

twenty-four hours, unless we feel the need to apply for an extension.'

'Can they do this?' I ask David O'Byrne.

'Unfortunately, yes,' he says, a grave expression on his face.

Another police officer arrives. He doesn't speak to me except for grunting, 'Follow me.' He leads me down a set of stairs, through two sets of locked doors made from bars, and then we're in front of a reception desk, much like in the bank where an officer sits behind a Perspex screen. My name and the time of my arrest are given, and then I'm led into another small room, where my photograph is taken, along with fingerprints and a DNA swab. I'm trembling with shock. How can this be happening to me?

He then takes me to a small room – a cell – on the right-hand side of a short corridor. He slams the door shut and locks it behind me. It's a tiny space lined with big white tiles. There's a built-in ledge with a thin plastic blue mattress on it and a toilet. Nothing else. I sit on the edge of the mattress and burst into tears, and then a wave of nausea grips me, and I'm violently ill in the toilet. It seems fitting somehow.

20

CARRIE

For the first time since meeting Leonie, I feel relaxed, as if the tricky pieces of my puzzle are at long last coming together. When the police turned up yesterday morning and took Leonie away, I wanted to jump with joy. If she is charged with Markus' murder, I will feel there is at least some retribution.

It's 8 am, and I'm sitting at my glass table, nursing a cup of coffee, watching the news on the television in the hope of catching something about the brutal murder of Markus Klausen. So far there's been a short bulletin stating a man's body was found at his home in South Kensington, but he hasn't been named. That's disappointing. The doorbell rings. I hope it's not Leonie, released. I go to the door and peer through the peephole. My heart plummets. It's the two police officers who were here yesterday. What the hell do they want from me?

I debate pretending I'm not at home, but if I don't answer them now, they'll only catch up with me at work, which could be so much worse. Reluctantly, I unlock the door and open it.

'Good morning, officers,' I say brightly. 'Any news?'

'Could we come in, please?'

Oh no. This is not good.

'Of course. Can I offer you a tea or coffee, perhaps?'

DC Matthew Ryan, the shorter of the two, declines.

'In which case, please take a seat,' I say, gesturing to my sofa. I turn away from them for a moment, trying to compose myself. My heart is racing, and I'm in danger of having another panic attack. Did someone see something? I grab a glass of water, but my hand is shaking too much to hold it. I put it in the sink, and the water spills over.

'Can't decide whether to have another coffee,' I say, all cheerily, as if it's perfectly normal for a couple of police officers to turn up at breakfast time. I paste an inane grin on my face and sit down opposite them.

'So, how can I help you?' I ask, placing my hands on my knees and leaning forwards.

'We're speaking to Markus and Leonie Klausen's friends, family and colleagues. We understand that you work for Leonie and you're a friend.'

'Yes, absolutely.' My voice sounds strained and unnaturally high. 'I'm the office manager at Castaway Property Search, and I've become a good friend of Leonie's.'

'Would you mind telling us where you were yesterday afternoon between 4 pm and 7.30 pm?'

'Absolutely. I was in the office at Castaway Property Search until, gosh, about 7.30 pm. I was working late. There has been so much to catch up on, due to Leonie having been away on honeymoon. Rearranging appointments, sending out invoices, updating the database and the like. I was the last person in the office, probably the last to leave the whole block, actually.' My smile feels forced, but I remind myself that I changed all the times on the clocks on my computer and on the office CCTV. And if the police investigate me, they'll be able to see I was sending emails at the precise time of Markus' murder. And when I left the office, I was wearing a hat and carrying an umbrella, so my face would be difficult to spot on street-level CCTVs.

'Is it normal for you to stay so late?'

'I probably stay late once or twice a week. There's a lot of admin for one person to do.'

'How well did you know Markus Klausen?' DS Chandry asks.

Now, this is a difficult question. If I tell the truth, then I will be opening Pandora's box, so I lie. I keep my gaze steady as I look into DS Chandry's dark, all-seeing eyes. 'Not well. I met him a couple of times through Leonie, and obviously I attended their glorious wedding. He seemed like such a nice chap, although from what Leonie mentioned, perhaps there was more to him than met the eye. Another side, you know how it is?' I let my gaze wander to the window.

'What do you mean by that?' DS Chandry asks.

I sigh and clasp my hands together. 'I don't want to talk out of turn, but their marriage did seem a little fragile. Leonie had her doubts even before they tied the knot.' I hesitate as if unsure whether to share this tidbit with the officers. 'I was wondering whether perhaps they'd had another of their arguments. Leonie does have a bit of a temper on her.'

The police officers glance at each other. *Bingo.*

'Where is Leonie, by the way?' I ask. 'I was expecting her back here hours ago.'

'Mrs Klausen has been detained for further questioning,' DC Matthew Ryan states.

'No!' I exclaim, my hand rushing to cover my mouth. 'I mean, there's one thing having arguments with your new husband; it's quite another...' I let my words peter out. 'Have you spoken to Zac yet?' I ask.

'Zac being?'

'Zac Robinson. He also works in the office and is Leonie's best friend from way back. They hold a bit of a torch for each other, although he was caught stealing money from the company recently. That really upset Leonie.'

'Was Zac working in the office yesterday?'

'Yes. He was there all afternoon until he left, I think, around 5 pm.'

'Could you give us his telephone number, please?' DS Chandry asks.

'Of course.' I search through the contacts on my phone and read out his number. 'I don't want to speak out of turn, but I don't think there was much love lost between Zac and Markus.'

'How do you mean?'

'Well, everyone knows Zac is in love with Leonie and has been for years. I think Markus realised that. It was a bit awkward that Zac was the only man at Leonie's hen party. Markus wasn't too pleased about that.' I'm spinning too much of a yarn here. I need to rein myself back in.

'Is there anything else that you can tell us about Markus and Leonie? Anyone else who might hold a grudge against either of them?'

I shake my head. 'I'm sorry, I don't know either of them well enough.'

'Thank you very much, Ms White. We'll see ourselves out.'

When they've gone, I do a happy dance. *Serves you bloody right, Leonie.* I'd have liked to have told the police the full story, but I can't explain who I really am. Never mind. Leonie will be going to prison for murder, which is sweet justice for what she evaded a decade ago.

I consider not going into the office, but decide I really should, if only to reset the clocks. Also, if the media get wind of what's happened, I could end up being the spokesperson in Leonie's absence. That could be fun.

I arrive late. It's nearly 9.30 am, and neither Zac nor Brenda have turned up. That suits me just fine. I make the adjustments to my computer and to the CCTV system and settle in for the day. The phones are quiet, and I have plenty of time to scour online news channels, disappointingly with nothing showing up. Shortly after 11 am, my mobile phone rings.

It's a withheld number. I answer cautiously. 'Hello?'

'Oh, Denise. I'm so glad you've answered. Where are you?'

What the hell? It's Leonie.

'Denise?' she repeats.

'I'm at the office.' Where else does she think I'll be on an ordinary Thursday?

'I'll come to you since I still can't go home.'

'What?' I say. What does she mean she'll come to me? Isn't she locked up in a cell? But she's ended the call.

I pace the office furiously. Why have the police let her go? And if they think Leonie is in the clear, who do they think killed Markus? I have been careful, haven't I? But careful enough?

Leonie arrives about thirty minutes later. She looks terrible. Dark rings under her eyes, her hair matted and unbrushed, clothes creased. *My* clothes, that is.

'What happened?' I ask, opening my arms out wide. I don't really want to touch her, but she looks so pathetic, waif-like even, I have a surprising jolt of pity for her. She leans into me, and her back quivers with sobs.

'You need to go home, have a hot bath and a drink of something strong. It's been a terrible twenty-four hours.'

Leonie pulls away from me and sits on Sam's swivel chair. 'I haven't told my parents yet, but the solicitor has probably said something.'

'Goodness,' I say, surprised. I got the impression that Leonie and her parents were inseparable. 'They don't even know that Markus has died?' I ask.

'The police still have my phone.' She buries her face in her hands. 'I can't bear the thought of talking to them,' she says. After a few moments of silence, she asks, 'Where's Zac?'

'I don't know. He hasn't come in today, and I haven't spoken to him.' I don't tell her that he's most likely talking to the police right now. 'Look, why don't we shut up the office, and I'll take you back to my place. You can clean up and relax a bit.'

'Thank you, Denise. You've been so kind to me. A real friend.'

I am rather pleased with myself, that I've proven to be such a fine actress.

'I could do with stopping off at a pharmacy.'

'No problem,' I say. 'So the police let you go?'

She nods. 'They found CCTV that showed me going home at the time I said I did. I've no idea who the witness was who lied about me getting home earlier than I did.'

I freeze. Someone must have seen me and thought I was Leonie. I was so careful, so very careful, but those damn video doorbells make subterfuge difficult. I was wearing Leonie's coat and a pair of trainers that she'd left at the office, and we're a similar height, so it makes sense that a neighbour might have been mistaken. But now what? Will the police still be looking for a woman of a similar build to Leonie? I'm a confused mixture of angry – because the police didn't pick up on my hints – and scared, but right now I have to put all of that out of my mind and focus on Leonie.

A few hours later, Leonie is wearing a pair of my old pyjamas and is curled up on my sofa under a blanket. We took a cab back to my place. Leonie popped into a chemist en route, whilst I stayed in the taxi. I didn't see what was in her carrier bag, but I presumed some basic toiletries. I was wrong.

'It's not quite wine o'clock, but I think we both deserve a glass, don't you?' I ask her. Leonie has been so quiet, wrapped up in her thoughts, not wanting to talk about Markus. Too soon, I suppose.

'Thanks, Denise, but I can't drink.'

I frown. 'Can't drink?'

She swallows and throws me a sad smile. 'I'm pregnant. I just took a pregnancy test.' She chokes back a sob. 'I'll never be able to tell Markus.' She pushes her clenched fists into her eyes and eventually murmurs, 'At least a part of him will live on though, and I suppose that might, in time, make his death just a tinier bit easier to bear.'

'Pregnant?' I whisper, sinking into the armchair. *No. No. No.* She cannot be pregnant! She doesn't deserve to be pregnant. How can Leonie be a mother when she took that vital part of me away for ever? I want to scream. Yell. *No!*

'Are you all right?' She peers at me.

'Sure. Yes. Wow! What a surprise.'

Every single time I think I'm destroying Leonie's life, the opposite happens. When I wanted her to be stood up at the altar, she married the man of her dreams. When I want her to be desperate and grieving for her husband, she takes solace in the fact she's carrying his child. When I try to create a wedge between her and Zac, it's only a half-hearted success. This is a total slap in the face for me. Why does Leonie get to live the perfect life when she ruined mine?

She must not have a baby. She cannot. I refuse to let this happen.

'Are you sure you're all right?' she asks me again.

'I've got a bit of a stomach ache. Perhaps something I ate. I'll be back in a mo.'

I hurry to the bathroom, locking the door behind me, and sit down on the floor. The bitch. She's got one over me yet again.

My mind freezes over, and I lose track of time. Leonie raps gently on the door. 'Are you all right, Denise? Can I get you a glass of water or something?'

'Yeah, fine. I'll be out in a tick.' My voice sounds thick and unnatural. There's one word that screams over and over in my head. *Bitch!*

'Goodness, I'm sorry,' I say. 'I've got a really upset stomach, and I need to be okay for tomorrow because my cousin is coming to stay. She lives in Australia, and I haven't seen her in two years. She's only in London for three days, and we've got so much planned.'

'Oh,' Leonie says, and I know what she's thinking. There is only one bed in this place and three people. 'You'll need me to leave.'

'I mean, I could put her up in a hotel, but I'm not sure she can afford it.'

'Please don't worry. If I could stay here tonight, then tomorrow I'll go to my parents'. I've got to face them sooner or later. It's so kind of you to keep them at arm's length for me.'

'I feel terrible about chucking you out,' I lie. I wonder why she's so reluctant to see her parents. But she's right: I have been keeping them away from Leonie. Brenda has been calling me several times a day, but I've reassured her that Leonie is fine – well, as fine as possible under the circumstances – and she'll be in touch very soon.

'I'm just grateful you've been here for me the last couple of horrific days.' Tears spring to her eyes again.

'I think you should have something to eat and then an early night. You look exhausted.' I stride to my kitchenette. 'How about pasta with tuna and a salad?' I ask. I'm not going to spend a penny more on Leonie than I have to.

'Thank you, that would be lovely,' she says feebly.

The next couple of hours are interminable as I wait for Leonie to go to bed. As soon as my bedroom door is closed, I fire up my laptop and go onto a private browser and research the best ways to make Leonie lose her baby. There are so many delectable choices. Poison, accidents, a break-in gone wrong. But is that enough? No. I want her to suffer exactly as I did. I want her to lie in a ditch in agony for two days, like I did. I want her to lose her child, know what it's like to be barren. And if she dies too, so be it. It's what she deserves.

And as I glance at the date, it hits me. We're approaching the ten-year anniversary of the devastation of my life. How fitting it would be for Leonie to suffer the same fate in the same place on the exact date! How very fitting indeed.

21

LEONIE

My parents already knew. Of course they did. The police had been in touch, and then when Mum couldn't reach me on my mobile, she was distraught. Denise has been the buffer between me and Mum, and for that, I'm really grateful. David O'Byrne had been in close contact with Dad, too, exactly as I'd expected. All my earlier resolve about distancing myself from my parents, not letting them take control, dissipated the moment I arrived at their home. Mum scooped me up, feeding me chicken soup and cake purchased from some fancy patisserie, none of which I felt like eating. I told Mum that I was pregnant then, and she sobbed, which made me sob, too. Dad, on the other hand, seemed abnormally uptight. It was only when I was lying in my single bed in my old bedroom, failing to sleep, that I realised how worried he must have been that I had spoken to the police. Yet he didn't mention a word about the past. It was all about the terrible misfortune that had befallen our family: mitigating the intrusiveness of the press, making sure that the horrific murder of his son-in-law had no impact on his business. I stayed at their house for three days; the moment the police said I could return home, I did. The problem is, I'm not sure which is worse: the oppression at my parents' house or the terror at mine.

It's the day of Markus' funeral. The day I've been dreading. I wear a black dress with opaque black tights and a long black coat that makes me look wan and washed out. I must have lost a stone in weight since Markus died, despite being pregnant. Zac, bless him, brings home-cooked meals into the office for lunch, telling me I'm fading away, which seems like an accurate description. I should be hungry, eating for two. I worry that I might be harming our child with the grief that has enveloped me like a cobra, wrapping and constricting itself around my torso, squeezing me so tightly I can't breathe. A foetus can pick up on their mother's emotions, yet I can't pretend to be happy. I'm distraught, as if my future has been swept away from me. I can't imagine being a mother, let alone a single mother, trying to juggle a business whilst taking care of a baby. Mum suggests I give up work, but work is the only thing that is keeping me sane. She says they'll support me financially, but that's exactly what I've spent the past few years trying to avoid: being in their clutches, being beholden to them both. The poor little rich girl.

The crematorium is packed, many of the faces that I recognise from our wedding. I'm standing with Mum and Dad just outside the main door, waiting for the hearse to arrive with my beloved husband, his pale wood coffin bedecked with the same pale roses and tulips that we had at our wedding. Mum has her arm around me, and every so often she squeezes my arm, tells me how brave I'm being. As if I have a choice.

And then an older couple arrive, by taxi. I watch as they get out of the car. The woman must be early seventies at a guess, arthritic and overweight, using a stick, wearing a black hat, like a fedora. The man helps her, and when he turns around, there's something familiar about him. The shock of white hair, the eyes, the stature. They hobble towards us.

'Is this Markus Klausen's funeral?' the man asks.

I nod.

'I suppose you're the wife?' he says. He doesn't wait for a reply. 'We're Markus' parents. Selina and Hans Klausen. We've flown in from Edinburgh this morning. The flight was delayed.'

I gawp at them. Markus said his parents were dead, yet here they are, and I have little doubt they are his parents. Markus looked so much like his father, it winds me.

'Leonie,' Mum says as I try to stop my knees from buckling. I sense a vehicle arrive behind me. There's the soft closing of car doors, low voices.

'We'll go in now,' Hans Klausen says. 'Perhaps we can talk afterwards.' They walk slowly through the open doors of the crematorium and disappear inside. I turn slightly. The coffin is being taken out of the hearse and lifted onto the shoulders of four men dressed in black suits. Inside that wooden box is the body of my darling husband, and I swallow a sob, burying my face in a white handkerchief.

My brain seems to shut down during the service, because I only hear fragments. The vicar saying what a dreadful shock it is that we're gathered here today just weeks after he married us. That sometimes God's ways are unfathomable to us mere mortals. Markus' parents are sitting across the aisle from us, and every so often, I glance across at them, yet they both keep their eyes firmly to the front. Dad stands up and gives a speech. I hear that, every word of it.

'Markus Klausen was everything we wished for when imagining a son-in-law for our daughter, Leonie. He adored her, as many of you will know, as you attended their wedding so very recently. The shock of him being taken from us so violently still ricochets through us, and will undoubtedly do so until the perpetrator of this horrific crime is brought to justice.' Dad's hands shake as he reads his notes, and it makes me warm to him just a little bit more. 'Markus was about to join our family business. With a nose for a deal and with all the qualities of an excellent salesman, he would have been the son we hoped for, the ideal person to step into my shoes when I retire.'

I inhale audibly. Dad already has a son. Sam wanted to come today, but I told him not to. It's such a long way for a funeral that's being recorded and streamed live. And what about me taking over the family business? Surely that was my role?

'Markus possessed an assuredness, a confidence that you can't be taught, so much potential.'

His mother makes a strange noise. A snort, even. I swing my head around to look at her, but her hat blocks out her features.

'Out of this hell, we do have a nugget of good news.'

'No!' I say out loud, because I'd expressly told Dad not to mention it.

He throws me a watery smile. 'Leonie didn't want you to know, as it's still early days, but Brenda and I thought you should, as it brings us all some solace. Leonie is pregnant. A piece of Markus lives on.'

There's an audible intake of breath. Someone claps, half-heartedly, and then stops.

My grief morphs into anger. How dare Dad tell everyone! This is my child, my story to tell. Now people will look at me with even more pity. I feel like getting up and walking out, but then I think of Markus. He would love for everyone to know that he's going to be a father. I can imagine him strutting around, his hand on my stomach, being almost overbearingly kind to me. Fussing. And so, I grip my fingers together and sniff loudly. I don't hear the rest of Dad's speech. And then the coffin is gone, and if I was bereft before, now I feel as if I have closed down completely.

Afterwards, Mum steers me to the exit, where we're meant to be getting in the big black people-carrier, but I need to stay, to talk to Markus' parents. They, like us, should have been the first to leave the funeral, but they've been swept up in the maelstrom and still haven't emerged.

'You go ahead,' I tell my parents.

'Absolutely not,' Dad says. 'You're the grieving wife, and you need to be in the first car to arrive at the hotel.'

'Just go ahead. I'll get a lift with Denise or Zac.'

Dad opens his mouth to object, but before they can physically restrain me, I hurry away from them, weaving between the scores of people leaving the crematorium, trying to block off all the condolences that are batted my way. When the Klausens appear, I step in front of them.

'I didn't know you existed,' I say. 'I'd have been in touch otherwise.'

'Your parents knew,' Hans Klausen says curtly. 'Your father invited us to the funeral. Imagine how that felt, being invited to your son's funeral. And the police knew. They told us that our son had been murdered.'

'I don't understand,' I say, because I really don't. Why did no one tell me about the Klausens? 'Markus told me you were dead.'

His mother scoffs. His father says, 'Come on, Selina. Let's find you somewhere to sit.' I follow these strangers as they hobble outside, into the bright daylight, which seems all wrong, because it should be miserable weather. They sit on a bench adjacent to two spindly trees planted in memory of someone, with a name plaque I can't read from here. I perch awkwardly next to them.

'We were estranged,' Selina Klausen says. She talks with a soft Scottish burr. 'We hadn't heard sight nor sound from Markus for the best part of five years. It was after he got fired from his job and got addicted to cocaine and then came running to us, desperate for money. But what were we meant to do? It's not like we've got thousands stashed away. We're living off our state pensions, and we're barely scraping by ourselves. And then he stole from us. Took my mother's engagement ring and the nice watch that Hans got from his retirement. God knows what he did with them; pawned them, probably. And so, we told him to leave and not come back until he was clean. I mean, he was a grown man, in his thirties, and we're pensioners. It was shocking.'

I'm struggling to match what Selina Klausen is telling me to the backstory Markus described of his life. His parents were upper-class aristocrats, asset rich, cash poor, with an estate in Scotland where he spent his long summer holidays as a child. He said he was addicted to oxycodone, not cocaine.

'Where do you live?' I ask.

'Glasgow.'

'Not in the Highlands?'

Selina's laugh is gruff. Hans sighs. 'We're in our two-up two-down, same as we've always been. What story did he tell you?'

I'm silent, struggling to process this.

'Look, love,' she says, patting my arm. 'Markus always thought he was better than us, and sometimes that can be a good thing. He wanted to achieve more in his life, and we supported that. He was very bright, top of the class in every subject, even though he barely did any work. He got a job in the city of London, and we were so proud of him, weren't we, Hans?'

Hans nods, his gaze somewhere off in the distance.

'But Markus must have gotten greedy. God knows why, because we instilled him with morals as a kid, but he wanted more and more. We never found out exactly what happened, but he got fired from his job in banking. And then came the drugs and the stealing and the lies, and we knew that tough love was the only thing that was going to work. We cut all ties for a few weeks, but you can't leave your child for ever. I made contact through friends of friends and said we'd welcome him home once he had ditched the drugs. But we never heard from him again. Didn't know if he was dead or alive. Didn't know if he was clean or living in squalor somewhere. Didn't know he'd sorted himself out and was married to you, a beautiful young woman.' Her voice breaks. 'Didn't know nothing until that policeman called us out of the blue.'

'But you said my parents know about you. I don't understand.'

'When you told the police that Markus' parents were dead, there was no reason for them to seek us out, so we were only contacted a few days ago, when they discovered we weren't dead after all. They gave us your name, and from there it was easy enough to find your business. Someone in your office gave us your parents' phone number. Your father invited us to the funeral.'

'But they didn't tell me,' I murmur. What is it with my parents trying to control the narrative all the time? I bat away tears, tears of anger and grief, tears of sadness for this couple who were never reunited with their son. Tears of frustration that Markus felt the need to concoct a fake back-story for himself. And tears of sadness that my child will never know his or her father, however flawed he may have been.

22

LEONIE

I bury myself in work because that's the only way I can cope. I put on an aura of efficiency and togetherness and just hope that no one can see through the veil of artifice to the terrified, desperate person that I am underneath. The police have not found Markus' murderer. The latest theory is he disturbed a burglar trying to enter the house from the passageway down the side of the mews, or more likely, a youth seeking drugs. Markus' previous addiction came to the notice of the police – I'm not sure how, because I certainly didn't say anything. From then on, it seemed to me that the police seemed less interested, almost as if Markus was somehow culpable for his own death. There were two theories. First, he had called his dealer, and they had a massive bust-up. Second, that he had gone out of the house to put the rubbish in the green bin, but there was an opportunistic burglar prowling around who found the door open, crept into the kitchen and grabbed the first implement he could, battering Markus over the head with my frying pan. Except the burglar didn't steal anything.

Perhaps my car scared him away. I don't buy into either of those theories. I think it's more likely Markus was killed due to his dealings in Turkmenistan. It was probably a professional hitman whom we'll never find. But the police aren't taking that suggestion seriously, or perhaps they don't think Markus' life is important enough to call upon Interpol.

I've turned my house into Fort Knox, with a state-of-the-art burglar alarm system, bars on the lower windows, floodlights outside and cameras inside and out. But I don't think I'll stay here. The interior still feels like home, and I have the happy memories of Markus in my kitchen, making love to me in my bed, but whenever I go outside the house, I am gripped by terror. I can't look at the place Markus fell, and I've moved the bins to the front of the house, by the garage.

It's ironic how I lived alone for the past five years and I never felt lonely, yet the past five months changed everything. Now it is hell being alone. Yet I can't stay with Mum and Dad, it's too oppressive, and I'm not keen on finding a flatmate. So I have no choice. And then, I remember that in a few months I will no longer be alone. I'll have a baby to care for. My days have taken on a uniformity. I barely sleep. I force myself to eat breakfast, if only for the baby I'm carrying. I'm early at work and spend all day in the office, sending Erin or Zac to viewings and external meetings, avoiding pity and awkward conversations with clients. The only time I feel tired is about three in the afternoon, when I want to lay my head down on my glass desk and fall into an uneasy slumber. Like now.

'Leonie.'

I glance up at Denise. She rolls her chair towards my desk. It's just the two of us in the office this afternoon. Mum doesn't work much these days; it's like she's preoccupied with other things. Not that I mind, because I'm more relaxed in the office when she's not there. Zac and Erin are both out. 'I was thinking,' Denise says. 'You need a break.'

'A break?'

'Yes, a few days away to completely relax.'

I sigh. 'I suppose I do, but I don't fancy being alone with my thoughts.'

'There's this stunning holiday house that I've stayed at a couple of times. It's in the middle of nowhere, with forest around, and it's got a jacuzzi and a cinema room. The walks are breathtaking. There's even a fancy spa hotel nearby that do the best massages. It would be the perfect place for you to rest and recuperate for a long weekend, and frankly, I feel like a trip out there, too.'

I'm not sure. I seem to be laden down with apathy for anything that isn't work, and as much as I like Denise, she's first and foremost a work colleague.

Denise continues, 'It's where I went after Mum died, and it gave me such solace. I'm not sure what it is about the place, but I was able to sleep there for the first time in months. The beds are like clouds.'

'Where is it?' I ask.

'In the northeast. Northumberland. County Durham, I think – can't remember exactly. But it's an easy run up the A1.'

'I'm not sure,' I say. 'It's a long way to go.'

'Actually, I've already booked it for this weekend.' Denise looks bashful. 'I looked in your diary, and you've got nothing on this coming weekend. And the forecast is good, which is important. I know it's a long way, but I promise you it's worth it. You'll come home a different person. Obviously if you really don't want to go, I'll take another friend, but I genuinely think it would be good for you.'

I smile wryly. Denise has been so kind, and yes, it would be good for me to go, but she said Northumberland. Do I want to go there? I haven't visited Northumberland for a decade; it's a county I vowed never to revisit. Yet that seems so silly now. County Durham and Northumberland cover an area of nearly three thousand square miles. That's huge, and the chances of ending up near my parents' old holiday home are slight.

'Please say yes.' Denise smiles at me.

'Okay,' I say eventually. 'Yes.'

I offer to drive, but Denise says that's out of the question. She argues that I'm much too tired, and this weekend is all about me relaxing. She says her car is only six months old, and although it's not as luxurious as my BMW, I'll be comfortable. And I have to admit that the thought of driving all that way is awful, so I happily accept.

The journey is long, and I find myself dozing off, waking with a start as we pull into a service station somewhere near East Midlands airport.

'I need a coffee,' Denise says. 'Do you want anything?'

'I'll come in with you. Need to stretch my legs.'

We walk companionably into the service station. 'The car was hiccuping a bit,' she says. 'It didn't start the other morning, so I took it into the garage on Saturday. They gave it the once-over and said it's fine. That's the trouble with buying a nearly new car.'

'Are you sure it's all right? Do we need to call out the AA or RAC?' I ask. That's the last thing we need, to break down on the motorway in the dark. So much for a relaxing weekend away.

'Don't worry. I wouldn't have suggested we bring it if I thought there'd be a problem.'

We're queuing up now for drinks. I insist on buying, and choose a hot chocolate for myself and an Americano for Denise. We perch at a table, and Denise stretches her arms up into the air, cricking her neck backwards and forwards. 'Are you all right to do all the driving?' I ask her.

'Yes, no problem. I enjoy driving. I find it quite relaxing, don't you?'

I'm not really sure how to answer her. It took me years to relax behind the wheel, and I only started to enjoy driving when I had a car with all the latest safety features. It's ironic that driving is such a big part of my job, because a decade ago I doubted I would ever really learn to drive. In fact, Dad had to force me to take lessons, to even sit my test. Of course, with hindsight, he did the right thing.

My phone beeps with an incoming message, saving me from answering Denise's question. It's Dad. I groan. Denise raises an eyebrow.

'I forgot to email Dad next year's budget for approval.'

'Look, I'm talking out of turn here, but your dad seems to control everything you do. Is Castaway your business or his? And you've been through so much recently. It just seems a bit much, you know?'

I pause before answering. Denise is right, of course, but she can't begin to understand why I'm under Dad's thumb, why I don't just break free.

'He's a workaholic and expects everyone else to be one, too. It's difficult to explain, but I owe him a lot.'

Denise purses her lips and then finishes her coffee. 'Shall we get going?'

'Wakey, wakey,' Denise says. I sit up with a start and

blink rapidly. It's pitch-black outside but Denise is pulling into a driveway. The gravel crunches as she edges the car forwards and then brings it to a full stop outside a beautiful honey-coloured stone house. There are topiary olive trees in neat balls standing either side of the pale green front door, everything lit up by uplighters the whole way around the house.

'It looks lovely,' I say, yawning. 'Sorry I slept most of the way.'

'It's fine. It meant I got to choose the music.'

I'm surprised I was able to sleep through any music; I'm normally such a light sleeper. Denise opens her car door, and the damp air hits me, making me shiver. We carry our overnight bags up to the front door, and Denise scrambles behind some creeping ivy to expose a key box. She punches in a code, and the box flicks open, revealing a bunch of keys and an alarm fob. Denise then uses the key to open the front door and quickly switches off the alarm using the fob.

'Welcome to Sesame,' she says as she switches on lights in the hallway.

'Sesame? Is that the name of the house?'

'Yes. Great name, isn't it?'

'Wow, this place is lovely,' I say as I step inside. The entrance hall has large limestone flagstones on the floor and a monk's bench on one side next to a grandfather clock, with a large console table in pale grey on the other side, on which stands a planter full of lavender. Next to the front door is a coat stand.

'Let's dump our stuff, and I'll show you around,' Denise says. We walk down the corridor and into a fabulous farmhouse kitchen with a double black Aga and cupboards painted in pale grey. It's tasteful and welcoming. On the island unit, there's a basket filled with a loaf of bread, a bottle of wine, a carton of eggs and some homemade scones.

'The owner always leaves goodies for her guests. Let me show you around the rest of the house.'

It really is very lovely, with large bedrooms and modern en-suite bathrooms and a vast living room with a pool table at one end. The property is much too big just for the two of us.

'I'm starving,' Denise says as we emerge back in the kitchen. She goes to the fridge and opens it up to reveal a shelf full of dishes. 'I organised for the owner to leave us food, so all we need to do is reheat it. What do you prefer, fish mornay pie or bean curry?'

'The fish would be lovely,' I say. 'It's so kind of you to do all of this.'

'There's no point us driving nearly five hours to then have to cook.' Her retort is a little sharp, and it surprises me.

'No, of course not.'

She takes the cellophane off the ceramic dish and places it in the microwave. She then uncorks a bottle of white wine and pours herself a glass.

Although I insist otherwise, Denise gives me the master bedroom. The king-sized bed looks small in the huge space, and even when I'm tucked into the bed with the duvet and a blanket over the top, I can't seem to get warm. I'm not sure if it's because the room is cold, or whether I'm going down with something, but it's as if my bones are chilled. I lie there in the comfortable bed for ages, missing Markus' arms around me.

When I wake up, a pale grey light seeps through the curtains, and even though it's only 6 am and I should probably turn over and go back to sleep, I feel fully awake. I tug on a thick jumper over my pyjamas and pad to the window. Pushing the floral curtains to one side, I sit on the cushioned window seat and look out over the lawn, the rhododendron bushes that edge the garden and the woodland beyond. The landscape is both familiar and strange, and I can't quite work out why.

Half an hour later, I've had a shower, dressed up in thick clothes and drunk a herbal tea. I'm as quiet as I can be so as not to wake Denise, who must be shattered after all of that driving. She's left the front door key in the door, so I unbolt it top and bottom and unlock the door, closing it behind me.

Not knowing where I am, I set off down the drive at a brisk pace, my breath creating clouds of condensation. At the road, there are no signs, but it's a country lane cutting through woodland, so I don't expect much traffic this early on a Saturday morning. I turn to the left and stride along the edge of the road. An uneasiness settles on me. Is this familiar, or am I imagining it, thanks to the tricks my memory likes to play? There's a small house sign just up ahead on the right. Once I'm near enough to read it, I let out a little whimper. The Wilds. I stumble just as a white van races past, so close to me I'm sprayed with water from puddles.

'Shit,' I mutter. How many other houses are there called the Wilds in Northumberland? With a sinking feeling in my gut, I take a few steps along the private drive, just far enough so I can see the house. It's been recently painted, the walls glaring white in the early morning light, and the garage door that was once black is now grey, but I'd recognise this house anywhere. I remember when Dad gave it to Mum. It was her birthday, and he said he was taking us all to stay in a hotel in Northumberland to celebrate. Mum was thrilled. She'd get to see her parents and the county that she loved so much. I remember Dad turning into the drive and Mum frowning and saying this isn't a hotel, is it? Dad had stuck a great big red bow on the front door, and after turning the engine off, he swivelled to face Mum and handed her a key.

'Happy birthday, love,' he said. 'Welcome to your new holiday home. I've called it the Wilds.'

Mum cried, great big sobs, and I didn't understand why she was so upset. Surely this was a nice thing?

'Go and choose your rooms,' Dad told Sam and me. It wasn't a hard choice. There was a room decorated in pink for me and a room with navy stripes for Sam. Every summer we would decamp to Northumberland for three weeks. I had happy memories of those summers: Gran and Gramps would take us to the wild beaches, Dad joined a local golf club, and soon we had lots of family friends. And so it should have continued, and perhaps it would have done if I hadn't had the accident. But the summer of my sixteenth year was our last in Northumberland. My parents sold the house, and that was the end of that.

I shiver as the memories come flooding back. What were the chances of ending up literally next door to our old home? Was it fate? Is this my past having at long last caught up with my present, forcing me to deal with the old ghosts? Did we drive past where the accident happened last night, or will we be driving past it today?

Suddenly a dog starts barking, and I back away, hurrying towards the road and striding briskly back to the luxury Airbnb where I'm staying. I want to leave right now, head back to the safety of London, but I know I can't. What would I tell Denise?

When I get back to our honey-coloured house, a property that, now I'm looking at it during the day, appears newly built, I open the front door, remove my trainers and walk towards the kitchen. There's the scent of frying bacon and newly percolated coffee. It makes my stomach rumble.

'You were up early,' Denise says as she turns away from the hob. 'Didn't you sleep well?' She looks really concerned, as if my lack of sleep might be due to something she's done.

'No, I slept fine, thanks. Just up early, so I went for a walk.'

'Found any interesting spots?'

'Um, no.'

'I can't wait to show you around later. I've got the day all planned out. We'll have a walk this morning, followed by driving to the spa, where we're booked in for a light lunch and various relaxing treatments. We'll come back here for an early night and supper. How does that sound?' She looks at me earnestly, and I force a smile.

'It sounds great. Can't wait.'

Except that's a lie. All I want to do is get back in the car and head south, far away from here.

23

CARRIE

Leonie looked pretty shaken when she returned from her morning walk. I wonder if she's worked out where we are, and I wonder if she's remembered that it's the ten-year anniversary of the accident this weekend, the moment that wrecked my life. Probably not. She's so wound up with herself, the nauseating grief over Markus, her damned business and following all of Daddy's instructions. It's probably never entered her consciousness that her actions have ruined another human's life.

The day goes interminably slowly. The spa hotel is one of those old-fashioned English country house hotels where everything is done oh so properly, and the staff walk around with soft-heeled shoes, in case footsteps might ruin the experience. The spa reception is lavish, with cocoon-like hanging chairs that dangle from the ceiling, piled high with soft cushions, and there's a strong scent of patchouli oil. We're taken to the changing area, where we're given fluffy white bathrobes and waffle slippers and told to lock all of our belongings away for the next four hours. Four bloody hours. I've booked Leonie in for a ninety-minute all-over body massage, as well as a rose-petal facial, and notified them that Leonie is pregnant. I thought that was exceptionally kind of me. Obviously, I'm not going to be having a body massage, as the last thing I want is for some masseuse to look at me in disgust, or, god forbid, for Leonie to catch a glimpse of all my scars. I'll have a pedicure and a facial.

And yes, the whole afternoon is costing a fortune. If Leonie thinks I'm paying for this, she's got another think coming. It's going to go through Castaway's books as vital expenses. I'm ninety-nine percent sure that Leonie doesn't examine the accounts, and even if she does, I'll bury it neatly so that she won't discover it for months to come. No, forget that. She won't discover it ever. Not with what I've got planned for this weekend.

Leonie is led away first, by an attractive masseuse with honey gold skin and her hair tied back in a high ponytail. 'Are you looking forward to being totally relaxed?' I hear the woman say. Stupid question.

My beauty therapist is overweight with white hair; she looks like she could do with a load of work herself. Typical, isn't it, that I get the dregs of the staff, whilst Leonie gets the best? She leads me into a small room with a treatment bed covered in fluffy towels.

'I'll leave you to slip out of your dressing gown and lie under the towels. Will be back in a couple of minutes.'

I'm not comfortable slipping out of the dressing gown, but I do as she instructed and slide in between the towels. The bed is heated, and I feel myself relaxing immediately. I pull the towel right up to my neck so the scars that run from my shoulders across my breasts are hidden.

She comes back into the room and turns the lights down. 'How sensitive is your skin?' she asks.

'Hypersensitive,' I say, although it isn't. My poor skin has been so battered it'll cope with anything.

'We only use natural products here and essential oils.' She puts two heavy and wet cotton wool pads over my eyes, and then she gets to work. I find it really difficult to relax. My mind is racing ahead to what I have planned on our way home from the spa. The minutes drag, and despite the firm but gentle touch of my therapist, my brain refuses to switch off. At the end of the interminable hour, she says, 'I'm going to leave you alone now, to come to slowly. Take your time. I've left you a glass of warm water on the side. Remember to rehydrate well today.'

I don't 'come to slowly', but immediately swing my legs off the bed and tug on my dressing gown. The scent of the aromatherapy oil is cloying, and I just need to get out of the therapy room. I tie the dressing gown tightly around my midriff, making sure none of my scars are visible, and walk back to reception. I've still got another two and a half hours to kill. Frankly, I could scream with frustration.

Why is it when you want time to speed up, it does the absolute opposite? I remember slipping in and out of consciousness and praying for time to speed up, for someone to find me, to hear my increasingly pathetic cries. Yet time dragged and pulled and tore up my insides. I find myself remembering more and more of those horrific hours as I sit curled up in one of the hanging cocoon chairs.

'Denise White?' a female voice asks. It still takes me a split second to remember that's me.

'Yes.'

'It's time for your pedicure.'

I choose black. A shiny black nail varnish with a minuscule fake diamond placed at the tips of my big toenails. I'm not sure why, but it gives me some inner strength.

Eventually, Leonie emerges. She looks completely spaced out, unable to walk in a straight line, yawning and rubbing her eyes.

'Feeling good?' I ask. I'm fully dressed now and desperate to leave.

'It was amazing,' she drawls. 'I'd like to stay here forever.'

'Well, I'm afraid they're turfing us out now we've done our four hours. I'll wait for you in the main hotel reception. We can go home, and you can put your feet up there whilst I make supper.'

'You're so kind,' Leonie says, and moves as if she's going to give me a hug. I slip away and say over my shoulder, 'See you in a mo.'

My heart is hammering as Leonie gets into my car. I am a bundle of nervous and excited energy. The light has faded, and shadows from trees cut across the road as I pull out of the hotel entrance.

'That was so good, Denise. I'm the most relaxed I've been in ages. Thank you for spoiling me,' Leonie says.

I have to swallow my chuckle. I'll certainly be spoiling her, just not in the way she's expecting. But I'm glad she's relaxed. It means what's about to come will be a greater shock. I turn the car confidently onto the road back towards our luxury home, but this time I don't take the direct route on the A road. Instead, I turn off onto a narrow lane, the far end of which is where *it* happened.

'Where are we going?' Leonie asks. 'Don't we need to take the signs to Hexham?'

'Shortcut.' And then I pause. 'Hey, I didn't know you knew this neck of the woods.'

She's silent for a moment, no doubt realising she's said too much. 'Actually, my parents used to have a house here in Northumberland. I came here as a kid.'

'Well, that's marvellous. Such happy memories. How come you didn't tell me before?'

She shrugs but doesn't answer. And now, whilst she's looking out of the side window, I pump the car's brake, causing the car to jerk.

'What's going on?' she asks, her voice a little higher than normal.

'Oh, for god's sake,' I murmur. 'Not now.' I bring the car to a shuddering halt as far over to the left of the road as I can manage. It's dark here, with all of the overhanging trees and the woodland on both sides of the road stretching a mile in each direction. 'The car has stalled. Must be that bloody fault that the garage promised me they'd fixed.'

'Can you try to start it again?' Leonie asks. She shuffles in her seat, the first visible sign of discomfort.

'I'll try,' I say, but I only turn the starter button halfway, and the car shudders but doesn't start. 'Shit. We're going to need to call for help. I'm a member of the AA, so I'm sure we can get someone to fix the problem or, in the worst-case scenario, tow us to a garage.'

Leonie starts rummaging in her handbag. She then takes out her wallet, a small bag of toiletries, tissues.

'What's up?' I ask.

'I can't find my phone.'

'Are you sure?'

She tips the full contents of her bag onto her lap now, and her phone most definitely isn't there.

'Did you leave it at the spa?' I suggest.

She runs her fingers through her greasy hair. 'It must have slipped out in the locker, and I didn't realise.'

'Don't worry,' I say. 'We'll go back and collect it. It's a classy joint, so I'm sure no one will have gone off with it.' I lean over to the back seat and grab my bag. 'I've got my phone, so no worries.'

I switch it on, but I get no reception. Of course I get no reception. I've had a little play in my settings, and my phone isn't going to work. I briefly turn the screen towards Leonie.

'Shit. There's no reception here. You'd have thought with 5G there would be reception everywhere these days.'

'I remember mobile coverage being poor around here years ago, but now...' Her voice fades away. 'What are we going to do?'

'Well, this is hardly the relaxing evening I was planning.' I sigh. 'I'm so sorry. Stuck on a country lane in the middle of nowhere, in the dark.' I pretend to think for a few moments. 'I saw a house a few hundred metres back. I'll walk back there, and hopefully there'll be someone at home, so I can use their phone. And if not, I'm sure I'll be able to pick up reception there, where more people live. It's probably best if you walk in the other direction, towards the Airbnb. If you get there before me, let yourself in. The door code is 3666933.'

I look in both directions, but there are no car lights coming from either way, and I doubt there will be. This is a quiet road, a cut-through only known by locals. I open my car door.

'You coming?' I ask Leonie, an edge of frustration to my voice.

'It's pitch black, and I don't have my phone, so I won't be able to see where I'm going,' she says hesitantly.

'Oh yes, silly me. I've got a torch in the front pocket.' I lean across and grab the small torch, handing it to her. I've made sure that the battery is nearly gone. She'll get perhaps ten minutes or so of light from it, if she's lucky.

'Walk along the grass bank at the side of the road,' I tell Leonie as she slips out of the car. 'It's probably only a mile or so that way to the Airbnb. If you get there before me, put the kettle on.' I laugh, but wonder if it sounds forced.

'Okay,' she says hesitantly. 'See you soon.' Leonie zips up her coat and sets off along the side of the road. She glances back at one point, and I start walking in the opposite direction, but once I'm sure she's turned the corner and is out of sight, I double back. I get into the driver's seat and sit there, forcing myself to wait a full five minutes. I then start the car and put my headlights on full beam. I drive slowly until I spot Leonie walking ahead of me. A surge of adrenaline rushes through my veins as I put my foot on the accelerator. My hands are gripped so tightly around the steering wheel, it feels as if my knuckles will burst through my skin. I let out a screech and drive straight towards her, faster. Faster. Faster.

Good luck, Leonie. Now it's your turn to lie in the ditch suffering just like I did.

24

LEONIE

I don't want to be here on this road, in the dark, today of all days. Denise was so kind in treating me to an afternoon at the spa, but this... well, this is my worst nightmare. Perhaps I should have just told Denise, explained that I had a horrible accident on this road a decade ago, and it's haunted me ever since.

But I didn't tell her, and instead I'm walking along the verge, the dim light from the torch bouncing up and down. And then I hear a car engine. I stand still. Perhaps I can wave the car down, get the driver to call the breakdown services. For a few moments, lights flicker through the trees. Then they are bright white, dazzling, coming straight towards me. It takes me a long second to realise that this car isn't just driving, it's speeding faster and faster, its engine roaring, the lights blinding me, searing my eyes. I wave my arms, but the driver doesn't seem to see me. It happens so fast. In a millisecond. The car is heading straight towards me, and if I don't move...

I throw myself to the side of the road, into the damp long

grass, rolling, rolling down a bank, scratching my face and my hands on spiky bushes. And the car just roars past. I think I'm going to be sick. That was so close, just a millisecond, a centimetre closer, and it would have hit me, sending me flying into the air, landing with a – landing dead, probably. My breath is ragged. I think I've just dodged being killed, and I lie in the damp grass, stunned, unable to move. I bring my hand up to my face, and it feels sore and scratched. I force myself to get up, wet knees in damp grass, my hands stinging. I sit for a long moment. It's pitch black around me; I've lost the torch in the fall. I'm stunned, can't think straight.

Except I can. I don't know the exact tree, the exact spot where I killed that person, but it was on this road. I'm sure of it. Is this karmic retribution? Was it always meant to be like this, for me to have an accident in the same place, for me to suffer like he did? I can hear Markus' voice, and tears spring to my eyes.

'Don't be silly, darling,' he'd have said. 'There's no such thing as coincidence.' And it hits me. This *is* no coincidence. It can't be. But how is that even possible? No one except Dad knew I was there.

I haul myself to standing, feeling wobbly, allowing my eyes to adjust to the low light, because the longer I stay here, the more I realise there is some light; it's just I need to adjust to the shadows. I clamber back up the bank carefully, my ripped palms stinging. I stay right by the edge, near the bushes, out of the view of the road. I peer in both directions. There's silence. Welcome silence. I limp a few metres, unsure if I even want a car to come past. And then I see a car parked up ahead of me, facing me, its indicators pointing to the side of the road. Its headlights are off, so I can't make out the model of the car, but it is facing the other way, so perhaps the driver of this car saw the other vehicle driving like a lunatic. Perhaps he or she saw me flying down the side of the road. I shout and wave, in the hope there's someone there, and in that instant, I realise I've made a terrible mistake. The lights go onto full beam, and the car is coming towards me. Faster and faster. The engine revving horribly. I glance to my side, but here there's a glinting metal barrier. In that split second, I know that I'm going to be crushed against the barrier, smashed, broken, squashed like a mosquito. And even though I miss my husband so very much, I want to live. I really want to live.

I scream. I launch myself over the barrier, somehow getting my head and shoulders up in the air and over the barrier with my hips catching the metal and my legs following in a manoeuvre I had no idea was even possible. There's the screech of metal on metal, the roar of a car engine, and then as I lie in the mud and grass, my hands over my head, the terrible noise fades. The car drives away and away until there's complete silence, my faltering breath the only noise. Everything hurts. My hips, my back, my torn hands. I realise I'm crying silent tears because, no, that was not a coincidence. Someone was trying to drive into me on purpose. Someone knows I'm here, and someone wants me dead.

I think back over the past twenty-four hours. Who knows I'm back in Northumberland? I didn't tell my parents, but Zac and Erin knew that Denise was whisking me away to a luxury house and spa. But what about the people at the spa hotel this afternoon? What if one of the masseuses somehow recognised me, or perhaps knew my name? But how would they have known it was me, that I was responsible for the death of their friend or family member?

Why have I buried my head in the sand all these years? I don't even know the name of the person who died. I looked for news reports – of course I did, in that masochistic way we have after being involved in something horrific. But there was nothing, just a single paragraph in a local newspaper saying that a car had been found following an accident. No other vehicles were involved. That was all it said. No name, no details, and I didn't understand why. At the time, I wondered whether perhaps Dad had pulled his weight and put an embargo on any reporting, but then he would have admitted his involvement, so it didn't make sense. Besides, I was sixteen, and I did what Dad instructed me to do: forget about it. Not that I was very successful.

None of this makes sense.

And then I hear Markus' voice again: 'You need to get the hell out of here!'

If someone is trying to kill me, driving into me on purpose, then they'll be back, won't they? They'll return to try again, to make sure that I'm squashed like a run-over squirrel. And if they don't find me on the road, they'll come looking in the woods. But at least I'll have cover there, won't I? I force myself to stand up, to move. Pain rushes through my left leg, but I can't stay here. My life is in danger.

I hurry deeper into the woods, totally confused as to which direction I'm going. I glance upwards through the branches of the trees and see the moon throwing shadows, lighting my way just a little. Yet I still stumble over fallen branches, catching my foot in a hole, a rabbit's burrow perhaps, sending searing pain up my ankle. *Keep going. Keep going.*

I peer at my watch, but the light is too low for me to read the dial. *Keep going.* I stagger forwards, pushing away branches, weaving between solid tree trunks, stopping every so often to catch my breath. I jump when I hear the hooting of an owl and then a horrific scream. I stand statue-like, swallowing a whimper. Has the murderer found another victim?

The scream comes again, and I realise it's not human. A rabbit, perhaps, in the clutches of a fox. *Keep going.* I force my legs to take one step in front of the next, my footsteps brutally loud from the snapping of branches and the crunching of leaves. Am I going around in circles? I've no idea. It seems as if I'm walking for hours, but perhaps it's just minutes. The moon disappears behind a cloud, and the forest becomes more oppressive, more silent. I feel a drop of wetness, then more. It's raining now, and I can see so little. And then, eventually... is that light?

I take cover behind a large tree and peer out. It's a light. Please, not a car light. I take a few steps forward, but every tread sounds so loud now. The cracking of branches as I place a foot in the wrong place. I pause every couple of steps and strain my ears, but all I hear is the gentle patter of rain on the ground. The light draws me nearer like a moth, and then I feel weak with relief. It's not a car. It's a house. A solid, square house with two windows lit up from within. It's a small house, not the Wilds, not Sesame, but somewhere that looks cottage-like, homely. I imagine an older couple opening the door to me, pulling me inside, making me sugary tea, calling the police. And I step closer and closer. And then I stop.

What if these are the people trying to kill me? What if this horror movie isn't anything to do with my past, but it's the same people who murdered Markus, and they're renting this house, luring me in so that they can kill me in the same way? I turn my face up to the sky, and the cold rain pours down my face.

Get a grip, Leonie, I tell myself. *Your mind is playing tricks.* I take a deep breath and stride forward, walking right up to the front door of the stone house. There's a brass doorbell, which I press. I must look a fright, and wonder if I'll scare off the homeowner. I'm formulating what I should say, waiting for footsteps, terror mingling with the prospect of relief. A dog barks from inside the house. It's a deep bark. What is it? A friendly Labrador or a terrifying pit bull? I press the doorbell again. The dog's bark is more frenzied now. There is no other sound.

I walk around the house, trying to peer into the windows. There are thick curtains across the rooms that are lit up. Around the back is the kitchen. It's dark in there, but I can just about make out an old-fashioned oven on the far wall. I walk all around the house and only then realise that there isn't a car here. Whoever lives in this place must have a car, yet there is no vehicle. I feel like slumping to the ground as I realise no one is at home.

What now?

I hobble down the drive of the house, keeping in the shadows, praying that I won't hear the sudden starting of a car engine, the roar as it races towards me.

I don't.

The rain patters on the tarmac, and I push my wet hair back off my face, blinking rapidly to see better. The drive belonging to this house meets the main road, and I shiver. I am going to have to follow the road to get help. Or I could stay here, perhaps, waiting until the owners come home, because I'm sure they will. They won't have left their dog there alone for too long. I hear a car and jump into the bushes. *Please don't come for me.* The vehicle is driving steadily, water from the road splashing up from the tyres, and it just carries on past the entrance to the small house, but its headlights catch a small sign on the other side of the road. A familiar sign. I wait until there is complete silence, no lights coming from anywhere, and I race across the wet tarmac. I crouch, every bone in my body searing with pain. It's a small white sign with black cursive letters. *Sesame.*

At last, I've got lucky. Despite being horribly lost in the woods, I've found my way back to our Airbnb. Relief makes me weak, but I force myself to run. I run and run, the lights of the beautiful, honey-toned house that is called Sesame beckoning me to safety. And only then do I remember I'm pregnant. How could I have forgotten? My body is so battered and bruised. Have I lost the baby? Have I failed this new life that is growing inside me?

25

CARRIE

I am fizzing with anger. Pure boiling rage that makes me see sparks and tenses up every muscle. My plan didn't work. At least, it didn't work exactly the way I hoped. Obviously, I didn't hit her the first time. She was too quick for me, throwing herself down the bloody bank. I knew that because I didn't feel the slightest jolt, so I turned the car around a few hundred metres up the road and slowly, stealthily, drove back towards the way I came. I sat there in the dark until I saw Leonie stagger towards me, and this time I was sure I had chosen a better location. There was a metal barrier edging the road, perfect for crushing her. But although the car scraped the barrier, I don't think I hit Leonie. There's no blood on my bumper, just a metal scratch. I just hope that she's severely wounded as a result of hurling herself over the metal barrier, perhaps banging her head against a rock as she tumbled down. Hopefully she's lying there right now, praying for help, as I did. I debated going back to look for her, but it was too risky. Instead, I'll return in the morning, perhaps for a morning stroll if the rain clears. I can imagine her looking up at me with glassy, begging eyes, blood seeping into the grass, desperately injured. I hope so. Whatever happens, I'll wait here for twenty-four hours and then ring Zac, asking him whether Leonie has returned to London. I'll pretend that Leonie went out for a walk and didn't return. I'm looking forward to that conversation.

I pour myself a large gin and tonic from the honesty bar. *Honesty.* That's a joke. Leonie wouldn't know it if it hit her in the face.

I light a fire with the logs and kindling that the owners of this house have kindly left us – although for the price of this place, I'm not sure why I think they've been kind. And then I settle down on a comfortable armchair, taking a big, welcome sip of my gin.

Suddenly there's banging coming from somewhere. What the hell? I jump up, spilling the gin. I stand still for a moment, and then it comes again. It's as if someone is hitting the front door. I race into the hall, and just as I'm about to lock the door from the inside, it swings open.

'Denise!' Leonie cries. She looks shocking. She's soaked through, her hair plastered to her head, and scratches dripping blood down her cheeks, her hands covered in mud and blood.

'What the hell!" I exclaim, stepping backwards.

'You're not going to believe it, but someone tried to kill me!' Leonie cries. 'They tried to run me over. Twice!'

I stare at her. She's meant to be dying in a ditch, not standing here making this perfect floor filthy. She's meant to be fatally injured. Ideally, dead. The fury is burning inside me, and all I want to do is reach over for that heavy vase and bring it straight down on Leonie's head. Except I can't. I have to be cleverer than that. Much cleverer.

'Denise?' She peers at me questioningly, and I realise I need to snap out of my wishful thinking. I've got a catastrophe to deal with here and now.

'Oh my God! Leonie,' I say, rushing towards her and slamming the front door shut. 'That's terrible. You look awful. Are you very hurt? Come into the kitchen; let's have a proper look at you.'

She's puddling mud on the beautiful floor. I certainly don't want to be clearing up after her. 'Actually, best sit down here in the hall, and let's remove those sodden clothes. I'll go and get you some towels.'

Leonie seems shell-shocked and does as I tell her, sitting down on the floor, tugging off her torn trainers, undoing the button at her waist. I hurry upstairs and grab two large white towels. She's shivering in her underwear, her teeth chattering, her body smeared with blood and mud. At least she's hurt. That's a little consolation.

'You need to take a hot shower, and then we'll have a look at those scratches. I'm sure there's a first-aid kit here somewhere,' I say. As if I care.

'I need to call the police,' she says in a quivering voice.

'Yes, of course.'

She's wrapped the towels around her, but is still shivering violently. 'Let's get you in the shower, and I'll call the police. Then I'll make us a nice hot supper so you can properly warm up.'

She nods and murmurs, 'Thank you.'

I guide her up the stairs and into the master en-suite. I turn the shower on, waiting until the water is hot. 'Don't lock the door, just in case,' I say. 'And shout if you feel dizzy or anything. I'm going to call the police now.'

'Thank you, Denise,' Leonie says, with such gratitude in

her eyes I have to bite the side of my mouth to stop myself from laughing out loud.

I'm sure Leonie is in the shower and won't hear me anyway, but just in case – and to amuse myself – I make a fake call to the police.

'I need to speak to the police,' I say, holding my phone to my ear and pacing up and down the hall, then walking into the living room. 'Yes, the police.' Pause. 'No, no one is in immediate danger.' A longer pause. 'The address here is, gosh, sorry, I don't know it offhand because we're staying in an Airbnb. Yes.' Pause. 'It happened on the back road near here. A car tried to drive into my friend Leonie Wilding. Oh sorry, she's Leonie Klausen now. Yes, twice. She had to throw herself to the side of the road to avoid it.' Pause. 'No, I'm sorry, I wasn't there.' Pause. 'No, I don't think her injuries are that severe.' Another longer pause. 'Of course. If you could come and take a statement in the morning, that would be great. Thank you. Goodbye.' I chuck my phone onto the sofa and grin.

As I walk out into the hallway, I hear the shower being turned off.

'Are you okay?' I shout up the stairs.

Leonie emerges in a pale grey dressing gown, her arms clutched around herself, her hair wrapped in a white towel. She looks very pale, the scratches on her face vivid against the white skin. 'I'm scared I might have hurt my baby,' she says in a croaky voice. 'What if something happened to him or her when I fell?'

In my mind, I'm pumping my fist and giving a cheer, but instead, I plaster a look of concern on my face. 'Have you had any bleeding?'

'No, but it's still early days. I'm wondering if I should go to the hospital to get it checked out.'

'Any cramping or pain in your stomach?' I ask.

She shakes her head.

'I think you'd know if you'd done serious damage,' I say, in what I hope is a reassuring voice. 'I think what you need is some warm food and an early night. If you're still worried in the morning, then of course, we'll find somewhere to get you checked out.'

'What did the police say?'

'That because it's not an imminent emergency right now, they don't have the resources to come out tonight, but they'll come over tomorrow and take a statement from you.' I watch her carefully to assess whether she doubts me, but she just sighs.

'That makes sense, I suppose. How did you get back here, anyway?' Leonie asks.

'Oh, I got lucky. I was walking towards that house when a man in a white van pulled up and asked me if I was all right. I explained that the car had broken down. Only turns out that he was a mechanic, so he tinkered with the engine and jump-started it. He was mucking around with it for a while and said something about the starter motor and plugs. Anyway, he reckoned he fixed it. Obviously, I offered to pay him, but he waved me away and said he liked helping ladies in distress. I didn't even get his phone number. I drove around looking for you, but when I couldn't find you anywhere, I came back here.'

'That was lucky,' Leonie says, without the faintest hint of suspicion in her voice.

'Right.' I clap my hands. 'I need to go and find some antiseptic cream for you and put the oven on. You get dressed.'

She throws me a weak smile and disappears into the bedroom.

All of this acting is doing my head in. I want to run back up the stairs, put my hands around Leonie's neck and watch as the life seeps out of her. But no, that's not true. I want her dying in that damned ditch, yet she's back here. What is it with this woman? Why does she have all the luck? Why does she manage to thwart me at every single turn? The anger is threatening to boil over, and I know I need to do something to thwart it, to keep my brain on track and not let my true feelings show. I stomp into the kitchen and find a ceramic dish. I hurl it onto the floor. It cracks with a satisfying thwack.

'Everything okay?' Leonie shouts from upstairs. Her voice sounds raw.

'Managed to drop a dish on the floor. Don't worry – I'll clear it up.'

I kick the broken shards to the side of the room. I know that I'm going to have to change my plan. I had been so desperate for Leonie to suffer on the exact ten-year-anniversary of the accident, which is today, but I suppose I need to accept that I might not achieve that. What is more important? The date or the place?

The place. I want her to lie incapacitated in that ditch. I'm damned if I'm going to deviate from the plan too much. I want her to experience the fear that her life is drifting away, that her baby is dying, that the world as she knows it is over forever. As I shove one of the ready meals into the oven and hear Leonie's footsteps coming down the stairs, I realise something else, too. Harming her is not enough. I might just have to kill Leonie outright.

26

LEONIE

The hot water goes some way to easing the aching of my limbs and the scratches all over my face, arms and legs. What it doesn't do is dispel the fear that sits in the base of my stomach like a lump of jagged ice. There are three possibilities. First, that it was an accident, that some idiot was driving crazily fast and simply didn't see me. As much as I wish this was the case, I don't really believe it. Secondly, someone knows who I am and what I have done, and I was their target. Yet how did they know where I was going to be? Thirdly, that the mercenaries who killed Markus have tracked me down. And that means I'm not safe anywhere.

As I hobble downstairs and hear Denise humming in the kitchen, I realise that she's the only person who knew where I was. But Denise has worked for me for months; she's been a genuine friend, supported me when Markus died, and look how kind she is being to me now. She knows nothing about my past. And that's the problem. No one knows what I did, other than Dad. As much as we have our differences, as much as I complain about his tight grip over my life, I know that Dad loves me. He was the person who saved me, so there's no way he would be behind this. But Denise – how well do I really know her?

'How are you feeling?' She appears silently from the living room, making me jump.

'Better, thanks. Sore and scared, but I don't think I've broken anything.'

She steps towards me and places a hand on my stomach. 'And baby?' she asks. I don't like that she's touching my stomach, and I step backwards.

'All good,' I say, wrapping my arms around myself awkwardly. I try to see Denise through fresh eyes. Is she really my friend? How well do I know this woman?

'Supper is nearly ready. Why don't you make yourself comfortable by the fire in the living room?' she suggests.

I nod, but then that icy fear settles on me, and this house seems too big. 'I'm scared, Denise,' I admit. 'What if they come looking for me here?'

'Don't be silly,' she says, with an annoying chuckle. 'How would they – whomever *they* are – know where you're staying? It was probably some drunken idiot driving too fast.' A strange expression briefly crosses her face, and I wonder whether she feels bad for minimising what happened to me, or whether there's something she's keeping from me. 'I'll be in with your food in a mo.'

I walk into the big living room with its sofas and armchairs covered in neutral colours, and the big windows that look out onto the pitch-dark night. I pull all the curtains, making sure that there are no gaps, and only then do I sit on an armchair in front of the roaring fire. Am I catastrophising? Yet I can't stop that nagging thought that it's ten years almost to the day, and I'm staying right next door to our old home. And why did Denise bring me here? We could have gone anywhere in the whole country, yet we're right here in Northumberland.

Denise walks into the living room holding a tray, which she puts down on the wooden coffee table. 'A glass of juice and a bowl of pasta for you,' she says, handing me a glass and a large blue ceramic bowl, with a fork balanced on top of it. She sits down on the sofa, with her socked feet curled up under her. 'It's cosy with the curtains drawn.'

'I didn't like the thought of anyone looking in.'

'Yeah, I know what you mean,' Denise says, fluttering her fingers melodramatically before shovelling some pasta in her mouth. 'I was thinking,' she says, her eyes on her food, 'You might be right. If they do know where you are, we're not really safe here.'

I shiver involuntarily. And I wonder, where has the confident, gung-ho Denise gone?

She looks at me, her eyes wide. 'Oh, don't worry too much. I'll make sure all the doors and windows are locked and bolted before we go to bed.'

But now I feel even more scared. When Denise seemed nonchalant about my concerns, that was so much better. And if she was behind all of this, why would she say she was scared, too? We eat in silence for a few minutes, but with every mouthful, fear curdles a little bit more.

'I'm wondering if I should call the police back,' I suggest. 'They might be prepared to do a drive past.'

'I doubt they will,' Denise says, wiping her mouth with the back of her hand. 'You didn't get the registration number of the car, did you?'

I shake my head. 'The lights were so blinding, and it happened so fast, I don't even know what sort of car it was.'

'Mmm,' she says. 'That's the trouble. Because you didn't get any details, and obviously there's no CCTV on these little country roads, the police officer said there's nothing they can do tonight.'

I suppose that makes sense, but it doesn't ease the knot of fear. Frankly, I'd like to get back in Denise's car and drive all the way back to London, this very moment. But I know I can't ask that of her, not when she's been so kind to me. Or should I call for a taxi? It would cost a fortune to get a taxi all the way back home, but at least I'd feel safe.

I place my bowl of pasta back on the tray. I haven't eaten it all, but my stomach is too tight. I'm taken back to the days straight after Markus died. If only I could hear his voice...

'Oh,' I say, remembering that I don't have my mobile phone, so I can't call for a cab even if I want to. 'Could I borrow your phone to ring the spa hotel, to see if they found my phone in the locker?'

'Gosh, I'd forgotten all about that,' Denise says, leaning over the tray and picking up her mobile phone. 'I'll call them right now.'

She's scrolling through her phone when suddenly there's a piercing alarm. I gasp. Has someone broken in? And then I catch the smell – the scent of burning.

'Shit!' Denise says, dropping her phone onto the sofa. 'I think I forgot to turn off the gas on the hob.' She races out of the living room. Instinctually, I stand up and grab her phone. I want to speak to Zac or Mum. I want to tell them what's happened, where I am. I want to make sure that Denise is the lovely friend she claims to be. The screen is still lit up on her phone, so I press the green phone button, and it goes straight to recent calls. I glance down the list, and it takes me a second to realise what's wrong. The first number at the top of the list should be 999. That was the last number that Denise called, wasn't it? Yet the last call that Denise made was yesterday afternoon. It takes a moment to sink in. Denise hasn't made a single outgoing call today.

What the hell!

I'm trembling as the full implications of this dawns on me. 'Everything all right?' I shout. My voice sounds like it belongs to someone else.

'I left the bloody pan on, and it's a burned mess.'

'Do you need a hand?'

'No. Just need to get all the windows opened and to stop the alarm.'

Her phone is burning in my trembling hands, but I know now is my only chance to have a look. I scroll back to the homepage and see an app called Notes. I click on it, and on the list is my name: Leonie. I click the folder, all the time listening for Denise, willing her to stay in the kitchen a bit longer. And then I see a photograph of a newspaper cutting. It's just two lines long, and I only manage to read the first line:

Carrie Denise White was found barely alive...

'God, what an idiot I am!' Denise walks back into the living room, wiping damp hands on her jeans. I quickly hold the phone behind my back, my heart thumping. Somehow, I've got to get the phone onto the sofa without her seeing, without her realising that the screen is still live. The fire crackles, and that gives me an idea.

'Does the fire need stoking? I'm crap at lighting fires.'

She eyes me suspiciously, but I edge backwards onto the sofa, dropping the phone behind me, hoping, just hoping, that it's lying with the screen facing downwards. I'm trembling, my knees actually shaking as I sit down on the sofa, watching this woman whom I clearly don't know at all. Carrie Denise White. Her first name is Carrie. And she was found barely alive. Dad talked about the 'man' who died, but what if we were wrong? What if it had been a woman in that car. Carrie Denise White.

What the hell am I going to do? I'm stuck in this beautiful prison with no phone, no car, no way out. And the more I think about it, the more obvious it all is. The only person who knew I was walking on that road was Denise – or Carrie, as perhaps she's really known. It was Denise who pretended her car had broken down. It was Denise who put her foot on the accelerator and hurtled towards me. Not once, but twice. And no wonder she looked shocked to see me at the front door just forty-five minutes ago. She must have hoped that I was lying dead or dying in the ditch.

'You all right?' she asks as she puts the bellows and poker back in their stand. 'You've gone all pale.'

'I've got a massive headache,' I say, which isn't far from the truth. 'Would you mind if I go to bed?'

'Not at all,' she says, her voice all saccharine. 'You need to take care of yourself. And try to switch off tonight. I'll double-check that all the windows and doors are locked and bolted, and I'll put the alarm on.'

'The alarm?'

'Don't worry. There are sensors on the windows and doors, so that if they're opened, the alarm goes off.'

'So if I want to get a drink in the night, I won't set it off?'

'No. You're safe walking about the inside of the house, just don't open the windows or doors.'

'And what's the code?' I try to ask casually. What did she tell me earlier? 3669 something? It's probably not correct, anyway.

'No need to worry yourself about the alarm, Leonie. You just have a good night's rest, and if you're not feeling well in the night, don't hesitate to wake me.'

As I walk out of the room, I feel her eyes on my back. The hairs on my neck prickle, and my stomach clenches. I realise how completely alone I am. Utterly vulnerable. I am the only person who can take care of me, and I've absolutely no idea how to do that.

27

LEONIE

Denise wants me dead. There is no doubt in my mind now that she has brought me here with the single aim of killing me. And now I am stuck in a locked house with her, with no way out. What just a few minutes ago felt like safety now feels like a prison. She has made it quite clear that all the doors and windows are alarmed, so if I try to get out, she'll know. What will she do? Get me back in her car, hurl me out of the passenger side and mow me down? It's not like I'm going to get into her car willingly. No, I need to get out of this house, but with the doors and windows alarmed, how?

And what if I stay in the house? Will she kill me whilst I sleep, cut my throat open or hold a pillow down on my face? Or perhaps she'll set fire to the place and watch while I burn inside? My mind is a terrifying whirl. Perhaps there's a land-line in this house; if I could find one, then I can call the police, but do rental properties have landlines? Unlikely, in the knowledge they could be abused by visitors. I stand at the bottom of the stairs, my legs so wobbly, I have to grip the bannister to keep me upright. Perhaps I should get a knife from the kitchen, something to defend myself with. I turn, to head in that direction, but in that instant, Denise appears from the living room, holding the tray of dirty dishes.

'Do you want a glass of water for the night?' she asks.

'Yes. Thanks. I was about to get one for myself.'

'No need. You pop upstairs, and I'll bring you up a glass.'

I open my mouth, try to come up with a reason why I can get one myself, but she's already disappearing into the kitchen. So I do go upstairs, forcing one foot in front of the other. I walk slowly to my bedroom, which is two doors down from Denise's, and then I climb on the bed and pretend to read my Kindle. When I hear her footsteps come up the stairs, followed by a creak on the landing, my stomach clenches, and I swallow, and the saliva gets caught in my throat. I cough. She walks into my room.

'Here you go,' she says, as if she hasn't got a care in the world, as if she's really the friend I thought she was.

'Thanks,' I say as she puts the glass on the bedside table next to me.

'Now you sleep well, and hopefully you'll wake up in the morning feeling like a new person.'

I smile wanly at her. Will I have a tomorrow? I look at the glass of water and wonder if I should chuck it in her face and then make a run for it, or smash it on the floor, leaving me shards of glass, shards that I can use to defend myself with. I pick up the glass, but it's light, and I realise it's made from plastic. My hand is shaking so much, water sloshes over the side. I place it back down again.

'Night then,' she says, and closes my bedroom door behind her.

I have no idea what to do, but one thing is for sure, I

won't be sleeping tonight. I hug a pillow to my chest and try to think straight. *Carrie Denise White.* Who is she? How I wish I had my phone or a laptop so I could look her up. Now I'm thinking about it, I bet I didn't really leave my phone at the hotel. Denise has probably got it hidden away somewhere. Then I think of the next sentence in the newspaper cutting. *She was found barely alive.* Could those boots have belonged to a woman, and was she perhaps not dead at all? Did we leave her there, dreadfully injured? Did Dad get it completely wrong?

The implications are too horrendous. I can't decide if that makes me a worse person for not insisting we call an ambulance, or if it relieves me of some responsibility. Is Denise that woman? As I let that dreadful thought percolate, I realise with a sinking feeling that I've been groomed. Denise has inveigled her way into my company and my life; she's probably been planning her revenge for months, if not years. What a terrible judge of character I am. What a terrible person I am.

But how did she find me? How did she work out that it was me and Dad who left her there? Perhaps I should just confront her, admit my role in the horror of the accident, and then maybe she'll let me go. I swing my legs off the bed, but I can't make myself move any further. If I admit it, then I'm throwing Dad to the wolves, too. We'll likely both go to prison. And how will Denise react if I say anything? She might just stab me there and then in a fit of rage.

I stand up, but I feel woozy, and my stomach cramps. I double over. *Please no, don't let me lose the baby.* I take a sip of water and force myself to breathe deeply. The cramping eases.

I can hear Denise now, footsteps coming up the stairs,

the creak on the landing. Is she coming for me? I hold my breath, frantically looking around for something to defend myself with. There's a lamp. But then the footsteps fade, and I hear the gentle clicking of a door closing. There's the faint gurgling of taps. Perhaps she's just going to bed? Perhaps she's not a killer after all?

I tiptoe to my en-suite bathroom and quickly brush my teeth, but I don't change into my nightwear. I can't risk staying here. I need to get out of this house, away from Denise. It's hard to think straight. Is she really getting ready for bed, or is she perhaps planning on having a few hours' sleep, but then waking early and doing something terrible to me before day breaks? I'm going to have to wait until she's asleep, and then somehow get out of this house.

I pad back to my bed and sit on top of it, my now dried-out parka covering my legs. Picking up my Kindle, I suddenly realise that it gives me access to the internet. My heart begins to pound as I click on the World Wide Web icon. But it just goes around and around and around before eventually saying *no internet connection.* Denise must have switched off the Wi-Fi, because I had connection on my phone last night.

The gurgling in the taps stops, and I hear a creak. But then there is silence. Where is she? I walk to my bedroom window and open the curtains, then switch off the bedroom light. It takes me a moment to adjust my eyes to the low light, but I can see the moon now, clouds passing quickly in front of it. The rain must have stopped. And then there's the glow of light from a room further along the house. Denise's bedroom. I stand there, staring out to the dark woods, waiting. Time slows, but eventually the light goes out, and the whole house and garden are plunged into darkness. Has Denise gone to sleep?

I pull my curtains again and stumble back to the bed, finding the bedside lamp, which I switch on. It's now 11.05 pm. I will wait until midnight, and then I will try to get out.

With bated breath, I ease open my bedroom door. The hinges squeak slightly, and I tense every painful muscle in my body as I stand still in my doorway. Silence. I'm wearing my jeans, two thick sweaters and my parka and have stuffed my wallet into the inside pocket. The rest of my belongings can stay here. I tiptoe as softly as I possibly can, easing myself along the corridor until I'm outside Denise's bedroom door. No light seeps from underneath it, and I just pray that she's asleep. I carry on walking, but it's dark here, and I have to feel along the wall. Low, insipid light pours in through a roof window in the hallway, lighting up the staircase. *Creak.* My heart races as I stand stock-still. There's no movement from inside the house, and for a moment I wonder if I should go into Denise's bedroom and try to find my phone, or even hers. But I discount that idea. It's much too risky.

I tiptoe down the stairs, and when I reach the bottom, I let out a quiet sigh. There are patio doors in the living room, and even though Denise said everywhere is alarmed, if I can open them, I'll have a good head start on her. Perhaps I can run to the neighbours, the people in the Wilds, our old house; how ironic that would be.

I try the patio doors. They're locked, and there is no key anywhere to be seen. The windows are also locked. How the hell am I going to get out? I try the front door and the back door, but everything is locked, no keys in sight. In the kitchen, I think about finding a knife, but could I really use it? Probably not, but I take a medium-sized knife from a drawer and shove it in my pocket anyway.

And then I remember the downstairs toilet. I'm sure there was a small window in there, above the toilet. Is that locked, too? I open the door, switch the light on and lock the door behind me. At least I'll be safe in here. Denise isn't a big person. I'm sure she'd struggle to knock down the door.

The window is square, small and quite high up above the WC. I put the lid down and clamber up onto it, gripping the window ledge. When I've got my balance, I try the handle to the window. It moves. But then I stop. Is it also alarmed? Will an alarm wail if I push it fully open and try to hurl myself out? I've got no choice, though; I have to get out of here. I tense myself and push down on the handle. The small window opens. I brace myself for the howl of an alarm, but there's silence. Perhaps this window isn't alarmed, or was Denise lying to me? I doubt it, because there definitely is an alarm to the property. She switched it off when we first arrived. I try to haul myself up onto the window ledge, but my left foot slips on the smooth plastic toilet lid, and I lose my grip, tumbling off the toilet, slipping down onto the ceramic tiled floor, catching my hip on the side of the seat. I let out an *ouch,* and then as I look down at myself, I realise that the blade of the knife has cut straight through the fabric of my pocket. I'm such an idiot. I could have stabbed myself.

Trying not to whimper with frustration, I haul myself to my feet and climb back up onto the toilet lid. My legs feel so feeble, my head light. This time, I throw the knife out of the window, hoping that the metal will glint in the moonlight, and I'll be able to find it outside. I have to ignore the burning in my arms, the yet-to-be healed wounds from this afternoon tugging and splitting. I've got to get out.

I edge my backside up onto the ledge, but the space is small, and for one horrible moment, I think my hips might be stuck. I wriggle, ignoring the burning from my earlier cuts and bruises, and then I'm tumbling. It happens so quickly. One second, I'm still on the window ledge, the next I'm on the ground, pain searing through my legs and hips. The moon swims in and out of view. I try to move, but it's like I'm caught in a nightmare where I'm frozen immobile. I force down a wave of nausea, and the blackness comes again.

Wake up; you need to wake up. The terror grabs my heart and my lungs. I squeeze my eyes and open them again. This time, I can see. No, it's more than seeing. There's a blinding light, and there is Denise's face right above mine. It shimmers and morphs in and out of focus like some terrifying hologram. I must move my arms. I must try to move. But I can't. It's as if an invisible force is holding me down. I try to speak.

'*Why?*' But I'm not sure the word is actually comprehensible.

Denise is staring at me. 'Glad to see the drugs are beginning to work,' she says.

'Help!' My mouth moves, but I don't know if any sound comes out.

'I don't think so.' She smiles, but it's cold and sinister, the features so different to those of the warm friend I thought I had. Is this really Denise?

'I'm going to make you suffer in the way you made me suffer.' Her voice is low and emotionless. 'You'll lose your baby. I'll break your legs, leave you in crippling pain, and then I'll return and kill you, slowly. Yours will be a slow, painful death.'

As the words hit me like bullets, Markus' face appears in my mind, his voice in my ears.

'At least I'll be with Markus,' I murmur. Did I say that out loud?

There's a cackle, and Denise grins at me, her face contorted like a gargoyle. Why did I ever think she was pretty?

'Markus wasn't who you thought he was.' She laughs. 'He was using you; we both were.'

'No. No, that's not true.'

'Sorry, Leonie. Actually, I'm not sorry, really. It's true. I've known Markus for years.'

My thoughts are muddling, her face morphing in and out of my vision. That can't be right. Why is she saying that about Markus? And why can't I move?

'Don't believe me?' There's a bitter edge to her voice. Suddenly a lit-up phone is shoved into my field of vision. A photo of several people sitting in a circle, the focus on two people in the middle of the photo. Denise and Markus. Markus with his arm around Denise, laughing, pulling a silly face, looking relaxed, his hair longer than I remember it. It doesn't make sense. Nothing makes sense.

A heaviness is pushing me downwards, and it feels as if my body is going to disintegrate into the wet earth. I need to hang on to reality, but I can't. I just can't. I try to keep my eyes open, but everything is a blur now, and my lids feel so incredibly heavy.

I'm sorry, I think. *I'm sorry, baby in my womb. I've failed to protect you.* I let my eyes close, my lids bringing blackness. I am going to die. My baby is going to die. And there is nothing I can do to stop it.

28

LEONIE

I wake up gasping, unable to breathe. Where the hell am I? Panic grips my neck, and my head is throbbing. My eyelids feel as if they're stuck to my eyeballs, so I scrunch my eyes and force myself to blink several times. They feel scratchy and sore, but they're definitely open now. Yet it's still pitch black. I'm lying down, so I feel around with my hands and sense I'm on some sort of fabric. Ignoring the pain in my arms, I press downwards with my palms to get myself into a sitting position, but I bash my head, painfully, and collapse back down. What the hell? It's noisy in here, and I'm being tossed backwards and forwards, from side to side. Then, as if in slow motion, my brain kicks into gear. I'm in the boot of a car. It takes several more long moments for me to remember what happened. But how long ago? Just now, hours or days ago?

Denise's car. I must be in Denise's car. The memories come flooding back; how I found that article on her phone; how someone tried to ram me with their car, twice. Denise. How I was locked in the house, until I wasn't. And then how

I couldn't move, my limbs incapable, my head like cotton-wool. And the story about Markus, how Denise knew him from before. Surely not?

Panic grips me. I need to get out, because now I know that I wasn't mistaken. Denise wants to hurt me, to leave me in that ditch to suffer a painful and horrific death. Twisted retribution, somehow, for how I left the scene of her accident. Yet I still don't know how she's worked out it was me. What I know for sure, though, is if I don't get out of this car now, I'm going to die.

The more I think about that, the harder it is to breathe. I'm gulping in stale air that stinks of petrol, and it's as if it can't reach my lungs properly. *Calm down!* I tell myself. I've got to stay focused, not just for me but the baby I'm carrying. *Calm down.* It's hard to move, but I feel around the boot area, trying to dislodge anything that isn't smooth, because surely it's possible to get to the rear lights of the car from the inside? But my fingers can't make out any catches, and it's pitch black in here. If only this were an older car, perhaps I would see a trickle of light, perhaps I could ease away some plastic casing. By contorting my sore limbs, I manage to turn my body so my feet are against the lid of the boot, hopefully near the catch. I push hard, but my body is still heavy, as if the synapses from my brain to my legs aren't firing properly.

At some point, this car is going to stop. Denise is going to come and get me, haul me out of the boot. Should I pretend to be comatose and limp, or should I try to attack her? I fumble around for anything that I can use as a weapon, but find nothing. She's not so stupid to leave anything in the car with me. I lie there for what seems like long minutes but probably isn't, my bones aching as the car swings around corners, juddering over rough land. And then we're slowing down.

The car comes to a halt. I hear a door slam. Then a click. Sheer terror courses through my veins. How is she going to get me out of the boot? She's slim, and I must be a dead weight. Or has she got an accomplice, perhaps? My thoughts freeze.

The boot lifts up, and the murky light of dawn reveals Denise's face, which is distorted into an expression of disgust. And in that instant, I realise I can't feign unconsciousness. My eyes are open, locked onto hers, and instinct kicks in.

I don't know how, but I hurl myself out of the car, rolling onto a grassy verge, pulling myself up to standing as Denise comes for me, arms flailing, screaming indecipherable words. Her sharp fingernails gouge at my cheeks, pulling my hair so it comes away in big chunks.

'I've lost everything because of you!' she shrieks.

The word *catfight* comes into my head, but this is more than that. She wants to kill me, and despite her slender frame, she's displaying an iron strength. Denise punches me in the jaw, and I stagger out onto the road, the tarmac slippery from the night's rain. I kick at her as she comes for me again.

'I'm going to kill you!' she shouts as she wobbles on one leg. And then, out of the corner of my eye, I see she's holding something. A rock? No, it's a piece of wood. She's holding it out in front of her like a sword, coming towards me as if she's going to stab me with a sabre.

And then I hear it. Coming from behind Denise, what starts as a low rumble making the road vibrate, getting louder and louder. But it's as if she doesn't notice.

'Get out of the way!' I scream as the blinding lights of a huge truck round the corner.

She laughs then, a manic, hyaena-like laugh, and in that split second, I see what she's trying to do. To hit me with that piece of wood; to push me into the path of the oncoming truck. As she brings the log down, I dart to one side, and my foot kicks out, catching Denise's left shin, and as she falls, I push her in the small of her back as hard as I can. A vicious wind sweeps straight by my face, propelling me backwards; a monster blinds my vision.

There's a terrible scream. Partly human, partly the screeching brakes of a gigantic timber lorry that has way too much momentum to come to a sudden halt. Denise has disappeared. Another scream that goes on and on, and it's only when I find myself on my knees at the side of the road, unable to breathe, that I realise the scream is coming from me. There's a gigantic hiss. Silence. Complete silence. There are no birds singing, no gentle rustle of leaves or tree branches, no airplanes overhead or the distant sounds of car traffic. Just silence.

And then footsteps. A burly man appears in front of me, big black boots that remind me of her boots from so long ago.

'What the fuck happened?' his deep voice croaks. 'You all right?'

He extends a hand, his arm covered in tattoos, black short-sleeved T-shirt straining around his large belly. I take his strong hand, and he pulls me up to standing, but my legs are too weak, and I fall into him, noting his face is paper-white in the low morning light. Despite the size of him, he's also trembling.

'I've never killed anyone before,' he murmurs. 'Haven't even had an accident.'

The full horror of it, the knowledge that Denise is dead and not me, hits every cell in my body. Once again, I pass out.

29

LEONIE

When I come to, I'm sitting on the side of the road, a scratchy blanket that smells of cigarette smoke wrapped around me. A solid arm is around my shoulders, and for one glorious moment, I think it's Markus. But then I hear the sirens and the gruff voice of a stranger, who simply says, 'Don't look.'

It's too late. I can see her feet sticking out from under the lorry, so small between the gigantic wheels of the truck, crimson blood smeared across the grey tarmac road. I yelp. The stranger puts a rough, nicotine-scented hand over my eyes, turning my head so that I bury it into his solid chest.

'Don't look,' he says again.

I've killed Denise. I have actually killed her. I thought I killed her ten years ago, but now I really have. I am shaking violently, a cold within me so bitter, it feels as if my body is made of ice. The sirens are deafening now, and then there are blue lights strobing across the trunks of the trees either side of this road, lights flickering against the metal base of the logging truck. People in black uniforms appear from every direction. The trucker, the stranger who was giving me warmth, stands up and leaves me a quivering mess in the very place where I was meant to die.

'I don't know what the hell they were doing,' he says. 'But they were in the road. I guess their car broke down, but the woman, she was right there, and I couldn't stop in time. God help me, I tried, but I couldn't.'

'It's all right, sir,' the police officer says, steering the truck driver away from me. Although, of course, it isn't all right. Not at all. Two paramedics crouch down next to me.

'What's your name?' the female paramedic asks. She has chestnut hair and pretty green eyes. Why am I even noticing that?

'Leonie,' I say. 'Leonie Wilding. No. Leonie Klausen.'

'Hello, Leonie. I'm Caitlyn. Are you hurt?'

I shake my head, because I'm not hurt from the run-in with the truck, but then I remember I *am* hurt. Denise tried to ram me off the road yesterday, and I'm covered with cuts and bruises.

'You look like you might have some injuries, Leonie. We'd like to check you over in the ambulance. Are you able to stand up?'

I nod, and the kind paramedic helps me to standing, then supports me as she guides me to the ambulance.

'She tried to kill me,' I murmur. I see the paramedic's frown, the realisation that this horror scene might not be a simple tragedy, and there's a coded look that passes between her and her colleague. Her colleague leaves us and strides towards a uniformed police officer, their heads together, voices low.

The light inside the ambulance is too bright, and it hurts my sore eyes. I lie on the hard bed, and with gentle hands, she checks me all over. I wince at the numerous bruises and cuts all over my body.

'I'm pregnant,' I say, my hands covering my belly protectively. 'Is my baby all right?' My voice wobbles.

'We'll get you an ultrasound scan to be sure,' she says, 'but from the looks of things, your wounds are superficial.'

I remember then how leaden my limbs felt, how when I fell from the bathroom window, I couldn't move. Had Denise drugged me, put something in my supper or in the glass of water she brought to my bedroom?

'I might have been drugged,' I say. My voice sounds strangely monotone.

'I'll have a word with the police officers, and we'll likely take some blood.' If this is an unusual conversation for her, she doesn't let on.

A FEW MINUTES LATER, I'm still sitting in the ambulance, a silver sheet around my shoulders, and it's all so very déjà vu. It was only a few weeks ago that I was sitting in an ambulance just like this for the first time, after I discovered Markus' body. And yet here I am all over again. Just a different body, a different location, a different ambulance service. Another interview.

'Leonie?' the police officer asks, his singsong Geordie accent strong. 'Can we ask you some questions about what happened here this morning?'

I nod.

'I'll leave you to it,' the paramedic says, jumping down from the ambulance. Yes, this really is a copycat of what happened before, except it isn't. When Markus died, it was such a terrible shock, and I still don't know what happened, or why. This situation is completely different. I know all the whys.

'Is she dead?' My voice is a whisper.

'Yes, I'm afraid so. Do you know the name of the deceased?'

'I knew her as Denise White, but I think her full name is Carrie Denise White. She was trying to kill me.'

The police officer's clear blue eyes widen slightly. 'Okay, Leonie. I'm going to take a few notes here. My name is Detective Alisdair Holden. Please tell me exactly what happened.'

And so I do. I tell him how Denise got a job working for me, and that despite everything, she was excellent at her job. How my new husband was found murdered at our home in central London just a few weeks ago. How Denise invited me up to Northumberland to stay in a gorgeous holiday house, and how someone tried to kill me by driving their car into me twice. I tell him how I discovered Denise's real name was Carrie and that she was seeking revenge, that her sole aim was to kill my baby, fatally injure me and leave me at the side of the road. How she drugged me and then got me in the boot of her car, and how against all odds, it was Denise who fell under the tyres of the logging truck, not me.

I start sobbing.

'It's all my fault,' I say. 'It's all my fault because I nearly killed her a decade ago. I was sixteen, a selfish idiot, and I stole my mum's car. There was another car coming towards me, and I swerved, but that other car crashed. And then my dad was there, and we looked at the wreckage, and he said the person was dead, that there was nothing that we could do. So he took me home and told me to forget about the accident, because if we told the police, my life would be over before it had begun. I spent the last decade riddled with guilt, believing I had killed someone. But it seems that Denise didn't die, and instead she's been plotting how to make me pay. She had a file about me on her phone. She wanted me to suffer as she did. It should have been me who died under that lorry, not Denise.' I dissolve into sobs then, because it's such a strange relief to tell the truth after so very long.

I lose track of the hustle and bustle, the questions, the way my life is now in the hands of others. I wonder if the policeman will believe me, whether I'll be arrested, shackled and taken away to some women's prison, where I'll give birth to this child in isolation. This is my penance. All I've done is delayed the inevitable by a decade.

Except it doesn't happen like that.

Detective Alisdair Holden tells me that the paramedics will be taking me to hospital for a checkup, and once I'm released, I'll be able to go home. That they will want to stay in touch with me and that they will interview me again, officially, but that might be done by the Met police, as I live in London. There will be a full investigation, and it will take some time.

At the hospital I'm treated well, taken for a scan where, for the first time, I see the tiny beating heart of my baby. How I wish Markus were here with me, but then I remember Denise's words, and I recall that photo of her and Markus. Did they genuinely know each other from before? Was Markus really after me for my money; was he using me? And was he really doing business in Turkmenistan? I question everything now. I recall how he paid for everything before our marriage, but afterwards we only spent my money. I remember how on our honeymoon his credit card didn't work. Was he playing me? What a terrible judge of character I am, so naive and gullible.

'You're good to go home now,' a nurse tells me. 'Is there someone who can collect you?'

And I don't answer for a while, because who have I got now? Zac, my best friend Zac, who Denise clearly set up to make me question his honesty. Or my parents. No, it has to be Zac.

I nod eventually, but I have no mobile phone. Denise took it. So the nurse takes me to a payphone, and I fumble in my pocket to remove my wallet, and I pay for the call with a debit card. But it's a Sunday, and there won't be anyone in the office. I don't know Zac's number from memory. But then I remember I have his business card, and right there is his mobile number. When I hear his familiar voice, my throat chokes up.

'Zac,' I say, 'I know it's a long way to come, but could you come and get me?'

'What's happened, Leonie?' he asks.

'There's been an accident. No, not an accident. It's been terrible, Zac. Can you come?'

'Of course I can. Where are you?'

'I'm in the accident and emergency department of the Royal Victoria Infirmary, the main hospital in Newcastle upon Tyne.'

'Are you all right?'

'Yes, sort of. I want to go home,' I whisper.

There's a pause. 'It's going to take me at least four hours to get to you, maybe more. Are you happy to wait?'

'I'll wait for as long as it takes. Thank you, Zac.'

I sit all alone in a waiting room for long minutes, my thoughts muddled as I try to piece everything together. And then I can't sit anymore. I ask someone where the nearest shops are, whether there's a mobile phone shop anywhere nearby, and I'm directed towards the centre of town. People stare at me, no doubt because I look a fright, my hair all messy, scratches on my face. I walk for fifteen minutes until I stumble across a shopping centre, bustling on this Sunday late afternoon, and I find a phone shop and buy a pay-as-you-go phone, because I need to be connected to the world. I stop for a coffee and drink the liquid when it's still too hot, it burns my mouth, and then I feel guilty, because should I be drinking coffee when I'm pregnant? I don't know whether to laugh or cry, because I shouldn't be alive right now. I should be dead, like Denise. And with tears pouring down my cheeks, I stumble back towards the hospital, a mishmash of confusing emotions.

Zac is good to his word. He arrives just under five hours after I placed the call to him. I throw myself into his arms, so grateful for the familiarity of him, so sorry for doubting my best friend. He squeezes me tightly, and then, with an arm around me, he says, 'You look terrible, Leonie.'

'Thanks. I feel it.'

'What's happened?'

And so, I tell him everything, about Denise and Markus and the sheer horror of it all, and the whole time he holds my hand and looks at me with an expression of dismay.

'I'm so sorry this has happened to you,' he says eventually. 'So sorry. Look, it's too much for me to turn around and drive us back to London tonight. Can we stay at that holiday house you rented?'

I look at him in dismay, because no, I will never go back there again.

'Let's stay at a Premier Inn,' I suggest. We find a cheap

hotel in the centre of town, and Zac is still holding my hand as we walk up to the reception desk.

'Two single rooms for tonight,' Zac says.

'I don't want to be alone,' I murmur.

Zac hesitates, but surely he must know that I just need a friend, nothing more? 'A room with twin beds?' he asks the receptionist questioningly.

'Thank you,' I say quietly.

Much later, when I've bought a change of clothes and some basic toiletries – because I have no intention of ever returning to Sesame to collect my belongings – we're lying on our respective beds, watching television. I've told Zac everything, including about the original accident, and he stared at me speechless. I apologise for not trusting him, for being taken in by Denise's ruse. And then I Google *Carrie Denise White* using my new phone, and I find just one article about her from a decade ago, which gives me no further information.

30

LEONIE

A few days on, I feel broken. I haven't been able to go to work, so Zac is holding the fort. I've done the one thing I didn't want to: move back into Mum and Dad's house. I was interviewed again, twice. Once by DC Matthew Ryan and DS Lloyd Chandry, and another time by Detective Alisdair Holden, who came down from Newcastle to interview me in London. I talked them through that fateful night a decade ago, how I took Mum's car, how Dad chased me, how I didn't hit the other car, but it went off the road. They have made it quite clear: I will be prosecuted, but for what, they haven't yet decided. And in a way, I want to be prosecuted. If I hadn't taken Mum's car all those years ago, Denise's life wouldn't have been ruined. I am responsible.

That first evening, when my parents discovered what had happened, Dad came storming into my bedroom, closing the door behind him.

'What the hell did you do?' He stood there with his arms crossed and fury etched across his jowly face.

'I told the police the truth. I told them about the accident.'

'You do realise that in your selfishness, you have most likely ruined my life. Did that even cross your pathetic little brain? After everything I've given you, you've just thrown your own father to the wolves.'

I stood up then and walked right over to him, standing in his personal space, so close, I could smell his beer breath.

'We should have told the truth in the first place. You were the adult. *You* should have told the truth.'

We stared at each other, but I am a different person now, and Dad held no fear for me. I knew he wouldn't raise a hand, that he's all bluster, like a typical bully. And my prediction was right. He turned on his heel, walked out of the room and slammed the door behind him. We haven't spoken a word since. But what makes me sad is Mum hasn't intervened. She hasn't asked why we're not talking to each other, what has really gone on. She seems to be out all the time. And I can't work out if it's because she knows the truth, or she's scared of knowing the truth.

My phone rings, and it's DC Matthew Ryan. 'I thought you'd like to know the latest development. We have matched Carrie Denise White's DNA to the crime scene at your house. We believe that she killed your husband, Markus Klausen.'

I gasp. 'But why?'

'We have found text messages between the two of them. This won't be easy to hear, Leonie; however, they hatched a plan well over a year ago. Markus was promised ten thousand pounds by Denise if he stood you up at the altar.'

'But he didn't!'

'Exactly. Based upon the messages between the two of

them, we think Markus went rogue, so to speak. He was no longer following Denise's instructions. We'll never know exactly why she killed him, but we think it was to make you suffer.' He pauses. 'I'm very sorry.'

'And the deals in Turkmenistan?'

'There was no business in Turkmenistan. Your husband had no money, just mounting debts.'

'But he sold his house on the south coast for a lot of money.' I think about Sandcastle House, where we first met.

DC Ryan clears his throat. 'We have studied Markus' bank statements going back several years, and we have found no indication that he bought or sold a house.'

I'm silent. Was anything Markus told me the truth? Or was Denise right, and he was with me solely for my money? He was so kind and loving towards me. Could he have kept up that charade for all of those months? Now I will never know whether Markus had any genuine affection for me, or whether our whole relationship was a mirage. Despite everything DC Ryan has told me, I have to believe that there was some genuine love between us. I think of Sandcastle House and his fancy Tesla car and realise he probably borrowed both. It would be easy to do that. Yet I honestly think I would have fallen for him if he'd told me he was penniless. So many lies, all for nothing.

Later that day, I put all the jewellery that Markus gave me into a bag, and I go to our local jeweller's shop. I lay the pieces out on the counter, and I ask whether I can have a valuation. The lady tells me that it'll take a few days and that they charge for the service. 'Fine,' I say.

The next morning I'm awakened by the sound of banging. It takes a moment to understand what the noise is. I jump out of bed.

'Police, open up!'

They've come to arrest me, and in a way, it's such a relief. Denise has paid with her life, and now it's time for me to pay, too. I tug on a pair of jeans and an old jumper, stuffing my feet into trainers, and take a last look around this room. I'm ready for this.

I walk down the stairs and come to a sudden halt halfway down.

'Angus Peter Wilding, we are arresting you on suspicion of perverting the course of justice, causing serious injury by dangerous driving and assisting an offender. You do not have to say anything. But it may harm your defence if you do not mention when questioned something which you later rely on in court. Anything you do say may be given in evidence.'

Dad roars, 'It's her bloody fault!'

I flinch.

They handcuff Dad and walk him out of the house. I stand there on the stairs, waiting for them to come back to arrest me, but the front door stays ajar, and I hear car engines start up and the crunching of tyres as vehicles drive away. Then complete silence settles over the house.

Where is Mum?

And then I remember. She isn't here. She was staying with a friend in London last night, sorting out some paperwork in the office, purchase orders and payroll that I need to sign, admin that Denise used to do so efficiently. I sink to my haunches. Thank goodness Mum wasn't here to witness that spectacle. But now I'm going to have to tell her everything, not least that her husband has been arrested.

For the first time since Denise died, I am back in the office, dressed in a smart suit, in my armour. This place is my responsibility and no one else's. Zac and Erin are in the office, both hunched over their desks. Someone has cleared Denise's desk; Zac probably. Mum is in the private meeting room, which is a relief, because it enables me to break the news to her in private.

'Dad was arrested this morning,' I say. 'And it's my fault.'

She slowly lays her pen on the table and holds my eyes. 'No, it isn't. You were a child. You shouldn't have stolen my car, but you were still a child. It was your father's responsibility to ensure justice was done, and he shirked that responsibility.'

I stare at Mum, open-mouthed.

'Have you always known?'

She shakes her head. 'No. He told me the truth after Denise died. I can't believe he made you lie all those years. I'm sorry for the damage it has done to you, love. David O'Byrne rang me earlier. He'll be supporting your father.'

'And you, what about you?' I ask.

'I think you and I have some businesses to run, don't we?'

Dad is bailed, allowed to go home, but with stringent conditions. He has to report to the local police station three times a week, his passport is taken, and he is forbidden from having any contact with me. The shame of it. I can't begin to imagine how he's coping. I suppose he's spending a fortune on the very best lawyers, employing KCs and planning his defence. Contrary to what Mum thought, Dad isn't using David O'Byrne. I speak to David, who tells me that Dad will likely get a custodial sentence, probably three years. I can't imagine Dad in prison.

Then DC Matthew Ryan requests that I attend a meeting at the police station. I ask David to accompany me. DC Ryan tells me with a look of sadness that I will be prosecuted, too. That despite all the mitigating circumstances, they have no choice. I am being charged for driving without a licence or insurance, for causing serious injury by careless driving and failing to stop and report an accident. But, he repeats, there were a lot of mitigating circumstances, not least that I was a child, that my father was chasing me, and that the driver in the other car had been drinking. Evidently Denise's – or rather Carrie's boyfriend of the time came forward with some details about the night of the accident.

Because of all that, there are no bail conditions. I am free until my trial.

'Will I also go to prison?' I ask the two men.

DC Ryan shakes his head. 'I very much doubt it. You'll probably receive a sentence of one year in custody, suspended for two years, and you'll lose your driving licence for twelve months.' Then he stands up and shakes my hand. David O'Byrne confirms what DC Ryan said. I feel like I've been given a get-out-of-jail-for-free card.

A COUPLE OF WEEKS PASS, and work is my solace, not that I achieve much. To my surprise, Mum comes into work every day, and she's decamped from her front desk to the office. When I ask her what she's doing, she tells me she's taking over the paperwork and bookkeeping that Denise used to do.

Zac is the one who supports me the most. He brings me lunch and checks that I've registered with a midwife. And then he interviews and appoints another office manager, a forty-year-old man called James, who wears thick-rimmed glasses and is pedantic in the extreme. We don't go out for drinks after work anymore, which is fine by me, because I'm shattered by the time I get home. For the first time in a decade, I sleep well: long, dreamless sleeps. But I know that will change soon, as my belly expands and my baby starts kicking.

Mum seems different somehow. I ask her whether she's going to stand by Dad. She throws me a strange glance and says, 'I'm formulating my plans.' I haven't got a clue what that means, and when I push her for more information, she manages to bat me away. I wish I had a warmer mother, someone with whom I can share my hopes and fears, but I don't. And I wonder if any gentleness in her personality has been leeched out by Dad over the long years of their marriage, because my childhood memories are happy ones: Mum chasing Sam and me around the garden, making a mess in the kitchen.

One evening, I'm the last person in the office, and I'm feeling so lonely, I decide to go round to Mum's London house. Dad is living in their Horsham house, but as far as I know, Mum is staying in London during the week and returning to Sussex at the weekends.

I've been thinking about my wedding and the dress that was sold to someone else and the floristry brief that was changed. Now I know all about Denise, I suspect it was her, but I need to look Mum in the eye to be one hundred percent sure.

As I drive at a snail's pace along their Marylebone street, looking for an elusive parking space, Mum's door opens, and she steps out. She's wearing a sequinned dress and has a stole around her shoulders. She's obviously going out somewhere, but with whom? Not with Dad, due to his curfew. With a girlfriend perhaps, to the theatre? But she didn't mention anything to me. She hops into a waiting taxi. For a moment I consider following her, like I did that time with

Markus, but then I decide Mum is entitled to her own life. I turn the car around and head back home.

I have also realised that the only authentic person in my life is Zac, and it probably has always been that way. He is my true friend, the only human being who knows everything about me, and from time to time, I think of that one occasion when we slept together. It makes me wonder, were Zac and I meant to have been together all along? Have I been ignoring what is right in front of my eyes? I let myself dream. Would Zac accept me with another man's child? Will he mind that I will have a criminal record? And is it too soon to jump into another relationship?

Today, I watch his face light up when I walk into the office. Mid-morning, he makes me an herbal tea without asking, and at lunchtime brings me a salad from Pret.

'Are you doing anything tonight?' I ask, trying to keep my voice casual.

'Ah, sorry,' he says, barely looking up from his laptop. 'I'm meeting a couple of mates for drinks after work.'

'Never mind,' I say. 'Another time.'

'Another time,' he repeats.

As normal, I go home, make myself a microwaved meal for one and lie on the sofa to watch television. Except I can't stop thinking about Zac and all those little kindnesses. We need to talk. I know it might make things awkward in the office, but I need to tell him what I really feel. A promise I have made myself: no more secrets.

The next morning it's a Saturday, and I hope that he'll be home and won't mind being disturbed before 9 am. I climb into my car and drive across London to Zac's flat. As I stand outside about to press a finger on his bell, I wonder if I'm doing the right thing. But then a woman comes out, talking on her phone, and I catch the main entrance door and walk inside. I take the stairs to the second floor, and before I can second-guess myself, I knock loudly on Zac's door.

I hear footsteps, and my heart starts beating faster. There's the sound of the chain being undone, and the door opens. And standing there in a silk floral dressing gown, with her bare ankles and feet underneath and too much of her cleavage on display, is Mum.

We stare at each other for a long moment, until eventually, I speak. 'What are you doing here?'

31

LEONIE

'What are you doing here?' I repeat the question.

'Come in, come in!' Mum stands to one side and ushers me through the narrow hallway.

My brain can't keep up. Mum is in Zac's apartment, dressed only in a silk dressing gown, a dressing gown that I haven't seen before, but clearly doesn't belong to Zac, because it's covered in a pink floral pattern. And it's 8.53 am.

'Zac!' she says as we emerge into the living room. 'Leonie's here. Perfect timing, isn't it?' Mum grins, and I'm totally confused. 'Have a seat, love,' she says, indicating the sofa. Zac shuffles into the room, wearing pyjama bottoms and a baggy T-shirt. He's holding a mug of steaming tea. Mum walks over to Zac and, to my astonishment, stands on tiptoes and places a kiss on his cheek. He slips an arm around her neck.

'We've been wanting to talk to you, Leonie. I'm sorry, love, that we've kept this a secret from you, but Gus would have killed me if he'd found out.'

I stare at both of them. Zac can't quite meet my eyes, but Mum... well, Mum seems completely relaxed, more relaxed than I've ever seen her.

'You and Zac?' I ask in a high-pitched voice.

'We've been together for a while,' Zac explains eventually. 'I'm so sorry, Leonie, but with all the terrible things that have happened in your life, we didn't want to add to your stress. I hope you understand.'

I don't understand. I know Dad is a jerk, but I never thought Mum would be the one having an affair. And with a man young enough to be her son. And not just any man, but my best friend. I can't process this.

'How long?' I ask eventually.

'A year,' Mum says, placing a kiss on the side of Zac's face.

'You've been having an affair for a whole year!' I can't stop the incredulity in my voice. *How did I not realise this?* 'And Dad?'

'I've told your father I'm leaving him. We're getting divorced. And we all know that your father will be going to prison.'

'But the age difference?' I exclaim, unable to process this.

'I realise it must be a shock,' Zac says. 'I've felt that you and your mum have been family for a very long time. And as trite as the saying is, age really is just a number. When you love someone, you just know. A bit like how you knew with Markus.'

Except I got that one wrong, didn't I? Just like I got Zac wrong, and Denise. But now, I think back over the past year, and I can see how I might have missed the signs. I was so swept up with my own grand love affair, I had no time for anyone else. And there I was thinking Zac was being so loving towards me, yet he was just being a good friend. I remember my hen party, when Zac appeared by Mum's side when the games got too embarrassing. Was he there to support me or her? And how Mum was so indignant when Denise accused Zac of stealing from the company.

Mum gets up now and ties the dressing gown a bit tighter around her midriff. 'What would you like to drink, love? A tea or orange juice? We have got orange juice, haven't we?' She addresses Zac.

'I don't want anything,' I say. My stomach feels queasy.

'In which case, take a seat next to me on the sofa.' Mum slips over to the sofa and pats the seat. I don't move. 'Zac and I have been discussing the business. Obviously, the future looks quite different now. With your father facing trial and no doubt becoming a felon, he's not going to be able to direct the business anymore. We've got two options. We sell up, or we move forwards, and after lots of discussion, Zac and I have decided we want to move forwards. Zac will take the helm, step into your father's shoes, so I can concentrate on acquisitions, and as you'll be taking a back seat, we might sell off Castaway.'

I can't concentrate on a word she's saying. I shake my head. 'Wait, wait,' I say, flapping my hands.

'Well, with a baby on the way, you're not going to want to work. I mean, look at me. I took fifteen years off to bring up you and Sam, and only then slipped back into the business. But of course, I started a lot younger than you. But we were thinking the sensible thing would be for you to transfer your shares to Zac, and Wilding Properties can pay you a nice big monthly retainer so you can be a stay-at-home mum and not have to worry about a thing except your baby.'

I have never truly understood the expression 'see red'

before, but now I do. Streaks of crimson and black streak across my vision, and the room feels totally claustrophobic, Mum's cloying perfume mingling with Zac's aftershave and the faint scent of burned toast.

I cannot do this. I cannot stay here a single second longer.

I get to my feet and throw one final look at Mum. How could she do this to me? How could she and Zac betray me like this? And then in a flash of perception, I realise I have allowed them to. They haven't betrayed me, really; I have just stood back and been my parents' puppet all these years. When Mum or Dad said *run*, run I did. For so long, I've felt I owed them, yet I don't. I owe them nothing. And right now, it's stopping. I grab my bag, take my coat off the back of a kitchen chair and stride to the front door.

'Leonie!' Mum says.

I don't look back. I open the door and run quickly down the two flights of stairs and outside to my car. As I'm driving back across London, like an automaton, I think of my brother and how clever Sam was to get out all of those years ago. How much more perceptive he was than me.

But it's not too late for me. To hell with Mum and Dad and Zac and all the people who took me for granted or used me for their own purposes. To hell with them all. I don't even feel sad, just weary. Yes, I loved Castaway Property Search, but it was undeniably stressful working there, and I was using it like an emotional crutch. If Mum and Zac want it, or if they want to sell it, good luck to them. Perhaps I'll set up my own search agency somewhere in the countryside, where I can live a more relaxed life with my baby. I certainly don't intend to be bossed around by Mum or Zac, or Dad, when he's out of prison.

The phone rings. I glance at the clock in my car. It's just turned 9 am. It's the jeweller who was valuing my jewellery.

'I'm very sorry, Mrs Klausen, but all of the pieces you brought in were fakes. The stones weren't even semi-precious; they're glass. Under the circumstances, we'll be waiving any valuation fee.'

And then I start laughing, a hysterical laugh that becomes so all-consuming I simply can't stop. A chap in a white van parked next to me at the traffic lights throws me the strangest look, and that sets me off even more. I've been a complete idiot.

But no more.

Most people's lives consist of the before and after, a line drawn by some major life event: a marriage or a death, the shock of finding out your mum is sleeping with your best friend or that your father is going to prison. The knowledge that I am being prosecuted, too. But I know what my before and after will be. The line is the realisation that I have been a pawn in everyone else's life. The after will be me standing on my own two feet, doing what I want to do rather than what I think I should be doing. It might not be a solid line, and it might waver, but my life is mine. And right now, I want to get the hell out of here.

When I get home, I go straight into the cupboard in the second bedroom and lug out the biggest of my suitcases. I start throwing clothes into it, a mixture of light summer clothes and thicker winter jumpers, because I don't know where I'm going. Then I find my passport and some dollars, euros and rands left over from past holidays. I turn down the thermostat in the house, make sure all the windows are locked, and take one last look at my home. I'll be back, but not until the date of my court hearing. I'll find a doctor and midwife wherever I end up, to make sure that my pregnancy is progressing to plan.

I lug the suitcase to the front door, turn off all the lights and lock the door behind me. I pull the case awkwardly along the cobbled lane and out onto the street. Glancing at my watch, I realise it's 1 pm. I'll have lunch at the airport.

A black taxi passes by with its light lit up in orange. I flag it down.

'Heathrow Airport, please,' I say. The taxi driver helps me with the suitcase, and I settle myself in for the journey. On my phone, I check out the live departures board and realise I have such a wide choice. I calculate backwards. I'll take whatever flight is leaving in exactly four hours.

Mauritius. There's a direct flight with Air Mauritius at 5 pm. That will be perfect. But when I get there, I won't stay in a fancy hotel. I will seek out voluntary work, do something that actually has some meaning. And perhaps I'll travel on to Africa and visit Sam. Maybe I'll give birth in a hospital in Cape Town with Sam by my side. Or perhaps I won't. This is my life now. A bubble of excitement rises up through me.

'It's you and me, baby,' I think to myself, placing both hands over my gently rounded stomach.

A LETTER FROM MIRANDA

I am dedicating this book to my godson, Sam Mason. (Sam – I'm sorry I don't have any truly nice characters to name after you!)

Thank you very much for reading *Make Her Pay*. When I first pitched the idea for this novel it was all about a wedding. Somehow, as we worked through the outline, the story morphed away from that and pivoted on the concept of guilt. How one tiny action taken in adolescence can have devastating implications for years to come. Leonie had everything: a loving family, friends, money, education, and yet she was weighed down by guilt for a decade. Rightly so, you may think. But she was only sixteen at the time... and heavily influenced by her dreadful father. Quite the moral dilemma!

I have had help with this book. Firstly, thank you to Graham Bartlett who is a police procedural advisor and author. I wasn't sure how Leonie and her father might be sentenced a decade after the accident and Graham pointed me in the right direction. All mistakes are my own. For this novel, my twenty-first psychological thriller, I've had help with naming my characters. Members of my Facebook Group, *Miranda Rijks Thriller Readers' Group*, got to nominate themselves or friends and family as characters. Thank you to: Melissa Borsey, Erin Crossway, Catherine Hester, Julie Howells, Selina Hutchison, Sheryl Hugill-Potts, Denise Little, Melanie Pleat and Carrie White Shields.

If you would like the opportunity to name characters in any of my future books, please join my Facebook Group where I post details of giveaways and bookish news.

https://www.facebook.com/groups/mirandarijks

None of this would have been possible without Inkubator Books. Thank you to Brian Lynch, Garret Ryan, Stephen Ryan, Claire Milto, Alice Latchford, Elizabeth Bayliss, Jodi and the rest of the team.

A huge thanks to the book blogging community who take the time to review my psychological thrillers, share my cover reveals and talk about my books on social media. I am so grateful for your support. A special call out to Dawn of the Facebook group, Psychological Thriller Authors and Readers Unite.

Finally, and most importantly, thank *you*. If you have a moment to leave a review on Amazon and Goodreads, this helps other people discover my novels and I'd be massively grateful.

My warmest wishes,

Miranda

www.mirandarijks.com

ALSO BY MIRANDA RIJKS

Psychological Thrillers

THE VISITORS

I WANT YOU GONE

DESERVE TO DIE

YOU ARE MINE

ROSES ARE RED

THE ARRANGEMENT

THE INFLUENCER

WHAT SHE KNEW

THE ONLY CHILD

THE NEW NEIGHBOUR

THE SECOND WIFE

THE INSOMNIAC

FORGET ME NOT

THE CONCIERGE

THE OTHER MOTHER

THE LODGE

THE HOMEMAKER

MAKE HER PAY

The Dr Pippa Durrant Mystery Series

FATAL FORTUNE

(Book 1)

FATAL FLOWERS

(Book 2)

FATAL FINALE

(Book 3)

Printed in Great Britain
by Amazon